Previously published Worldwide Mystery titles by
MAGGIE BARBIERI

THIRD DEGREE
PHYSICAL EDUCATION

Extra Credit

Maggie Barbieri

W⬤RLDWIDE®

TORONTO • NEW YORK • LONDON
AMSTERDAM • PARIS • SYDNEY • HAMBURG
STOCKHOLM • ATHENS • TOKYO • MILAN
MADRID • WARSAW • BUDAPEST • AUCKLAND

In memory of my good friend Neil Ferraiolo.
I hope this book is as slammin' as you were.

Recycling programs
for this product may
not exist in your area.

Extra Credit

A Worldwide Mystery/September 2014

First published by Minotaur Books, an imprint of St. Martin's Press

ISBN-13: 978-0-373-26912-9

Copyright © 2012 by Maggie Barbieri

Printed in U.S.A.

Acknowledgments

Thank you, as always, to the wonderful team at Minotaur Books: Kelley Ragland, Matt Martz, Elizabeth Lacks, Sarah Melnyk, Hector DeJean and Andy Martin. I am lucky to have one of the kindest and most astute editors in the business editing my series—Kelley—and I am grateful every day for that gift.

Thanks to my fantastic agent, Deborah Schneider, and her equally fantastic contracts/rights/account manager, Cathy Gleason, both of whom bring good cheer, humanity and great business sense to everything they do.

A big thank-you to my gals at NYU, as always: Anna, Kathy, Rajni, Crystal, Caroline, Rosie, Nurse Joanne, Queen. Keep fighting the good fight.

And to my family, Jim, Dea and Patrick: Thank you for the support, encouragement and the willingness to overlook the take-out containers that accumulate when I'm knee-deep in a book.

ONE

I WISH I HAD seen that coming.

By "that," I mean a beautiful crystal vase, one that my mother had lovingly carried across the border from her native Canada, rocking precariously after being knocked into by one of my party guests. My best friend, the former Father Kevin McManus, jumped to his feet, the muscle memory from his days as a boxer coming in handy as he leaped, one foot extended behind him, and caught it before it crashed to the dining room floor.

I mouthed a thank-you to him. The party was getting out of control, and as I try to live the most boring life possible, that was at odds with my usual Saturday nights in my small Westchester County village.

"Sing it, everyone! 'And you look like one, too!'"

That's my friend Max's customary coda to "Happy Birthday," a joke that never gets old. Well, maybe a little old. Thankfully, she was singing it at a birthday party for two nineteen-year-olds who were not above a little song, a little dance, and a little seltzer down your pants, as Chuckles the Clown used to say, but the rest of the partygoers were a little perplexed. Nobody really ever gets used to seeing a grown woman who is the size of a large child standing on a chair at the dining room table, wearing a paper party hat and Kanye West novelty sunglasses, singing at the top of her lungs.

But that's Max and that's how she rolls, as she reminds me every few days, when I try to point out that we're getting past the age of wearing miniskirts, thigh-high boots, and blousy shirts with sayings on them. The closer we get to forty, the more she has begun dressing like a sixteen-year-old. Her husband, the gargantuan Fred Wyatt, didn't seem to mind—he apparently preferred his wife to dress like a hipster going to an Arcade Fire concert than like the savvy businesswoman she used to portray and actually is.

My husband, Bobby Crawford, had brought two children into our marriage, twins Meaghan and Erin, both of whom looked a little shell-shocked to be surrounded by so many loved ones at one time, particularly on their birthday. Their mother, Christine, was in attendance with her second husband and family of four young stepchildren, two of them just past toddlerhood. In addition to the twins' birthday, it was her return to the States after the family had lived in London for the past few years that was the occasion for this celebration. The girls were beyond thrilled; their mother had been gone too long for their liking, and they were happy to relieve me of my duties. Although I was not as close to Erin as I was to Meaghan, Erin and I had reached détente and she no longer referred to me as a word that rhymes with "witch." I was just as happy as they that their mother had returned to mother them, allowing me to retire from my temporary career as "Alison Bergeron, Evil Stepmother."

Christine's brothers were also in attendance, including the girls' inexplicably named Uncle Chick; they hadn't laid eyes on him in a few years, but he had reappeared in the not-too-distant past and wanted to reconnect with his family. He rivaled Max for the title of "life of the party." Chick, clad in bright red pants, white bucks, and a tight white T-shirt that gave new meaning to the expression "painted on," gave a little bump and grind at the end of the song, knocking into the dining room table so hard that the cake jiggled in the center. I righted a bottle of wine that tipped perilously close to the edge and gave Crawford a look. In a case of "no good deed goes unpunished," I had agreed to host this party and invite the two families together, not entirely sure what I had gotten myself into. Now it was clear: I had gotten myself into a raucous gathering of two very disparate tribes and wasn't really prepared for what would transpire.

Chick held up an almost-empty bottle of Chardonnay and waved it in my face. "Do we need to make another run?" he asked.

If so, it would be our third run to the liquor store that night. The Stepkowski clan, Christine's side of the family, had drunk every ounce of vodka, tequila, and wine that we had in the house. I'm married to an Irish cop and can drink with the best of them myself, but the Stepkowskis took the cake. Maybe that was what years of hanging around their father's Upper West Side bar had done for them; they were hollow-legged, one and all. I looked over at Crawford, my eyes begging for a little help. "I think we'd better wrap it up on the liquor runs, Chick," he said, a suggestion that Chick seemed to take in stride. It wouldn't have surprised me to learn that he had his own stash of booze in his car or even planted somewhere in my house, just in case of emergency.

Christine's other brother, Pavel, a.k.a. Paulie, wasn't quite as accepting of that news. "You always were a killjoy, Crawford."

Crawford, ever stoic, accepted this pronouncement with far more grace than it called for and disappeared into the kitchen. Kevin, bless his heart, attempted to engage Paulie in conversation, and Paulie's attention was momentarily diverted. One thing I've found is that even if you aren't a priest anymore, the fact that you were, to old-school Catholics, is enough. Nobody has the cojones to ignore— never mind disobey—the defrocked Kevin McManus.

I followed close behind Crawford, leaving Fred to cut

the cake and shovel it onto paper plates so that we could call it a night.

It wasn't that long ago that Crawford had put in his papers to retire from the police department, thinking that a life of leisure would suit him just fine. His "retirement" had lasted exactly two days and one house project gone horribly awry. (Suffice it to say that you shouldn't attempt to replumb the basement for a new bathroom if you have spent your entire adult life solving homicides.) A mere forty-eight hours after he had turned in his badge—a development that I was overjoyed to see—I was begging him to reverse his decision and don the blue blazer, white shirt, rep tie, and dress slacks that he wore every day to a very dirty and very dangerous job. The saggy gym shorts and soiled T-shirt, his new uniform, just weren't cutting it for me. It was shortly thereafter that we had learned that Christine would be coming back to town, and his decision was made; his girls would have their mother back in their lives, leaving him guilt-free to return to the job that really was his reason for being, although he was loath to admit it.

I joined him in the kitchen. Beyond the house, in the backyard, the children of the various family members were all hell-bent, it appeared, on torturing my dog, the wonderful Trixie Bergeron-Crawford, by denying the animal her favorite tennis ball. I opened the back door and whistled for her to come in. She raced past me and flew up the steps to the bedroom, where she took refuge under my bed, if the thump above my head was any indication.

Crawford was wiping the same spot on the counter over and over and gazing out the window over the sink. "They don't have matches out there, right?" he asked, throwing his chin toward the kids playing on the grass.

"I don't know," I said, alarmed. "Why?"

"It just looks like they are trying to start a bonfire," he said, sounding far less concerned than I thought he should.

I guess that's what twenty-plus years on the police department, half of them as a homicide detective, does to you. If dead bodies were commonplace, what was a simple bonfire, assembled by the combined broods of your ex-wife's extended family?

"You still want more kids?" I asked, harking back to a conversation that we had started the night before but never finished.

He looked less sure than when he initially brought it up. I looked at him. "I love your girls, but this party is over," I said, pulling open the screen door and going outside. "Hey!" I called to the group of kids huddled together over a pile of sticks. I hadn't bothered to learn their names, figuring such information would take up too much space in my already overloaded brain. I decided right then and there that I hated other people's kids, a quality that was probably not really desirable in a teacher, my chosen profession. I flashed on Crawford's eager and earnest face every time he held a baby and decided that was just one more thing that separated us; he loved kids and I could go either way, my opinion of children having been shaped by these types of experiences. The kids looked up and dispersed, something they seemed used to doing with regularity. It came very easily to the multiaged crowd.

I put my hand over the pile of sticks, thankfully cool, and turned to confront the remaining children, but the backyard was empty. Satisfied that we were out of danger for the time being, I went back inside, where Crawford was handing Paulie his jacket.

"So good to see you," he said with fake cheer, clapping his former brother-in-law on the back. He had confessed to me earlier that he had banked on never seeing any of the Stepkowskis again once he and Christine had divorced, so entertaining them was a huge sacrifice that he was willing to make for his girls.

"But I didn't finish my cake!" Paulie protested, taking the coat and marching toward the back door. Crawford followed him with a plate of cake in his hands.

"Here." Crawford shoved the cake into Paulie's solar plexus. "You can enjoy it on the way home."

"But it's ice cream cake," Paulie said.

Crawford thought about that a moment. "Fine. Come back in." He took Paulie's coat again. "But after you eat it, the party is officially over."

Chick came into the kitchen. "Wait. We didn't do presents yet," he said, pulling two envelopes out of his back pocket. "I want to give my nieces their presents."

Everyone went back into the dining room, where Meaghan and Erin were still lapping up ice cream cake and Max was regaling the group with a story about the off-camera goings-on for her show *Hooters: PIs*, a program that had become a ratings juggernaut. I'm not going to explain what it is; the title says it all. All I heard was "popped implant," which really was all I needed to hear. I pulled a finger across my throat to signal to Max that discussing the ins-and-outs of shooting a show about big-breasted waitresses who investigate cheating husbands really might not be acceptable cocktail-party conversation, but she wasn't having it.

"And Miss Downtown Abbey over there thinks it isn't high-brow enough," she said, shooting me a look.

"It's Down-*ton* Abbey, and no, I don't think shows about waitresses beating up cheating husbands is highbrow," I said. "Call me crazy."

"You're crazy," she said. "Tell that to the Nielsen people. You should see our ratings." She turned back to her rapt audience, a group who clearly didn't think they'd see the two of us throw down about a show with such high drama, if Max's description of it was any barometer. Max claims that I don't think what she does is "art." It's not. It's titillating and salacious and possibly entertaining, but "art"? Hardly. She shook her head. "She's so dismissive of what I do."

I took a seat at the head of the table while Crawford grabbed the presents off the sideboard and handed them to his daughters.

The girls whipped through them. To everyone's credit, the twins each had a pile of individualized, personal gifts to open. There were Uggs boots for Erin and a ski pass for Meaghan from her mother and her husband, Tim; Paulie and his wife, Ava, gave them both gift cards to a bookstore chain; and Crawford and I had sprung for Tiffany charm bracelets for both. Chick waited a few seconds before ceremoniously handing each of them an envelope, their names written on the front in chicken scratch only he could read. The girls looked alternately at the envelopes in their hands, then their uncle, and then their mother, who had a grim expression on her face. Her history with her brothers obviously telegraphed something to her that none of the rest of us could see, and judging by the looks of it, it wasn't going to be good.

"I love you guys more than words can say," he said, tearing up a bit, "and I'm sorry I haven't been in your lives more than I have."

I looked over at Crawford, who was studying a scratch on the sideboard with great intensity. Emotional oversharing was not his cup of tea, and it looked like that was what we were in for. Kevin, on the other hand, was eating this up. This was the party he never would have been invited to or able to attend if he were still the chaplain at St. Thomas University, ministering to a bunch of reluctant students at a Catholic college.

"The last few years have been hard for me," Chick said. "Life has not been easy, as you might have guessed. But I'm back, and I want to be with you and be there for the big days in your lives. Your weddings! Your first babies!"

Now it was the girls' turn to look away. They were barely halfway through college and not thinking about husbands, weddings, and babies. Christine walked over to her brother and put her arm around his waist. "It's getting late, Chick," she said gently, obviously not the first time she'd extracted one or another of her brothers after he had overstayed his welcome.

I attempted to communicate with Crawford telepathically. "You owe me big-time," I shot toward him, hoping that he could read my mind. He turned and looked at me. Apparently, he could.

Chick leaned into his sister. "I had to go away for a while. You know that," he said, looking at the girls again. "After what happened in my life, things just kind of fell apart."

It was a story almost all of the people in the room had heard before, judging from the sympathetic sounds and soft groans coming from them. Now, though, I had a feeling that we were going to get more details than we really wanted.

From behind her novelty sunglasses, Max chimed in. "What happened?" I heard Fred grunt in his wife's direction. "What?" she whispered. "I don't know what happened. It sounds good." With that, Chick fell apart, a combination of too much booze and too much sadness building up inside until he could no longer hold it together. Great, heaving sobs came out of the sturdy, barrel-chested man, the weight of what he was thinking too much to bear. "What happened?" he asked rhetorically, tears in his eyes, staring at a spot over Max's head. "Well, I lost everything. My wife, my best friend, my business, my staff. It all went to hell in a suitcase."

"Isn't it 'handbasket'?" Max whispered to no one in particular. Fred grunted again and this time added a little muscle. "Ow!" she exclaimed, rubbing the arm that her husband had just pinched to shut her up.

"My Sassy!" Chick cried. "My dear, sweet Sassy. I just wish it had worked out."

I looked over at Crawford, who mouthed, "I'll tell you later."

In my mind, I figured it was a pet. A cockatiel, a lovely Maltese. What else could a being named Sassy be?

Kevin leaned against the dining room wall, his arms crossed over his chest. Finally, a family that was as dysfunctional as his own, he seemed to be thinking. That, or he was planning how to make a quick getaway. It was hard to say.

Chick rubbed a hand over his florid face and tried to compose himself. "Sorry...sorry. Like I said, I'm back, and I want to say that I love you all very much and I'm sorry for what I put you through. All those years when you weren't sure where I was, weren't sure what I was doing." He paused dramatically. "I was just trying to survive."

Christine, obviously the recipient of a batch of recessive genes that allowed her to be beautiful, smart, and poised, unlike her roughneck brothers, kissed Chick's cheek and rubbed his back. "We're glad you're back, too, Chick. Now why don't you give the girls their presents?" she asked.

He nodded. "I need to make amends," he said.

"Oh, boy," I telegraphed to Crawford, whose face had turned white.

"To you, Bobby," Chick said, gesturing toward Crawford, who was now busy staring at a hole in a window screen at the back of the dining room, his hands shoved deep in his pockets. Why he hadn't tackled that little home improvement job while he had been retired was anyone's guess, opting instead for a plumbing project that was clearly beyond his skill set. "Look at me, man. I'm trying to say I'm sorry."

"It's okay," Crawford said quickly. "No need to apologize."

"No, I want to, brother. I want to tell you how sorry I

am that I never accepted you into the family. How I never thought you were good enough for my little sister. How I always thought you were kind of a big stiff."

Max couldn't resist another interjection. "He *is* kind of a big stiff," she said. Fred, Crawford's partner on the PD and his closest friend, glared down at her from his perch on the edge of the sideboard. "Well, he is…" She trailed off.

"Really, it's fine," Crawford said. He's actually not a stiff, just what I would call "measured" in his response to things. If that made him a stiff, I was completely in. "Thanks for coming," he said, moving toward Chick to usher him from the house.

"I'm not finished."

Crawford froze.

"Alison, you seem like a very nice lady. I never saw this guy here," he said, hooking a thumb in Crawford's direction, "with a professor, but hey, life's a funny thing, right?"

And getting funnier all the time, if Kevin's stifled guffaw was any indication.

"I hope the two of you are very happy in your life together."

"Thank you, Chick. It has been so nice having you," I said, getting up and going over to give him a parting embrace. Before I got to him, he started again. Apparently, he wasn't finished.

"Christine, I love you, sis. All the best to you and Tim," he said, nodding toward Christine's husband. Tim was kind of a stoic sort and so far seemed to have only one facial expression, a cross between concerned and confused. I was relieved to find that indeed he did have another expression, although fear wasn't the one I would have chosen. Chick let out a huge exhale and threw his arms wide. "I'm back! And I'm happy to be here. So open your presents, girls!"

The girls looked at their father, still dumbstruck like the rest of us. Crawford nodded his assent, and they ripped into their envelopes, taking out identical cards and opening them up at the same time.

Meaghan was the first to speak, and what she said came out in a hoarse whisper. "It's some money." She had better manners than that, so I knew something had to be wrong.

Erin looked at her mother, and then her father, catching a hundred-dollar bill before it fluttered to the floor. "It's not *some* money. It's a *lot* of freaking money."

TWO

FIVE THOUSAND DOLLARS *was* a lot of money for one person to receive.

Times two, at ten thousand dollars, it was even more for someone to give away.

Ten thousand dollars, in one-hundred-dollar bills, bestowed upon two nineteen-year-old girls by an uncle they hadn't seen in almost a decade. It was a bizarre capper to an even more bizarre get-together, the likes of which I hoped never to have to host—or endure—again.

Christine and Crawford had lobbied mightily for Chick to take the money back, but he refused. He was out the door before anyone could reason further with him. After he left, Crawford conferred with his ex, and they decided that we would keep the money here until one of them could convince Chick that a five-thousand-dollar gift was a little too generous for the girls on their nineteenth birthday.

Something else was niggling at Crawford, I could tell, but I didn't have a chance to ask him what it was. I suspected it had something to do with the origins of the money, but don't ask me how I knew that. All I gleaned from our evening together and subsequent conversation about it was that Chick had been gone for a long time. Maybe he had struck it rich while on a great adventure far away from his family.

Or maybe the truth was far more nefarious and that's where Crawford's mind was going. Either way, even if it hadn't been stolen from an orphanage or been liberated from an offshore bank account, the money was going back.

I was in bed by the time Crawford returned from driving Meaghan, a sophomore at St. Thomas University, the school where I teach, back to campus. Erin had her mother's spare car for the semester, and although she didn't enjoy driving a 2000 Honda Odyssey that had seen its fair share of cheddar Goldfish and juice-box meals, she liked having her own transportation and the ability to come and go as she pleased. Where she went was anyone's guess and, now that her mother had returned, something I didn't have to worry about anymore. Her school was about an hour and a half north, so she had set off fairly quickly after the Stepkowskis, promising to text as soon as she arrived back at her dorm. Meaghan's and my school was about thirty minutes south, so Crawford made that journey, hoping that he could catch up with his older-by-a-minute daughter and find out what was going on at school and in her life.

Good luck with that, I thought. Although the girls were close to their dad, Meaghan and her father shared the same gene that allowed both of them to wall everything off from everyone else. I suspected the conversation would be an interrogation on Crawford's part with few answers coming from Meaghan. Did that make them both "stiffs"? I didn't think so, but apparently Chick was of a different mindset.

The party had been the most time I had ever spent with Christine, and despite her brother's emotional unraveling after dinner and the behavior of the pack of wolves she called Stepchildren, nieces, and nephews, my feelings about her were confirmed: I liked her. I could see why Crawford had fallen in love with her but understood, too, why they had broken up. They had married young, had two children soon after that, and had tried to endure the pressures of his very stressful job, all of which weighed heavy on their unstable union. They had drifted apart and, to their credit, in much less dramatic fashion than I had from my first, philandering, late husband. (God rest his soul.) She seemed incredibly happy with Tim, who seemed to be the yin to her yang, and while I didn't think the four of us would go so far as to vacation together, dinners that revolved around Meaghan and Erin were certainly not out of the question in the future.

I was going to draw the line at the rest of *la famille* Stepkowski, though, and would be clear with Crawford on that.

It was close to ten when Crawford got home. I heard him greet the dog as he walked through the kitchen. He looked surprised to see me awake, tucked under the covers, a hardcover open on top of the quilt.

"Fun night!" I said.

"Not really," he said.

"I was being facetious."

"I wasn't." He pulled his belt out of its loops and took off his shirt. At almost six and a half feet, Crawford is what I call a "tall drink of water," a formerly skin-and-bones bachelor who had put on a few pounds since we had gotten married, something that served his physique well. Before moving in with me, he had existed on a diet of bad Chinese food and beer, and despite that, had stayed almost gaunt. A few years with me and he had filled out around the middle, but not in an unattractive way. He stripped off his pants and jumped into bed next to me, and we nestled together. I was grateful for the warmth of his bare skin against mine.

"What was that all about?" he asked. I assumed he was referring to Chick's outburst at dinner.

"You're asking me?" I replied. "He's your ex-brother-in-law."

He leaned back and turned the light off on the nightstand on his side of the bed. We lay in the dark, holding each other. "It's strange. I don't know where it came from."

"Obviously he feels pretty bad about the last several

years. It seems clear to me." I adjusted my arms so that I could hold him tight. "When exactly did he leave?"

"He left one day in the fall of 2001. No one knows where he went." He made a noise, and I wasn't sure what it meant. "For days, we thought he was dead. He finally called and left Christine a message a week later saying that he was fine and not to look for him."

"And she did that?"

"Not really," he said. "She tried to find him but gave up after a while. Then he turned up a week or so ago."

"What happened? Why did he leave?" There had to be a reason. No one just up and leaves his entire family, never to be heard of for years. At least no one in my family does that; my entire extended family still lives in Canada, my father being the only guy with a traveling jones—and even he didn't get that far, settling about eight hours due south in New York State.

"From what we could piece together, things went sour quickly for Chick. Lost his job, divorced his wife, maybe other things?" I could feel Crawford shake his head. "Who knows? It was right after 9/11, so I really wasn't all that concerned with where Chick Stepkowski had ended up. I was more concerned with..."

"Moving on?" I asked.

He remained silent. We had never spoken of that day, and I wondered if we ever would. He had spent time at Ground Zero, and aside from a comment every now and again, I had no details beyond the fact that he never wanted to speak of it in any detail ever.

"What was his business?" I asked.

Crawford chuckled. "You'll never believe it."

"Try me."

"Porta-potties."

"Really."

"Really." He shifted a little, moving his arm out from

under my shoulder. "He married into the business and did okay for himself, but it was kind of a joke in the family."

The click of nails on the hardwood floor announced Trixie's arrival. She fell heavily on the floor next to Crawford's side of the bed, letting out an odiferous exhale that smelled suspiciously of leftover chicken. I waited for a few minutes and thought that Crawford had fallen asleep, but he started talking again.

"I thought we'd never see him again. This is just weird."

"And what is a Sassy?" I asked.

"The ex-wife."

"Her name was Sassy?"

"Yep," he said, but I could tell that he was drifting off and the conversation was ending.

It wasn't the name I would choose for any of our maybe eventual children—the jury was still out on them after the kids that I had encountered that evening—or even any future pets, but I tended to go for the more mundane and Christian when it came to the naming of living beings. That's how my first goldfish, won for me by my father at the annual fire department carnival, had ended up with the name Frances Xavier. Also how the turtle that I eventually killed through neglect had been called John the Baptist.

The silence stretched on, and this time I realized he had fallen asleep for good. I detached myself from his arms and turned toward the window, watching the rain pelt the screen, feeling the cool, moist air coat my face. I don't know how long it took, but soon I was asleep, too, in a slumber that was dreamless, soundless, and devoid of the stress of the day.

THE NEXT MORNING, Crawford and I finished cleaning up the kitchen, still a mess from the night before. As soon as the last load of dirty dishes was loaded into the dishwasher, we headed to the backyard. It was a gorgeous autumn day, the sky blue, the air mild, the rain from the night before having taken with it the humidity that had lingered the previous week. Using the leftover vodka, somehow hidden from Chick and Paulie, I mixed up a pitcher of Bloody Marys and brought them to where Crawford had divided up the Sunday papers and left my favorite sections, the book review and Arts and Entertainment, on the chaise longue beside his. I handed him a drink. "Where're the chips?" I asked, the one item I had charged him with bringing outside.

He looked at me sheepishly. "Inside?"

I launched myself off the chaise and went back inside, muttering about having to do everything myself, sending a boy to do a man's job, etc. I was just about to return to the comfort of the chaise when the phone rang.

To answer or not to answer? That was the question. I considered the phone, ringing away on the wall, and decided to ignore it. By the time I got outside, however, Crawford's phone, always tucked into the front pocket of his jeans, was ringing, seconds after the house phone had stopped. When he answered, I knew it was Christine.

"Sure. Come by," he said. "We're just sitting here having a drink."

Christine had moved to Connecticut upon her return to the States, so it didn't take her long to get to our house in Westchester. She was alone when she arrived, looking sheepish about bothering us on a tranquil Sunday after the raucous goings-on of the night before.

I held up my half-empty glass. "Bloody Mary?" I asked.

"No, thanks. I'm on my way to take Meaghan for a mani/pedi. I promised both girls some quality time," she said, taking a seat at the picnic table. "I just wanted to talk to you about the money." Crawford sat forward on the chaise longue. "What about it?"

"Well, what to do with it," she said. "I'm sorry I took off before we could really discuss it."

Crawford shrugged. "Nothing to discuss. First chance I get, I'm bringing it back to Chick. Where's he living exactly?"

She gave us an address in a not-very-desirable section of Mount Vernon, a small city a bit south of us. She sighed. "Of all my brothers, Chick was the one I thought would end up on the straight and narrow. The rest of them?" She looked at Crawford. "Now that's a different story."

"I remember," he said. "Those guys were the embodiment of the Dead End Kids."

She smiled. "So you know what I mean," she said. "It seemed like things were going well until…well…you know."

"He left." It didn't need to be said, but he said it anyway.

She looked down at the patio. "Yeah."

"He was gone a long time," Crawford said.

"Did he leave right after losing his job? After his marriage fell apart?" I asked. Christine and I shared Crawford, and in turn, he shared everything with me. I didn't think it was impolite to let on that I knew what had gone on with her troubled brother.

"We guess he did, but we don't know." Anticipating my next question, she said, "He didn't tell anyone where he was going or for how long. He was just gone."

I didn't intend to make a sound, but I did. In that sound was my disbelief that they had not seen him for over ten years, yet he had turned up all of a sudden, out of the blue, without any warning whatsoever, or any explanations.

"We looked for him," Christine said, a little defensive, "but he was gone. We knew he was okay, so we didn't pursue it. You can't make someone come back. You can't make them do something they don't want to do."

I looked at Crawford, incredulous. Did this sound as weird to him as it did to me? Or did everyone just expect that given whatever emotional state he had been in, Chick had left town and everything he had here with the intention of not returning? Maybe he didn't want to be found, but it sounded like they hadn't looked very hard, either. Maybe they hadn't wanted to.

"You're looking at me like you don't agree with how we handled this," Christine said.

I was going to try to be as tactful as possible, a strategy I would have to employ a lot more if it meant peace with my husband's ex-wife. "I wasn't in your position, Christine. I don't know what I would have done."

The damage was done; she was hurt. "Yes, you do. By the way you're talking, you're thinking that you would have moved heaven and earth to find him." She shook her head. "Trust me. He didn't want to be found."

"Crawford said you got a call not long after he left. Did you hear from him at all after that?" I asked.

"One letter," she said. She opened her purse, a soft leather satchel, and pulled out a worn and tattered letter, one that she had obviously kept with her the entire time he was gone. She waved it toward Crawford. "You already saw this."

He nodded.

"I just don't want to rock the boat," she said. "You know…about the money."

"I'll handle it, Christine. I know how happy you are that he's back." Crawford reached over and patted her leg with a familiarity that made me just a wee bit uncomfortable, but I let it go. They had a lot of history. That's what I told myself.

She stood and looked up at the sky and then at me. "Life is really strange, you know?"

Did I know? I could write a book about my exploits that nobody would believe. I smiled to show her that I did know. I thought we were done, but she surprised me by bursting into tears. It was my turn to jump up and comfort her.

"This is not the family I would have chosen for myself," she said. "Or for anyone, for that matter. But it's the one I got."

I didn't have a family to speak of anymore, being an only child and having lost both of my parents far sooner than I should have. Before Crawford, Max had been my only family, and she had started out as my college roommate. Her family had adopted me, her father taking me under his wing particularly, and while I appreciated it, they weren't blood. However, after the events of the previous night, I was starting to think that being on my own for so long was a bit of a blessing, despite the fact that I missed my parents every single day.

She broke from our embrace. "You laughed about it all those years," she said to Crawford, "but it was never easy. It was never easy being from that family. Having those brothers." She reached into her bag and took out a tissue, wiping under her eyes. "It's just that they're all I have, and I'm just stupid enough to try to make it work again."

I felt for her; I really did. I was ready to put the Step-kowskis out of my head once and for all, though, and would be happy when the money was returned to Chick and Crawford and I could go back to pretending that our lives consisted of the two of us, Trixie, and the twins. It seemed like adding anyone else—even Max and Fred sometimes—disrupted the natural ebb and flow of our daily lives and our relationship. Then I thought of growing old, Crawford hopefully by my side, and no one else. No rambunctious kids, no doted-upon grandchildren, just us. Was that what I really wanted?

AFTER CHRISTINE LEFT, Crawford took the money and put it into a larger sealed envelope. "I'll get rid of this as soon as possible," he said. "This week. I'll go see him this week."

The sooner, the better, I thought.

THREE

I LOVE FALL semester at St. Thomas University. Well, maybe not the teaching part so much, but the campus itself. That Monday morning, a couple of weeks into the semester, was a gorgeous sixty-degree day that made walking through campus a joy, not a chore, despite the hills and valleys that make winter treks treacherous. Today, the river was in front of me, the sun overhead, and the leaves on the trees beside me beginning to burnish gold and red.

Plus, it was taco day in the commuter cafeteria. What could be better than that?

Nothing, I tell you. Taco day has lifted me out of many a depressed state over my years at St. Thomas.

I swung my messenger bag back and forth as I walked down the back steps to the office area; they had been fixed over the summer after a hundred years of neglect. Once, those steps had been my daily Waterloo, making it a challenge for me, a confirmed klutz, just to get from my car to the office without falling. Now, they were a study in pristine masonry. I still marveled every day at how having this one stress taken out of my work life had made things go so much more smoothly in this new school year. It's the little things, my mother used to say, and in this instance, she was correct.

I locked my office every night, something I hadn't started doing until I got a talking-to from Crawford about regular theft, identity theft, the difference between robbery and burglary, and a host of other police things that I had no interest in but could happen if someone decided to let himself or herself into my inner sanctum after I left. These were the kinds of dissertations that he found fascinating and·that put me to sleep; when all was said and done, it was just easier to do what he wanted. It was a good plan, if I put my keys in the same place every night, but I didn't. Hence, part of every morning was spent digging around in the bottom of my bag, my pockets, and anywhere else that keys might be stored, all while greeting various nuns who also kept offices near mine. Sister Perpetua wanted to borrow my iPad to play Angry Birds. (I said no.) Sister Dolores Marie complimented me on my skirt; I suspected she wanted my iPad as well. Sister James Patrick thought that we were going to get rain based on her creaky knees. Sister Anna Catherine wanted to know if I was going to coach the basketball team again. (I wasn't. My coaching days were definitely over.) Sister Louise, finally, wanted to know if taco day in the cafeteria was as good as every-one said it was. It was, I assured her.

Finally, I unearthed my keys from my bag and entered my office, closing the door behind me. Out in the office area, I heard the booming voice of Sister Mary McLaughlin, my boss and occasional nemesis. Judging from the few words I could decipher and the sound of her footsteps on the ancient hardwood floor, I discerned that she was coming my way and that she wasn't alone.

The day was off to a good start, and nothing was going to ruin that, even a cranky six-foot nun with a penchant for assigning me really horrible tasks that supposedly would benefit our entire department. I didn't see how counting the number of words in a particular stanza of an obscure poem was benefiting the entire department, but I did what I was told until I figured out that she was screwing with me, albeit in a very intellectual sort of way. Now I usually tried to make an end run around her if I could.

I picked up the phone and dialed Max. When she answered, I said, "We're having a very important conversation, and there will be times you don't understand what I'm talking about, but just stay on the line." I realized, too late, that I could have pantomimed this phone call without anyone on the other end, but I'm more of a Method actor when it comes to deluding and evading my boss.

"You got it. Can I eat while you talk?" she asked, even though I could hear she hadn't stopped eating since answering the phone. My guess? Bacon and egg on a bagel, one of her favorites. My mouth started watering, the quick-cook oats I had eaten an hour earlier a distant reminder of today's latest culinary disappointment.

"Of course," I said, then raised my voice so that it could be heard on the other side of the door. "If you don't submit the paper by day's end, it could result in a failing grade for you. Let's talk about what's wrong with this paper." There was a forceful tap on the door, followed by Mary calling my name. "I'm on the phone," I called out.

That meant nothing to her. She swung the door open, releasing the knob and allowing the door to swing into the bookcase behind it, causing a copy of *The Elements of Style* to plummet to the floor noisily. "Are you busy?" she asked, the implication being "You're not busy."

I pointed to the phone.

"How long will you be?" Mary favors an all navy blue wardrobe. If *The Elements of Style* offered sartorial advice for her monochromatic tendencies, I would surreptitiously leave a copy on her desk; alas, it was all about grammar. Today was no exception for her; she was in head-to-toe navy, right down to her sensible, one-inch-heeled pumps. Even the pendant dangling around her neck, a Miraculous Medal, was blue.

I put my hand over the receiver. "At least twenty minutes." I figured that would buy me enough time to get rid of her and cruise right into my first class, a place she certainly couldn't bother me.

She looked disappointed. Behind her was a woman as tall as she was, but impeccably turned out in a black pencil skirt, silk blouse, and heels. Her bag alone probably cost a thousand dollars. Her hair was the quintessential rich-Westchester-lady cut: expertly layered with highlights that certainly hadn't come from a bottle purchased at the local drugstore. I slid in closer to my desk so no one could see the run that had sprung from the toe of my pantyhose and now ran up the side of my leg; I dragged a hand through my own tousled mop. Mary turned to her. "Dr. Bergeron isn't available right now, but I'm sure you'll meet her at some point." The woman poked her head into my office and offered a big smile; I gave her a little wave. Without saying goodbye, Mary pulled the door closed and went on her way with the mystery woman.

Max was still eating. "What did the old hag want?"

"Not sure," I said. "She had a very attractive woman with her. Probably somebody looking to get her kid in here."

"More attractive than me?"

How does one answer that question? "Completely different type."

"So not as attractive as me."

Okay. If you say so.

"Kid with her?" she asked.

"Nope," I said, swinging my chair around so I could look out the floor-to-ceiling windows that took up one whole wall of my office, offering a view of the sisters' cemetery in the distance. "You'd be amazed. A lot of people look at schools without their kids these days and just send them wherever they've chosen."

"Really?" Max asked between bites of whatever she was devouring with gusto.

"I know. It's strange. It seems to be the trend, though."

Outside, the woman who had been with Mary was making her way up the same steps that I had traversed just minutes earlier. From my current vantage point, I could see that she had a school catalog in her hand. Yep, definitely an interested parent.

"You need me for anything else right now?" Max asked. "Because I've got a production meeting in about thirty seconds."

"Nope. We're good. Talk later?"

Max is the kind of friend for whom explanations are worthless and unnecessary. If I need her, she's generally there. She acts first and asks questions later, and while a misstep or two isn't uncommon in our dealings with each other, for the most part, she is true and loyal and our friendship is unwavering. I've put the time that she left me in the closet for a body to fall on top of me out of my mind.

Almost.

I packed up for my first class and was almost in the clear when I ran into Sister Mary on the landing between the fourth and fifth floors of the building, the smell of her Jean Naté enveloping me in the close quarters. Students flooded past us, pushing us closer together than either of us would have liked to be, with Mary backed up to the window that I wished weren't painted shut. I wondered how long I could hold my breath.

"Alison, it's unfortunate that you weren't available. The woman with me is interested in enrolling in a few courses, nonmatriculated, of course, with a concentration in creative writing." She gave me a look that would indicate that I smelled particularly bad, but that's just the way her face looks when I'm around, I've discerned. "Obviously, I thought of you."

Obviously. I had been handed the onerous task of teaching Creative Writing I this semester, a course that I had taught in the past and not enjoyed particularly. What was passing these days for creativity didn't mesh with my own definition, and that caused much consternation among the students in the class, all of whom had eked out C's with one exception. That kid had gotten a D.

My grading had garnered me a good talking-to from Mary as well as a trip to the academic dean for my division. Parents had complained, seeing their children as creative geniuses whose efforts needed to be admired and graded accordingly. Now whenever I heard "creative writing," my stomach did a flip; I much preferred Senior Seminar, where students were committed to their work and had learned how to write long before they got to me. "So she'll be in my class?"

"She's still deciding between St. Thomas and Dominican College in Rockland County." Then she said the words that struck fear in the heart of every creative writing teacher. "She's writing a novel."

I tried to remain impassive. If I had a dime for all of the first-draft great American novels that I had read in the past fifteen years of teaching, well, I'd have a lot of dimes. "That's great," I said, the required hint of enthusiasm leaking into my voice.

"I think it is," she said, agreeing heartily. "She's led a very interesting life."

I looked at my watch. "Look at the time," I said, starting off. Mary called something after me, but I lost myself in the throngs of students streaming toward their respective classrooms, hoping that she wouldn't spot me towering over the group I had the misfortune of falling in with, none of them over five feet tall.

On my way to my classroom, I spotted Meaghan. She was in her usual uniform of pajama pants, hooded sweatshirt, and flip-flops, but curiously, that ensemble or lack thereof didn't seem to faze the guy she was sucking face with right outside the classroom where I was about to teach a unit on Dante's *Inferno*. What happened to making yourself look as nice as possible for your boyfriend or girlfriend? The guy was in droopy athletic shorts and a wrinkled T-shirt. The outfits they were wearing were the domain of married couples in my opinion, but what did I know? I recognized her make-out partner as a kid on the lacrosse team for whom the term "dumb as a sack of hammers" was a particularly applicable turn of phrase. On the plus side, he was taller than the almost-six-foot-tall Meaghan. On the minus side, he was what I call a "super senior," a kid who should have graduated years ago but had returned to finish up the credits he had failed to amass as a result of either failure or neglect. From what I heard, he was a bartender at Maloney's down the avenue and, even with a college degree, might not go on to anything more secure than a lifelong bartending career. To say that Crawford was a little disappointed in Meaghan's taste in men was a serious understatement.

As I walked past her, I loudly cleared my throat. "Good morning!"

The couple broke apart quickly. "Oh, hi," she said, nervously smoothing her hair back. Mr. Lacrosse Player bid us *adieu* and slithered off, not interested in a conversation that would take place between a professor/stepmother and his girlfriend/her stepdaughter. "I'm on my way to class."

"How's Forensic Psych going?" I asked, having heard through a little birdie—namely her professor—that she had been late handing in one paper and had missed a homework assignment completely. So far, I had managed to keep this situation from Crawford, but the guy worked hard to keep his girls in school, Meaghan's sizable academic scholarship notwithstanding, and he expected results.

Her face took on that look that showed me what she must have looked like as a five-year-old. She didn't necessarily go pale, but it was close. "Fine," she said, packing a combination of defensiveness and nervousness into that one word, and letting me know that things were, indeed, not "fine."

"Listen," I said, moving in close. "Here's the deal: catch up on your work and turn everything in, and your father doesn't have to know. However, if Professor Larkin and her cat sweater come by my office again complaining about how disinterested you are in her class and the work involved, all bets are off." I didn't enjoy parenting like Don Corleone, but there you have it. Sometimes, intimidation, threats, and recriminations are the best form of keeping everyone on the straight and narrow. "Do you need a study group? A homework tutor?" I asked, more gently, knowing that St. Thomas made provisions for everyone to do well, not just their student-athletes.

Meaghan threw a thumb over her shoulder. "That's who he is," she said.

"Mr. Super Senior?" I asked, dumbfounded. "Well, that explains a lot."

"It started out that way," she protested, "but then... well...he's cute."

Yeah, if you like your guys big, dumb, and unable to interpret a college catalog. "Whatever," I said, realizing that I was late to class. "Get it together on Forensic Psych or you're going to have your father bringing a large can of whoop-ass down on you." I sighed more dramatically than the situation warranted. "I'm just trying to help."

"What's whoop-ass?" she asked.

I translated my eighties street talk for her. "A whole heap of trouble." She still looked confused. "Like you'll be living with us every weekend and be the saddest you've ever been."

That got her attention. She stiffened. I guess there was nothing worse than spending your weekends with your cranky detective father and his equally cranky professor wife while wondering what the difference was between symbolic interactionism and conflict theory.

She decided to switch gears to throw me off the scent of her bad grades. "I still don't understand why we can't keep the money."

"Haven't you been over this with your parents? You don't need a five-thousand-dollar birthday gift from an uncle you haven't seen in a decade," I said, getting right to the point.

"It's my money," she whined.

"No, it's really not," I said. I was sick of talking about it and told her so. "Take it up with your father. He's headed over there this week to give it back and explain to your uncle that while generous, it was completely over the top and unnecessary." I reached around the back of her hoodie and tucked in the tag that I had spied sticking out when I originally approached her. "Look at it this way: He'll probably get you something else. Something more appropriate to the occasion. Like socks! Or new pajamas that you can wear to school!" I said pointedly, full of fake cheer.

Meaghan was not amused. She looked dejected as she slunk off to her next class. I guess she didn't need new socks or pajamas. We were about the same size; if Chick took Crawford's suggestion for a better gift, maybe I would make out, too.

I went off and taught my class. After it was over, it was technically still too early for tacos, but that didn't mean I wasn't hungry. I was delighted to find my go-to guy, Marcus, behind the counter in the cafeteria. "Too early for tacos?" I asked, holding my hands together in hopeful prayer.

He looked at his watch and then at me. "It's ten thirty."

"Your point?"

"It's too early for tacos."

"Again, your point?"

He smiled and reached to a shelf above the stove and

took down a small package wrapped in tinfoil. He handed it to me across the counter and put his other hand to his lips. "Shhh. If anyone finds out that there were tacos at ten thirty, I'm in big trouble." He accepted the money I handed him. "Especially Sister Theodosia. She's a taco addict."

I stuffed the packet into my messenger bag and told him that his secret was safe with me. I hustled out of the cafeteria and down the hall toward the staircase that led to the sisters' residence, knowing that that part of the building would be empty at this time of day. I could eat my taco in peace, the only sign that I had procured it before the official lunch hour being the lingering smell of Marcus's perfectly seasoned ground beef in the convent stairwell. I climbed up a few steps and sat just below the first landing, unwrapping the steaming packet of Mexican goodness, touching it with my tongue to gauge how hot it really was before diving in. A previous, unfortunate dining experience—thanks to my inability to exhibit any patience whatsoever—had given me a tongue so burned that I had conducted my afternoon classes with a severe lisp, leaving all of my students perplexed and more than a little amused. I kept the foil wrapped around the taco so that the juice inside the tortilla shell didn't leak out all over my hands and clothes.

I took a bite and almost exclaimed with joy.

That joy was short-lived, though, because as I sat chewing, in a state of near ecstasy, I heard footsteps and voices below me. I hustled up to the next landing and pressed myself against the wall, not wanting to be found out. It really was no big deal to me that I had a taco before lunch service, but it could mean trouble for Marcus, and that guy had had my gustatory back so many times that I was wary of getting him into any kind of hot water.

The thing about these old buildings is that they are testaments to late-nineteenth-century construction, filled with enough marble, granite, and stone to withstand any kind of disaster. That kind of construction and building material also makes sound carry. Just ask anyone traversing the halls during a change of class. It sounds like a herd of cattle asked a herd of water buffalo to join them as they stampeded the hallways. In my case, taking a bite out of a taco sounded like I was crushing glass underfoot.

It also made the voices of the two people below me, engaged in a very serious exchange of goods and services, travel up to me with crystal-clear clarity. I quickly swallowed what was in my mouth and gingerly placed the remainder of my midmorning snack on the windowsill behind me.

The exchange was simple and pleasant. For the price of one hundred dollars, student X (a male with a deep voice) gave student Y (a female with a deep voice as well) a midterm for a class that he had taken, which he guaranteed was the same test that a certain professor gave every year, with little to no modification. He identified neither the class nor the professor, which would have made my job much easier. How did he know that the test rarely, if ever, changed? He'd taken the class twice himself, having failed the first time, and had gotten confirmation from his sister, an alumna, who had also taken the class a few years prior. I found that whole scenario a little hard to buy, but I kept listening to see if student Y, the purchaser, would fall for the sales pitch.

She did.

Cheating at St. Thomas carries the hefty punishment of immediate expulsion, if proven. I had all the proof I needed; after all, it was my word against theirs, and I had no reason to concoct a story about two students I probably didn't know. I was all set to scamper down the stairs and confront them when the door at the bottom of the stairs opened and a new group of students, fresh from some sort of intramural sporting event on the front lawn, burst through and flooded the area. I grabbed my taco off the windowsill and hurried down the stairs, trying to figure out who in this new thatch of young adults might be the cheaters, but there were too many of them, moving too fast.

Like a herd of cattle accompanied by a herd of water buffalo. But from my perch on the third step, just above the throng, I could see that I knew one student.

And his name was Mr. Super Senior.

FOUR

LATER THAT DAY, the remains of my taco still tucked away in my bag and emitting a stench that made me think taco day wouldn't be quite as enticing in the future, I texted Meaghan to find out how her paper was coming along. As I threw the sad-looking foil-wrapped taco into my garbage, I waited for her to write back, the vision of Mr. Super Senior still in my head. He was a jock, so maybe he was innocent, simply part of the intramural crowd that I had seen streaming through the front door. Or maybe he was student X, selling a midterm that had been used ad infinitum.

I was just about to call it a day when I spied Crawford coming down the stairs behind the building. Crawford's so used to surprising people, since it's the best way to get them to tell him what he needs to know, that he sometimes uses the same tactic on me. Instead of sending me an e-mail or a text, or God forbid, actually calling me, he chooses instead to do the surprise drop-in as if I'm a perp with a shaky alibi. I heard Dottie, our spectacularly inept department secretary, giving him some sugar in the form of a giggly greeting when he arrived on our floor.

I stood up behind my desk, waving my hands frantically to dispel the stench of spoiled taco. Remember those floor-to-ceiling windows? They don't open, so whatever air is in my office has been there since the school welcomed its first students in 1892.

"Taco day?" he asked, leaning across my desk to give me a kiss.

"Yeah," I said, deciding at that moment not to tell him about Meaghan's boyfriend/psych tutor and his possible connection to a cheating situation. "I didn't get to finish before my next class and carried its remains around, unfortunately, for the rest of the day." I pointed to my garbage can and crinkled my nose. "This may be my last taco day for a while."

"This may be *my* last taco day for a while," he said, "and I don't even eat here." He picked up the garbage can and put it outside my office door. When he came back in, he sat down, settling in for what, I didn't know.

"I was getting ready to go home," I said, pointing to my paper-stuffed messenger bag.

"Change of plans."

I waited. "Good change of plans or bad change of plans?"

"Before you answer, I want you to take a deep breath. You can have no reaction whatsoever."

When he told me what it was, I couldn't help myself. I let out a loud groan and peppered my response with a few four-letter words that brought Sister Perpetua, with whom I shared a wall, barreling into my office.

"Dear!" she said. "We don't use that kind of language at St. Thomas."

I dropped my voice to a whisper. "I'm sorry, Sister." I motioned toward Crawford. "I don't think you've met my husband, Bobby Crawford."

He stood and took her hand, charming the wizened old nun as only he could. "Pleasure to meet you, Sister. Perpetua is one of my favorite saints. She had a fascinating story."

I could have sworn I saw her wrinkled cheeks turn slightly pink. If he kept this up, he would give the old gal a heart attack.

"Have you read any of her diaries?" Sister Perpetua asked, her hands going under the folds of her habit.

I knew he was lying, but she didn't. "A long time ago. I remember reading her prison diaries and being very moved." Okay, maybe he wasn't lying after all. Who knew that Saint Perpetua had been in prison, let alone had diaries to prove it?

Perpetua was rapt, staring up at his handsome Irish face. "You're very well read, Mr. Crawford."

"Please. Call me Bobby," he said, bending slightly so that the little nun didn't get a crick in her neck from the angle at which she was holding her head.

I could have sworn I heard a giggle emanate from deep in her throat. First Dottie, now her. "Bobby it is." She turned to me, still irked by my outburst. "You, dear, need to keep it down. Some of us are trying to work. Oh, and by the way, you also need to open a window. It smells like rotten tacos in here." She scuttled off, but not before giving Crawford a winning, denture-filled smile. When she got back to her office, she slammed her door, I guess to show me who was in charge.

"What do you know about Saint Perpetua's prison diaries?"

"Nothing," he said. "I took a chance. Nine out of ten Catholic saints went to prison, so I figured the odds were in my favor."

"You're a smart one, Crawford." I kicked my door shut. "Sorry for my initial reaction, but before Perpetua interrupted, I could have sworn I heard you say that you wanted me to take a drive with you to Mount Vernon to return the money to Chick." I glared at him. "Didn't you say that you were going to do that first chance you got?"

"You just answered your own question," he said. "This is the first chance I've had."

Sometimes, he can be painfully literal. A little stiff even. I let out a huge breath, and he waved the air in front of his face. I blew into my hand. "Taco breath?"

"Taco breath," he confirmed.

I crossed my arms over my chest and considered his request. It would be an hour out of my life, but he promised me dinner at my favorite riverside restaurant afterward. What was an hour when it had that reward tacked on at the end? I sweetened the deal. "You're driving. I'm leaving my car here, so you have to drive me to work tomorrow." I went over to the filing cabinet where I kept my purse and dressier shoes and grabbed both, taking off my pumps and putting on the high heels. "Plus, you have to walk Trixie tonight and tomorrow morning."

"I'll see you the ride to and from school but will not do the morning walk."

Crawford hates to get up in the morning, and who could blame him? Once he was awake and at work, chances are he would be looking into the cold, dead eyes of the latest murder victim the Bronx had to call its own. I thought about that for a minute. "Okay, I'll take the morning walk, but you have to do the two nighttime walks. Tonight and tomorrow."

He held out his hand. "Deal."

I lowered my voice. "So, you've got ten thousand clams in your pocket?"

"In the glove box."

"Even safer," I said. "You really feel safe with that kind of money in your glove compartment?"

"Not really," he said, holding the door to my office open for me. "I should have put a rancid taco in there to scare everyone off."

I was amazed at just how close Chick Stepkowski lived to St. Thomas; after just a quick car ride, we were in front of his rundown apartment building, even more nervous about seeing him now that we were toting a large sum of money. It was times like this I was glad that Crawford looked exactly like a cop should look: tall, irritable, and Irish. There was no mistaking him for anything else. He carried himself in a way that suggested that he was in charge and nothing would get in the way of him getting to his destination or achieving whatever goal he had set for himself. The street was pretty empty, and I wondered if that was because we looked so out of place we might as well have had "law enforcement" stamped across our foreheads, or if it was just one of those neighborhoods where nobody came out until after dark.

Either way, it was disconcerting.

Crawford gave me a look that suggested he was a little uncomfortable; he took hold of my arm to keep me close. He didn't say anything, but his body language told me he might have regretted his decision to ask me along on this little caper. Leaving me in the car wasn't an option; the neighborhood wasn't the kind where you would want to sit, alone, and wait for your companion to return. Me accompanying him was the only solution.

The front door to the building was broken, so we didn't need to ring Chick to let us in. Come to think of it, we didn't even know if he was home, so we were taking a chance. Crawford, in an uncharacteristic show of forgetfulness, had failed to get Chick's cell phone number from Christine, but he had his address, so our showing up would be a complete surprise to his ex-brother-in-law, which really was the way Crawford wanted it, I thought. I looked at the row of mailboxes in the lobby and saw that Chick lived on the fifth floor. I didn't see an elevator.

"Looks like we're hoofing it," I said, immediately regretting my choice of footwear. I saw Crawford look at my shoes. "Not. One. Word." Crawford has determined that my footwear is always wrong for the occasion, the weather, or the circumstances, and based on this situation alone, he would be correct.

Anxious to get this little chore crossed off the to-do list,

I started up the stairs ahead of him, taking in the smells and sounds emanating from each apartment. Someone was making curry on the second floor; someone else seemed to have a septic problem on the third. By the fourth floor, sweat breaking out on my forehead, I determined that there may have been close to a thousand children living in the building, the sound of crying a growing cacophony the higher we got. We finally reached the fifth floor and looked for Chick's apartment, which turned out to be at the far end of the hallway.

The floor, once a beautiful old mosaic tile pattern, was now cracked and dingy. The sound of my heels echoed off the walls, which were so close together that if I stretched out my arms, I could touch both sides. I heard Crawford huffing and puffing behind me. "We're starting an exercise program," I said, "but not until I have the crème brûlée after dinner tonight."

"Sounds like a plan," he said.

If the second floor was a culinary trip to India, the fifth floor was barbecue heaven. Someone was cooking ribs, and the aroma was making my mouth water. We reached Chick's apartment; the door was nondescript and had nothing to identify him as its occupant. I looked at Crawford. "Want me to knock?" I asked.

"Either that or we can just stand here staring at the peephole together."

"You're a regular Jackie Mason tonight," I said, tapping lightly on the door.

"That's how you knock?" he asked. He lifted his hand and banged on the door.

No answer.

"Chick!" he called, banging again.

"He's obviously not home," I said, anxious to get out of Mount Vernon and this septic-scented, barbecue-flavored apartment building. My stomach was now protesting with a vengeance. Not finishing that taco had been a huge miscalculation on my part.

I started to walk away, but Crawford leaned in and put his ear to the door. "What are you doing?" I asked.

"Shhh," he said, holding up a hand to silence me. "Chick?" He banged again. "Chick!"

I started back toward the apartment. "What's the matter?" I asked, taking in his worried demeanor.

"He's in there." He turned to me and looked around frantically. "Go get the super," he said.

So here's the thing about me: I was raised the only child of very doting parents who grew up in a lovely one-family home in a quaint little town set up on a hill high above the Hudson River. I knew what a super was in theory—I had watched my fair share of *One Day at a Time*, after all—but I didn't know the first thing about finding one. I stared blankly back at Crawford. "Super?"

He spied a fire extinguisher half hanging off the wall about two feet behind me and grabbed it. "Yes, the super," he said. "First floor. Knock on doors until you find someone who knows how to find him."

I watched as he hoisted the fire extinguisher above his head and brought it down on the doorknob, hoping to disengage the lock. His first attempt at gaining entry was unsuccessful. He looked at me still standing there and said, "Go!"

I started down the stairs, listening as Crawford bashed the door again and again. When I got to the third floor, though, I heard him break through, so I started back up the stairs. By this time, the hall was flooded with the people who lived behind the other doors, and I pushed my way through until I reached the last apartment on the left.

There was a lot of blood; I remember that. I don't remember much else because as soon as I saw Chick Stepkowski, still sitting at his desk, blood pouring from a wound in his head, the room spun out of control in front of me and I ended up on the floor, wondering how I got there and if the screaming in my head would ever stop.

FIVE

CRAWFORD HAD THE unenviable task of breaking the news to Christine; she, in turn, would let the girls know. While I wanted to be with him to lend some moral support, I had to beg off, letting him know that after the experience of finding Chick like that, I was just about done for the day, if not the week. I had a full-fledged migraine, the likes of which I had never experienced, from my fainting/falling incident in the apartment.

I lay in bed with the curtains drawn and a cold rag on my head, the image of an almost-dead Chick seared in my brain. There was a suicide note, but according to Crawford it was practically unreadable. Not that I spent a lot of time trying to decipher why this eccentric man had taken his own life; that was for his sister and their brothers to try to come to terms with. The story itself was so strange that nothing about it surprised me anymore—his disappearance, his reappearance, the money. It was all outside the realm of what I considered normal behavior, but then again, I was an only child, and the majority of my extended family was hundreds of miles away in Canada making cheese and dealing with their own share of familial eccentricities, the likes of which I would never know beyond Aunt Isabelle's propensity for wearing men's overalls with high heels. We shared the annual Christmas card and the occasional e-mail and that was about it, so what did I know? Any day now, I could be getting a visit from a long-lost cousin who had decided to reconnect with family, only to find out that said cousin was a complete nut job along the lines of Chick Stepkowski.

Chick was still alive when Crawford broke down the door, sitting at his desk, having just finished a letter in which he explained what had gone through his mind when he decided to take this drastic step. I didn't see the letter, but Crawford made out a few of the words that weren't obliterated by the vomit that Chick had brought forth after taking enough prescription painkillers to keep ten good-sized men out of pain for a long, long time. The wound on his head had come from when he passed out, hitting the corner of the desk with great force. At least that's what everyone thought. Throwing up once wasn't enough to save him. By the time the ambulance arrived, he was dead, despite Crawford's best efforts at keeping him alive.

When I had finally gotten my wits about me, I found Crawford sitting on the twin bed pushed against one wall in the apartment, his head down, his arms dangling between his legs, his breath coming out in short chuffs, still exhausted from giving Chick CPR and mouth-to-mouth. He wiped a hand shakily across his mouth and looked at me; he looked sadder than I'd ever seen him look. Sure, homicide and death are a daily part of his life, but to see someone he had once known seconds before his death had unnerved him. The fact that he hadn't been able to do anything to save Chick was even more devastating, something that I had learned while sitting next to him on that dirty bed in that squalid apartment in Mount Vernon.

Crawford wandered in close to midnight, and even in the dark of our bedroom, I could see from the way he was moving that he was sad, defeated, and exhausted. His shoulders slumped as he took off his jacket, then his tie, and finally his shirt, kicking his shoes into his closet and putting the contents of his pockets on his dresser. He had the same routine when he came home every day, but tonight, I could tell by his shadowy movements that the events of the afternoon and evening had taken their toll on him. I called to him to let him know that I was awake.

"How is your headache?" he asked.

"Better," I said and reached out for him in the dark. He took his pants off and slid in next to me, letting me wrap him in my arms, the two of us lying there for a long time listening to Trixie, in her usual spot next to the bed, breathe.

"Jesus," he finally said.

"Yes?" I replied.

He sighed, not really in the mood for humor. "Sorry about this."

"About what?"

"Inheriting my crazy family is one thing, but getting the family of my ex-wife, an even crazier bunch, is not something you should have to deal with."

I couldn't disagree, but for the sake of marital harmony, I protested ever so slightly. "No. It's fine. She's the mother of your children."

"Still…"

I pulled him tighter. "None of us could have anticipated this turn of events, Crawford. We'll deal with it, and then we'll go back to the way things were."

"How were they?"

"Boring. Lacking dead bodies."

"I hope you're right," he said, just before drifting off to sleep.

In the morning, after I showered and dressed, I went outside to pick up the papers that we had delivered, looking through them as I brewed a big pot of coffee. Both of us had to work today, in spite of the previous day's events, and neither of us had slept very well. As was often the case after I had a migraine, my head felt hollow and my stomach a little queasy; I mentally took stock of what my day might bring in terms of stress and determined it should shape up to be pretty calm. I would beg off office hours after my last class, a two o'clock Senior Seminar, and book it back home to spend some time on the couch with Trixie and a book that I had started over the summer and never finished. If any day called for playing the couch potato, today was it.

Crawford looked worse than I felt, but he was up, showered, and dressed at the normal time, taking his gun out of the kitchen cabinet where he stowed it and affixing it to his belt before heading to the precinct. "How fast for coffee?" he asked.

"About three minutes," I said. "You okay to go to work?"

"Don't have a choice," he said, turning his phone on and looking at the screen. "Message," he said, dialing into his voice mail. He looked at me while he listened, an expression crossing his face that told me he didn't really understand what was being said. He hit a button and played the message again.

I took an insulated coffee cup from the drain board beside the sink and made him some coffee to go. He snapped his phone shut.

"Remember when you said that we would deal with this and then go back to the way things were?" he asked.

I nodded, the smell of the coffee all of a sudden becoming unpleasant.

"You were wrong." He put his phone back in his pocket. "Mount Vernon PD found two hundred and fifty thousand dollars in Chick's mattress."

SIX

JAROSLAV "CHICK" STEPKOWSKI was buried from the chapel at St. Thomas. Raised Catholic but not really a churchgoer, Chick was without a place to call his own spiritually. That's when having a best friend who is a former priest comes in handy; one call to my dear friend Kevin McManus and not only did we have a church, we had a priest to officiate, as well as a few altar servers who made sure the church was prepared for the funeral. Other celebrants might have had a problem with suicide, but Kevin and the guy he pressed into service did not. Nor did Kevin or his friend care that Chick hadn't been inside a church since his confirmation thirty years previous. Father Bracca, who was a friend of Kevin's from the seminary and now sat on the board of a private Catholic high school in Manhattan, had taken the time to drive north to the Bronx to give Chick the send-off the tortured man deserved and provide the family some solace during a difficult time.

The president of the college, Mark Etheridge, an old nemesis of mine who was now something just shy of a friend, had given us permission to have Chick's funeral on a weekend when students wouldn't be in the building. In recognition of my service to the school, he also sprang for a vast array of gorgeous flower arrangements and the use the organist from his own church, who blew the doors off with her rendition of "Precious Lord, Take Me Home." There wasn't a dry eye in the place, except maybe for Crawford, who looked like he was having an out-of-body experience, an expression he had been wearing since we had discovered Chick.

It had been a tough week, to say the least. I had gone to school, but Meaghan and Erin had taken the week off to spend with their distraught mother, surrounded by Stepkowskis, who in the light of day didn't seem as raucous or unruly as they had at my house. Another brother, Gabriel, flew in from Savannah, his home for the past twenty years, with his wife and two grown sons, all of them staying close to Christine so that they could mourn together.

We stood in the rotunda outside of the chapel watching as the funeral director brought the casket down and put it into the hearse. His assistant, a guy who had ex-cop written all over him, instructed us to follow in our cars to the cemetery, ten miles or so north of school. I turned to look for Crawford and spied him off to the side with another cop-looking guy, deep in conversation. I caught his eye and gave him the high sign that we needed to leave. As he separated from the man and the conversation, I overheard him say, "Keep me posted."

I wouldn't expect anyone to understand why I had a friend in the Westchester medical examiner's office, but I did. His name was John "Mac" McVeigh, and he was an old-school gentleman, someone who felt very comfortable at funerals and who always knew the right thing to say. I saw him in the throng of people walking down the rotunda stairs and ran to catch up with him, leaving Crawford to follow behind me. We were between the second and first floors when I grabbed his arm.

"Mac!" I linked my arm in his.

"Good to see you, Alison," he said, quickly amending, "but not under these circumstances, of course."

We got to the first floor of the building, and I lowered my voice so that the other mourners couldn't hear us. "What are you doing here?"

"Mr. Stepkowski was one of mine," he said, and by that, I knew that he had performed the autopsy. "When I read the obituary in the paper and saw that he was the uncle to Meaghan and Erin Crawford, I did a little digging until I found out the connection." He laid a hand over mine. "I'm so, so sorry."

"Thank you, Mac."

"We took exceptionally good care of him," he said, but he didn't need to. Mac took exceptionally good care of everyone who came through the morgue; I was sure of that.

Christine drifted by, and I watched as Crawford put his arm around her slim shoulders. She was shattered, and I didn't know if she would be able to put the pieces back together, knowing that prior to his death, she carried a heavy burden where her brother was concerned.

"Suicide?" I asked, still not convinced.

Mac nodded sadly, his blue eyes kind.

"Well, thank you for coming, Mac." I leaned in and gave him a kiss. "We need to have that lunch we keep talking about."

"You know where to find me," he said and walked off, his head bowed.

I found Crawford outside of the building on the front driveway, helping Christine into the limousine. Tim was idling in his minivan behind the limo that would take Christine and the girls to the cemetery. Crawford and I walked to his car and fell into line behind the hearse.

"Was that Mac?" he asked.

"Yes," I said. "Who were you talking to?"

"Lead detective on the case. Name's Minor."

"He have anything to say?"

"Nothing that I haven't heard already," he said, his eyes on the road leading off the campus.

It took a few seconds for it to dawn on me. "Why is there a lead detective? Why is there a case?"

Crawford angled the car onto a narrow side street, getting out of the funeral queue. He knew where he was going, obviously, and didn't need or want to be in a line of slow-moving cars. "It's about the money."

"Seriously?" I asked.

"It's always about the money," he said, something I didn't understand. "The fact that there is so much of it and that it was hidden? That's a problem."

I guessed that made sense, but what if Chick was just a strange guy who liked to carry his money around with him? He wouldn't be the first person to have done that. My uncle Guillaume, according to my late mother, had once hid four thousand dollars in American quarters in a barn way out in eastern Quebec. Yes, Uncle Guillaume now resided in an assisted-living facility for people who couldn't take care of themselves from day to day, but maybe he was on to something. Maybe the American quarter would become extinct, going the way of the Susan B. Anthony dollar and other arcane bits of currency that we all remembered but none of us had. Maybe, once he died, I would inherit a huge fortune, all in quarters.

"I can see your wheels turning over there," Crawford said.

I was staring out the window. "Who, me? No, no wheels turning here," I said, but I was lying. I wondered if those four thousand American quarters had been found and if so, if there was more where that came from. My mother wasn't around, so I couldn't ask her, and Uncle Guillaume thought that it was 1967 and that he was still harboring one of my cousins from the States who was avoiding the draft. Mr. McLaughlin, Uncle Guillaume's next-door neighbor, didn't appreciate being called a draft dodger every day, but to my uncle, Mr. McLaughlin looked no different than my cousin Tommy from Traverse City, Michigan, and that was presenting real problems for my cousin Jeannette, Uncle Guillaume's daughter.

We pulled into the cemetery and lined our cars up one in back of another, all of the doors opening almost simultaneously as we emerged to stand by the gravesite. We gathered in a semi-circle around the casket and the open grave into which it would be placed, which was covered with a white blanket. Tim had his arm around Christine; thankfully, none of their children were with them today, and Tim could attend to his wife without having to enlist the help of my ever-gracious husband, whom I needed at the moment. The remaining Stepkowski brothers, cut from the same stocky genetic mold, stood shoulder to shoulder while the priest recited some prayers, commending Chick to the gates of heaven. Behind them, at a safe but watchful distance, was the cop I had seen at the funeral, along with some of his compadres, who had appeared out of nowhere to witness the burial.

It was strange; I had to admit, even with the precedent of Uncle Guillaume and his hoarding of quarters. First the ten grand and now a quarter mil in a mattress in a fleabag apartment in a bad part of Mount Vernon. What had Chick been up to for ten years? The years before that? Christine's recollections were sketchy, and I couldn't tell if that was on purpose or not. Selective memory? She was definitely the odd man out in that clan and had created a lovely life for herself, first with Crawford and then with the somber and silent Tim. Did she avoid thinking about the upbringing she had endured in the midst of a brood of ruffians? Or did she really not know?

I had no leg to stand on. I had endured a long marriage with my eyes closed, figuratively, thinking that my husband's lack of interest in me was due to our busy schedules and our pursuit of academic standing at St. Thomas. What I knew deep in my heart, but refused to acknowledge for the longest time, was that I had married a scoundrel, a cheating one at that. If Christine was indeed deluding herself into thinking that Chick had gone underground for a ten-year spa retreat only to reappear for precisely no good reason whatsoever, who was I to judge or deny her that little fantasy?

The prayers concluded, and we started to go our separate ways. Christine caught up to us. "Would you join us for lunch?" she asked, her eyes beseeching us. We were about to decline when she played her trump card. "I know the girls would love it if you came."

I looked at Crawford; this wasn't my decision to make. I could almost see his mind working; he wanted out of here and fast, and he was trying to figure out a way to say no. Apparently, Christine figured out what he was thinking, too, having been married to him long enough to know what the look on his face meant at any given time. She waved the suggestion off. "Forget it. Another time. I'll get the girls back to school," she said, and although I wanted to detect a hint of passive-aggressiveness so I could do something to make her less than perfect in my mind, there was nothing there, just a sensitivity to the fact that we would want to get out of there as quickly as we could.

I held my breath, hoping that Crawford wouldn't capitulate, and he didn't disappoint. "Thanks for understanding, Christine. It's been a long week," he said.

She stood on her tiptoes and kissed his cheek, then turned to me and hugged me tightly. "Thank you for coming," she said.

Crawford and I walked back to the car, and I wondered if this would be the last time we would have to endure the company of the Stepkowskis. I thought of asking Crawford but then thought better of it. I looked out the window as we drove through the rolling hills of the cemetery, spotting a lone woman sitting on a hill beside a soaring stone statue of an archangel, her face obscured by a large black hat, her long blond hair cascading down her back, hair that you would see on a Barbie doll or a woman who was in a certain kind of "show biz," for lack of a better term. She was tall and voluptuous, her curves not hidden by her black pants and gray shirt. She was leaning nonchalantly at the foot of the angel, Michael the archangel, if I had to guess, studying alternately her manicure and something in the distance. I turned my head to see what she was looking at, but it wasn't necessary.

The only thing in the distance was Chick Stepkowski's casket, all alone, waiting to be put in the ground.

SEVEN

I DROVE WITH Meaghan back to school on the Monday after the funeral, as she'd stayed with us on Sunday night. She was a bit more circumspect in her reaction to Chick's death than her sister, whose only question to us as we put her cranky little ass back into her minivan was "Now do we get to keep the money?"

Crawford had slammed the door shut, but not before asking her which charity she'd like to donate it to, just to mess with her head. She had driven off in a purple rage, muttering undoubtedly about all the things she could do with five grand, starting with declaring her independence from the parental units in her life.

Crawford went back to work, investigating the untimely deaths of people he didn't know, which was just the way he liked it. I returned to my slate of teaching, including the creative writing class, determining who had talent and who didn't; I wasn't expecting anything in the way of surprises, and that's just the way I liked it.

I grabbed my messenger bag and made my way up to the fourth floor of my building, where I was met by Sister Mary and the woman she had brought by my office over a week earlier and about whom I had promptly forgotten. They were waiting by the door of the classroom, expectant looks on both their faces.

Mary was all piss and vinegar, just like always; the smell of her Jean Naté was particularly pungent today. "Alison, thank you for joining us," she said, insinuating that I was late. I wasn't. "This is Ms. Bannerman—"

The woman interjected, "Please. Call me Mary Lou."

Mary didn't seem to mind her interruption; God forbid I should jump in with any germane information, though. Her head might explode. "Mary Lou is the new student I told you about who would like to audit your creative writing class."

"Audit?" I asked. That was the first I heard of that. It meant Mary Lou was using the creative writing course at St. Thomas as her own writing workshop. If she wanted to workshop her stuff with a bunch of kids, there was no one stopping her, but I wondered why a nattily turned-out woman who was closer to my age than that of the other students would choose our little university rather than a Gotham Writers' Workshop class or even an online critique group.

She anticipated my question or saw the puzzled look on my face, because she had an answer for all of that. "My kids are in college, so I have a lot of free time on my hands, and my mother was a 'Tommy.'" She smiled at some memory that she didn't share. "I have a lot of fond memories of St. Thomas. The annual Visit with Santa in Memorial Hall, the Easter egg hunt on East Lawn…I love it here."

This woman really knew her St. Thomas fun facts.

"And I'm writing a novel," she proclaimed with so much joy it made my heart hurt.

"Great!" I returned in kind, noting that Mary was looking at me like if I made one false move—or didn't respond in the way she thought was appropriate given the situation—she would devour me whole. "I'm thrilled that you're in my class," I said, channeling my inner Lee Strasberg. I motioned toward the classroom. "Please. Join us."

Mary seemed satisfied by this incredible acting display

and stomped off in her old-lady nun shoes, giving one backward glance that was both intimidating and hilarious at the same time. I stifled a giggle as I followed Mary Lou Bannerman, the next great American novelist, into the classroom. She took a seat right in the front row, just as I knew she would, and turned around to smile at the rest of the students, who wouldn't have noticed if Chewbacca had entered, let alone a middle-aged dilettante who was the daughter of an alumna.

"Good morning, class," I said. "This is Mrs. Bannerman—"

"Mary Lou," she interjected.

"Mary Lou," I said, "and she will be joining us for the semester. Let's all give a warm welcome to Mary Lou."

There was a mixture of "good morning, Mrs. Mary Lou," and a bunch of other interesting non sequiturs, but that was as good as it was going to get. I got down to business.

Mary Lou was an apt pupil, just as I knew she would be; the older students usually are. I talked about our plan to generate a short story by the end of the following week, highlighting some of my favorites to give them guidance as they thought about their own. I asked a few students what they thought they would write about and got some interesting answers.

Mary Lou raised her hand. "So we *will* be doing novels at some point, right?" she asked.

"Well, we'll start with short stories," I said, "but if you find you have something there that can be turned into a longer work, feel free to keep going with your plot and characters."

She jotted some notes down in a Vera Bradley notebook; her pen was a very expensive and very large Montblanc. She looked up at me expectantly.

"Would you like to share what you'll be writing about?" I asked.

She nodded and turned toward the class. "I'll be writing about my husband's murder."

EIGHT

I SEEMED TO be the only person in the classroom who had any kind of reaction to Mary Lou's topic, but I tried to remain impassive, muttering a noncommittal "ohhhh" in response to her statement. When I got back to my office, though, I threw every permutation of "Bannerman" and "murder" into Google and tried to find out who her husband was and how and why he had been murdered. I came up empty, which was even more of a surprise to me than the fact that she had lost her husband violently.

All kinds of possibilities existed for why her name didn't lead to anything on Google. She had remarried. She had moved here from somewhere else. She was in the Witness Protection Program. Did I really care, though? That was the question. I guessed the details behind the event would be revealed through her novel and my curiosity would be satisfied eventually. Until then, better to keep my nose to the grindstone, keep Meaghan out of trouble, and try to reestablish equilibrium in my own life after the events surrounding Chick's reappearance and death.

In response to Erin's parting question to us— "Now do we get to keep the money?"—the answer was that we still weren't sure. Crawford thought about putting it into each of their college accounts, while Christine thought we should just keep it handy in case of some unknown development, like someone else claimed it or it was impounded by some probate judge, neither of which seemed likely to us, but hey, I'm just the second wife. Nobody really listens to my opinion. Except when they do. We were all still a little uneasy about accepting the money, given that we weren't sure of its origins. Why would someone who had so much money— two hundred and fifty thousand dollars in the apartment alone—live in such dire conditions when he could obviously better his situation? It just didn't make any sense.

I could tell that Crawford was torn up about it. Since we had missed the opportunity to have dinner at my favorite restaurant the night that Chick died, we'd decided to do it tonight. We were seated at a table by the window, the Hudson just a few feet away. I had a perfectly prepared martini and he was drinking a beer while we waited for a plate of oysters. "Did you talk to the detective who was at the funeral?" I asked. "That Minor guy?"

"That's the first thing I did this morning."

"And?"

"He said to keep it."

I looked out the window. "So there's your answer."

"It just doesn't feel right."

"I know what you mean," I said, "but there are worse things in the world than being told you have to keep ten grand." I pulled a thick chunk of bread from the basket on the table and tore into it. "What happens to the two hundred and fifty thousand?"

"It goes to someone called a public administrator who will evaluate any claims on the money."

"Who might claim it?"

He shrugged. "Don't know, but I suspect once word gets out, a few people will materialize."

"Like the brothers?"

"Maybe."

"Christine?"

"Doubtful." He looked in the breadbasket and saw that I had made short work of its contents; I handed him half of what was left on my plate. "Can we talk about something else?" he asked. "And don't ask me about work."

"So ask me about mine," I said, polishing off my drink. "How's work?"

"The usual. Sister Mary hates me, the kids are bored already," I started. "Oh, but I've got this lovely middle-aged lady in my creative writing class."

"That's great. Now you have someone your own age around to play with."

I cocked my head to the side and gave him a look. "You think I'm middle-aged?"

"What would you call yourself?"

"An adult. With a bangin' bod."

"Who's middle-aged," he added. "Do the math. If you live until you're—"

I put up my hand. "Stop right there. Let's leave it at this: She's a little bit older than I am." I looked out the window again and muttered, "*You're* middle-aged, but I am—"

"Middle-aged," he repeated.

A drink magically appeared in front of me. "Do you ever want to sleep with me again?"

He raised an eyebrow questioningly. To him, that was a rhetorical question, but I meant business.

"Then stop referring to me as middle-aged."

Our oysters came and we dug in, him dousing his with way too much hot sauce, and me making mine just the way I liked them with a lot of lemon and a little horseradish. We finished them up in record time, and he leaned back and rubbed his stomach.

"So," he said. "Who's the lady, and why is she taking your creative writing class?"

"She wants to write a novel."

He sucked in some air; he knew how much I hated working with budding novelists. The buds usually never flowered into anything resembling a beautiful novel, let alone a decent grade. "I'm sorry."

"I'm trying to have a new attitude about it. Maybe she's the second coming of Virginia Woolf."

"I hope she is, for your sake." He signaled the server for another beer. "Any idea what the novel is going to be about?"

"Her husband's murder," I said and watched as he had the same reaction I'd had. "Funny thing is that I did a Web search on her name to see what came up, but there's nothing. Zilch. Nada." I eyed the bread on his plate. "You going to eat that?"

He responded by sticking the whole thing in his mouth. "Maybe she has a different name than her husband did?" I wondered aloud.

"Maybe," he said. "Did she say what happened?"

I shook my head. "Nope, and I didn't ask."

"But you're curious."

"Of course I'm curious," I said. "Have we met?"

He held out his hand. "I don't think we have." We shook. "My name is Bobby Crawford, and I'm a middle-aged stiff."

"Alison Bergeron. Adult with a bangin' bod."

He leaned over the table and gave me a very uncharacteristic public kiss. "Are you easy?"

"The easiest."

"Then I think we'll get along just fine."

NINE

With everything that had gone on, I had almost forgotten my concerns about Mr. Super Senior and his relationship to Meaghan and a possible cheating scandal, or Meaghan's close-to-failing grade in Forensic Psychology. Or maybe I was just employing selective memory, trying to forget that this situation hung over my little world like a black cloud. I hadn't thought of it much until the Forensic Psych professor, Joanne Larkin, showed up in my office a few days later, a smile on her normally pinched and pained-looking face.

She poked her head in as if she were a flamingo taking a drink. "Alison?"

I stood. "Hi, Joanne." I gestured toward one of the chairs across from my desk. "Please come in."

"Don't mind if I do," she said. She plopped down in the chair, crossing her legs. It looked as if she would be staying a while. "I just had to stop by and tell you how well Meaghan is doing in my class. I'm thrilled with her turn-around."

"Meaghan Crawford?" I asked. There had to be some mistake. The Meaghan she'd described a few weeks earlier was in danger of flunking the class, despite it being early in the semester, and the girl I had spoken to about this dire situation didn't seem terribly concerned. To think that she had been able to execute some kind of miraculous 180, given the fact that she had missed almost a week of school after her uncle's death, was a stretch. "Really?"

Joanne nodded vigorously, making the helmet of hair she

usually sported move just the tiniest bit. "It's truly amazing. She got a perfect score on her midterm."

My stomach did a little flip. "She did?"

Joanne peered at me from behind the most unflattering glasses I had ever seen on a person; big and round with the outdated half-moon bifocal at the bottom of each, the top half making her eyes look the size of an owl's. "You don't seem happy, Alison."

"I don't?" I asked, wondering where she had gotten a sweater with three-dimensional jack-o'-lanterns sewn on it. That had clearly taken some investigation. It made the workmanship on the cat sweaters look like child's play. "I am. Happy, that is. I'm thrilled. Her father and I will do a celebratory dance of joy tonight."

She pursed her lips together in a way that suggested disapproval. "Alison, you know, I think more people would like you if you dropped the sarcasm every once in a while."

"People don't like me?"

She stood. "The sarcasm. Drop it."

Ouch. I stood as well. I tried to put on my most sincere, least sarcastic voice. "Thank you for coming by, Joanne. I appreciate your letting me know earlier about Meaghan's failure to perform in your class, and now I thank you for taking the time to let me know that she's doing better."

She regarded me coolly. "Go back to the sarcasm. The sincere thing isn't working for you either."

"I'll be honest with you, Joanne: Without the sarcasm, I'm an empty husk." I smiled sincerely. "I don't really have a personality to speak of."

This didn't impress her. "Interesting," she said.

I decided that in addition to some children, I didn't like psychology professors very much.

She left in a huff, clearly not satisfied with my strange reaction to her news. Had Meaghan studied really hard to get a good grade, or had Mr. Super Senior—her *tutor*—

provided her with a test from years gone by to help her boost her score?

I sat down and took a deep breath. First, I didn't even know if Mr. Super Senior was involved in the cheating caper, and second, I didn't know if Joanne was the professor who was too lazy to vary her tests from year to year. One thing I knew for sure, and that was that Meaghan wasn't one of the students I had overheard. I talked myself down, something I'm getting better and better at the more time I spend on the proverbial ledge.

Still, I needed some confirmation. I don't know why I called Max; she's notoriously contrary. "Hi," I said after she picked up and let it be known that she was doing several things at once, "quick question."

"Shoot."

I thought of a way to phrase the question so that I could get an honest answer from my sometimes obtuse friend. "Does the fact that I use sarcasm ever make it difficult to like me?"

"Yes," she said without hesitation.

The alacrity with which she answered took my breath away. "Seriously?"

"Yes," she said. "Sometimes all we want is an honest conversation instead of one filled with your ironic asides and sarcastic nonsense. It's annoying. We hate it," she said, speaking for the masses, it would seem.

That was pretty much to the point.

"You'd be doing yourself, and all of us, a favor by not trying to be so funny all the time," she said. She was, as she liked to say, as serious as a heart attack.

I was stunned into silence.

"Kidding!" she hollered into the phone. "Got you!" Her guffaw was as annoying as the sound of a buzz saw at six o'clock in the morning. "Had you going, didn't I?"

"That wasn't very nice," I said, my voice husky with the weight of uncried tears.

"Oh, lighten up," she said. "What's this all about?"

"One of my colleagues told me that nobody likes me because I'm too sarcastic."

"Well, that may be true, but don't change. You work with a bunch of cadavers who wouldn't know sarcasm if it bit them on their dead, numb zombie asses."

"Thanks, I guess."

"Who is this person, anyway?"

"Meaghan's Forensic Psych professor."

"Oh. Well, maybe you should tone it down a bit until Meaghan gets out of the class."

"Thanks, Max."

She put something in her mouth and then attempted to talk. I couldn't really understand the specifics of her next question but knew that it had to do with Chick's money.

"It's with the public administrator. From what I understand, that person decides who gets the money."

When it came to business—or money—she was as sharp as a tack. "Did he have a will?"

I didn't know.

"That would clear up a lot. Anyway, why did he keep that much scratch in his apartment?"

"Not a clue."

"What did you do with the girls' ten g's?"

"Crawford put it in a safe deposit box at the bank, just in case it turns out it's not ours after all." I tapped my mouse and saw that in the space of a half hour, I had twenty new e-mail messages. "I've got to go, Max."

"Hey, I didn't mean to mess with you," she said.

"Yes, you did, but it's okay. Thanks for reminding me that I work with a bunch of zombies."

"*De nada.*" She paused. "That means 'I've got your back.'"

No, it doesn't, but I didn't tell her that. Before we hung up, she jumped in with one more little detail.

"I forgot!" she said. "My parents are having a little get-together at their house on Sunday afternoon."

I didn't know if that qualified as an invitation, so I waited.

"For my birthday?" she said, as if I were supposed to know. "You have a birthday coming up?" I asked, just to get a rise out of her.

She didn't take the bait. "Two o'clock. Early-bird special. There will be cake."

"Well, as long as there's cake, I'm in," I said. "Anything in particular that you want?"

"Just your smiling face next to me as I blow out the candles." We hung up, and I turned my attention to my e-mail. Just to let her know that I was still paying attention, despite the fact that her mother was back in town, I shot Meaghan a message. It was short and sweet: "Good job on your Forensic Psych mid-term!" Hopefully, by the next time I saw her, I would have more information on this situation and be able to discuss it with her. For now, creative writing students awaited, and I was in danger of being late.

I raced up the stairs, and I found Mary Lou Bannerman waiting for me outside of the classroom; all of the other students were in their seats, all of them looking at some kind of handheld device and busily working their thumbs into a frenzy. If only we could harness that kind of energy for good. Mary Lou smiled at me as I approached. She was in a pair of expensive-looking jeans, soft leather driving moccasins, and a cashmere turtleneck. She dressed like I would if I had money. Or any fashion sense whatsoever.

"Hi," she said. "I wanted to catch you before we went into class."

I shifted my heavy messenger bag from one shoulder to the other. "Everything okay?"

"Everything's great!" she said. "I'm really enjoying your class."

"Good. We love having you," I said, and it was true. The kids seemed to have grown to like her in the few days she had been in class; she was familiar enough, like someone's mom, yet she was one of them, having a tough time with plot and structure just like they were. I was proud of my mixed class of sophomores and juniors and happy that they had brought her into their postadolescent fold.

"Thank you for saying that," she said, seemingly touched. "Listen, can I buy you lunch? After class today?"

"It would have to be in the cafeteria downstairs because I only have fifty minutes. Would that be okay?"

Her face lit up. "That would be perfect."

We went into class, and I started my lesson. I thought about Mary Lou inviting me to lunch; in all my years of teaching, a student had never done that.

Maybe Crawford was right. Maybe I would enjoy having another middle-aged person to pal around with; I had worn out my welcome with my colleagues, obviously. Maybe I'd get really lucky and Mary Lou would be the kind of woman who appreciated some good sarcasm.

I didn't have high hopes.

TEN

MARCUS WAS SURPRISED to see me on a non-taco day accompanied by someone he had never seen before. I introduced Mary Lou to Marcus, the head chef, and I have to say, she was quite impressed that I had such an in at the cafeteria. I noticed a new guy behind the grill, tall and handsome, filling out his chef's coat in a way that suggested that there was a nice body beneath it.

In all my years teaching here, I had never seen anyone new. I asked Marcus, "Who's the new guy?"

He called over the counter to the grill. "Briggs! Say hi to one of our most valued customers!"

The guy, a strapping blond who looked like he had just gotten off the boat from somewhere in Scandinavia, put a finger to his chef's hat and gave me a little salute. "Ma'am."

The grill was fired up and making a bit of noise. I leaned over toward Marcus. "Please tell him to drop the 'ma'am' stuff. I hate that. 'Alison' will suffice."

Marcus grimaced. "You know we can't do that." Our president was very formal and insisted that college staff refer to each other by their titles and nothing else. "How about 'Professor'?" he asked, knowing I was really a "doctor" of letters.

"I guess," I said, hating that the cafeteria staff were made to address professors by their titles rather than their given names. Marcus usually didn't call me anything, except what I ordered. One day I was "Hey! Ham on Rye!" and the next I was "Chicken Parm!" It worked for us.

I looked at Briggs and thought that with his steady job, good looks, and ability to cook, he'd be perfect for my step-daughter Meaghan, who seemed to have been born with seriously bad taste in men.

"So, do we order?" Mary Lou asked, interrupting my daydreams about having a line cook as my son-in-law. She was obviously unaccustomed to moving down a food line with a tray. I wondered where this woman had gone to high school; hasn't everyone experienced a meal or three hundred in a cafeteria over their lifetime?

"I prefer to let Marcus surprise me," I said, hustling past an old, stooped nun whom I recognized as Sister Frances from the Nursing Department, frantically counting the number of croutons on her plate. Nuns take a vow of poverty when they enter the order, and believe me, teaching at St. Thomas does nothing to relieve the financial burdens that they face. Salad was weighed and charged by the ounce, so the more croutons Sister Frances took, the heavier—and more expensive—her lunch would become.

"Don't worry, Sister," Marcus called from behind the grill. "It's buy twelve, get twenty free on the croutons today." Marcus had been here long enough to know that the sisters were famous for their frugality, and it was not often that they ate in the cafeteria, all of their meals generally being served in the adjacent convent.

"Thank you, Marcus," Sister Frances said. "We were having Salisbury steak in the sisters' dining room today, and I just can't abide that many onions in one meal. Not to mention that lunch is nearly over by the time I can get back to the dining room from my last morning class." She harrumphed a bit more while heaping some more croutons on her plate, adding some ham, and dispensing herself a hefty diet cola from the soda machine. The cup was almost as big as she was.

I was so busy watching Marcus flip our burgers on the

grill that I didn't notice that Mary Lou had wandered down toward the end of the line. When I realized she was gone, I looked around, spying her talking to the cashier, Maria; she slipped her several bills, all of which Maria quickly stashed in the register.

Marcus handed me two plates, each with a cheeseburger and fries, and I waited for Mary Lou to return before moving down the line. Sister Frances was in front of us and exclaimed in delight when Maria told her someone had picked up the check for her lunch. Maria professed not to know who it was or where she had gone but mentioned that the lady had said "bon appétit" after she had paid. I turned and looked at Mary Lou.

"Shhhh," she said as we moved down the line.

Sister Frances scurried off, a big smile on her face, her croutons dancing merrily atop her healthy salad.

Mary Lou and I took a seat at a table by the window, one that had a full view of the Hudson in all its resplendent beauty. "That was awfully nice of you," I said, plucking a fry from the stack on my plate and dipping it into some ketchup. "You made Sister Frances's day."

Mary Lou cut her burger into several smaller pieces, removed the top half of the bun, and salted the whole thing. "How can they serve lunch if she can't even make it in time, poor thing?"

"You'd be surprised what goes on around here," I said. "I have a lot of respect for the nuns. Many of them went into the convent as teenagers and have been here ever since." I took a big bite of burger. "I agree, you'd think that the least they could do is keep a plate warm for the old gal." I pointed toward Mary Lou's burger. "Good?"

"Wonderful," she said, taking a dainty bite. "I'm trying to take some weight off, so I'm cutting down on carbs."

"You? You're a rail."

"Thank you," she said, blushing slightly. "I haven't always been. It's such a struggle to keep it off."

It was hard to imagine this sylph of a woman any heavier; she had a fabulous figure and wore clothes like a fashion model. I looked at my burger and decided that eating half was plenty. I pushed my plate away, but not before grabbing a last handful of fries. "So, you're enjoying the class?" I had never gotten the sense that many people enjoyed my classes, or maybe that was just my paranoia presenting itself. I wanted confirmation from Mary Lou that indeed, what she was getting from the class was what she expected.

She took a sip of soda and looked out the window before answering. I didn't take that as a good sign, but she was more enthusiastic once she started talking. "At first, it was hard, what with being with a bunch of young people, but now, I'm loving it."

"Your writing is quite good," I said. I had read the beginning of one of her short stories the night before, and although it was rough, it was headed in the right direction.

"You think so?" she asked, a smile spreading on her face.

I nodded. "I do. It could do with a couple of minor tweaks, but it's definitely a good start." I couldn't resist the burger sitting on my plate, so I pulled it back in front of me, my waistline be damned. "Have you started your novel yet?" The class wouldn't be starting the outline process on a longer work for several weeks, which I'd let her know on her first day. "Because if you have some ideas, you can start sketching them out. I don't think that will take away from what you're doing with the short stories." I didn't want to sound too curious about her husband or his murder, so I stopped talking for fear of sounding like a nosy-body. Which I am.

She looked pensive. "Do you think?"

"Whatever you want to do." She seemed reluctant to

take my advice, so I delved a little deeper. "Is it because of the subject matter of your novel?" I asked. "The death of your husband?"

She looked down at her plate and nodded.

"Are you sure you want to write about something so painful?" I asked.

She crossed her arms on the table and went back to gazing out the window. "I'm not sure," she said.

We sat in silence for a few minutes. "Listen, take your time," I said. "You may have another story to tell. It's a few weeks before we start that unit, so think about it."

She smiled, but I could tell that she was troubled; about what, I wasn't sure. All I knew was that writing about murder was heavy business and she didn't seem to have the strength to do it, as much as she told herself she wanted to.

"For now, just enjoy the class," I said. "Without you, I'm not sure what I would do. You seem to be the only one who gets my jokes."

"You *are* very funny," she said.

"Not too sarcastic?" I asked, still feeling the sting of Joanne Larkin's criticism.

"Sarcastic? You?" she asked, smiling. "I don't believe I know what you're talking about."

It was right then and there that I decided that I really liked Mary Lou Bannerman. The woman obviously had very good taste.

ELEVEN

DON'T ASK ME how this group came together, but it was Saturday night and I found myself in a dive bar that was a midpoint for everyone in attendance, drinking cheap white wine from a glass that may or may not have been clean, sitting on a bar stool that was losing the stuffing from its cushion. Surrounding me were Crawford, Fred, and Max, and Christine and Tim, and much to my growing surprise, we were waiting for a table to open up so we could sample the fine culinary delights offered by this sketchy establishment. Who'd have thought there would be a wait? Not I.

Max, clad in leggings and a baggy Ramones T-shirt that drooped off one shoulder, was looking around suspiciously. This from a woman who thought that Maloney's, the bar where we spent the better part of our senior year at St. Thomas, was fine dining until at least the late nineties. I took in her outfit, her leggings going down into a pair of throwback Doc Martens. Yep, still having a tough time with her upcoming birthday. She looked like the Max that I had carted out of CBGB back in the day, the one time I had seen liquor get the better of her. The most disturbing thing was that she had accessorized with a pleather pocketbook, not her usual thousand-dollar bag. Something was definitely afoot, and I wasn't sure it was just her birthday. I wondered if she was having some kind of psychotic break; it just wasn't like her not to look stunning at all times.

She leaned in and I got a whiff of her perfume, which, mixed with the smell of peanut shells and cheap beer, was not a pleasant scent. "What are we doing here?" she hissed. "And with these people? I thought it was just going to be us."

"I told you that Christine and Tim were coming."

She was not pleased. "Well, I didn't think they'd actually show up. Her brother just died, for God's sake."

When Max had one thing in her head, and things went another way, it was trouble. She was clearly in a pissy mood.

"This is worse than Maloney's."

"I thought you loved Maloney's."

"Sure, in the nineties when I didn't know any better."

"Just pretend that it's the nineties, then," I said, not bringing up that she looked as if she had dressed for a nineties frat party. She'd have fit right in in that outfit.

Fred looked cranky, but that's his general mien. "I want food."

Max looked at him. "Well, why don't you go ask the maître d' if we're going to be seated soon," she said, looking at me. "Oh, right. There is no maître d'."

Christine, who had gone to the ladies' room—and I use that term loosely—returned. "It will just be a minute," she said. This had been her idea. She had read about this place on some Web site where it had been deemed the "best rib joint this side of the Mississippi." That, coupled with the fact that it was exactly the same distance from Connecticut, Westchester, and New York City, made it a good suggestion, at least until we had actually walked in.

Christine took in Max's reaction. "We can go somewhere else," she offered.

"No, it's fine," Max said kindly, but the passive-aggressiveness was in full display for me, her oldest friend.

After another round of cheap hooch, and a third glass of seltzer for the designated driver, Max, we were led to a red vinyl booth, complete with nail heads to hold in the Naugahyde, and seated around a large round table. The sides of the booth went up so high that no one could see over them to the next table. It was cozy, to say the least. So cozy that I could feel the muscles in Fred's thigh pressing against my own; it felt like I was sitting next to a two-by-four.

"Alright, so bring on the barbecue," Max said, turning the flimsy menu over in her hand, looking at both sides, unimpressed. "Did this article you read talk about what we should order?" she asked.

Christine scanned the menu. "Try the mac and cheese and the spare ribs."

Satisfied with that suggestion, Max put her menu down. I had to admit that even though we were all making our best effort to make this outing not weird, being together was still new to everyone, and it was bordering on the absurd. Christine was definitely hell-bent on illustrating the fact that she had once been married to my husband, and had two children with him, was a nonissue. I wasn't sure what to make of her attempts to make us all friends; it seemed forced and a little unnatural, but I was giving it the old college try, if not for Crawford—who didn't seem remotely interested in having a relationship with Tim—then for the girls, who would be better off knowing that we could all get along. As for Fred and Max, we had invited them along as our "buffer couple," Christine having known Fred for far longer than I did. I had explained that to Max when we made the plan. Crawford and I figured that if the conversation lagged, one of those two would pick up the slack. We hadn't taken into account Max's black mood, nor the fact that Fred rarely spoke.

All in all, the whole thing was hurtling along toward a miserable end, so I tried to change the subject, asking Tim if he could explain exactly what a hedge fund manager did and why so many people did it. The first part seemed to be inexplicable, because when he was done, I still wasn't any closer to an understanding of the occupation, but the second part was far clearer. They did it for the money.

"Ah," I said, nodding. "Definitely a lure."

Apparently, Max picked up something in his tone that suggested that all wasn't peachy-dandy at Westcore Financial Trading. "What do you really want to do?" she asked.

He looked at her, surprised that she had picked up on a little shred of dissatisfaction that the rest of us had missed. "I'd love to open a sandwich shop," he said.

"Really?" she asked. "I'd like to be an exotic dancer."

We all turned toward her, waiting for her explanation. We knew one was coming. She was a ditz sometimes, but she gave things a lot of thought when she was hot on something.

"Work nights, all cash, exercise every day," she said. "Flexible hours. What could be better?" She looked around for our server. "I need another drink."

No, you don't, I thought, remembering then that she was drinking soda and saying a silent prayer of thanksgiving.

"But back to this sandwich thing," she said. "What's the deal?"

Tim blushed, unaccustomed to the interrogation stylings of Max Rayfield. "I love to cook, but I love sandwiches the best," he said.

"Duh," she said. "What is it about a sandwich shop in particular that makes you think you'd like it?"

He considered for a moment, not having given this as much thought as Max had given her imaginary career as a stripper. "The creativity. Figuring out different ways to put ingredients together to make a special sandwich." He shrugged. "Not sure, I guess. It just sounds like it would be a great way to spend my days."

"You need a hook," Max said, ever the marketer. "You know, like bread baked on the premises, or all-Italian, or salad mixed with sandwiches. Or guys who work shirtless."

"I think that's against the Health Department guidelines," Tim said without a trace of irony.

Max waved a hand in the air. "Whatever. You need something to set you apart. It can't just be a regular old sandwich place."

Tim leaned in, all ears.

"You've got to make sure you have a story and a concept all worked out before you dive in." She waved her empty glass around, hoping, I guess, that someone would take pity on her and refill it. "Otherwise, you'll fail."

"Fail," he murmured, saying a word that he hadn't had a lot of experience with, if his hedge fund was doing as well as he said it was.

Max let it go. In an uncharacteristic show of sensitivity, she changed the subject and asked Christine how she was doing after her brother's passing.

Christine's mood changed at the mention of Chick. She dropped her head and stared at the table. I looked over at Max as if to say, "Good going." She shot me back a silent "What?!"

When Christine looked up, her eyes were wet with tears. "I don't know if I'll ever get over it," she admitted.

Max wisely kept her mouth shut.

"He was so happy to be back," she said. "I just can't believe that he would take his own life."

I thought back to my brief conversation at the funeral with Mac McVeigh. He seemed pretty sure that it had been suicide, but his final report hadn't been rendered. I had been in that apartment; the note and the drugs seemed to point to suicide even if Christine couldn't believe that it was.

"I know what you're thinking," she said, looking at me. "He was a strange guy. I know that. But he was just so happy to be back with us, and I'll never forget that. I don't think he came back just so he could leave again," she said, and with that, her crying began in earnest.

Our server, a tattooed fellow with a scruffy goatee, came by, nervously took in the scene, and told us he would give us another minute before taking our order. I reached across the table and gently squeezed Christine's hand. "This must be really hard for you."

"You have no idea," she said sadly. Then she seemed to gain strength from my show of sympathy, quickly becoming defiant, a side of her I had never seen. "My brother did not kill himself. I know that."

I resisted the urge to raise an eyebrow at Crawford, preferring instead to keep my eyes trained on Christine. Crawford, as was his way when the emotional chips were down, kept his mouth shut, something he'd be hearing about later in the evening.

"You're looking at me like I'm crazy," she said, directing her comment to everyone at the table, thankfully not just me. "Chick was happy to be back. He was happy to be home."

If he was happy to be in that fleabag of an apartment with two hundred and fifty thousand dollars stuffed in his mattress, the guy was crazier than I initially thought. Honestly, the one evening I had spent with Chick had left me thinking that he was capable of just about anything, and even though suicide wasn't one of the things that would have crossed my mind, it didn't surprise me a bit. The guy had been gone for a long time. Who knew what he had done, what he had seen? I was sure Christine didn't know the half of it.

She continued to look at all of us crowded around the table. Finally, when it appeared that no one was on her side, she crawled over her husband and left. He peered around the high banquette and watched where she went.

"Ladies' room," he said. He got up and put his napkin on the table. "I'll be back."

The four of us looked at each other; it didn't seem proper

to go back to discussing the menu, so we did the only thing that seemed appropriate under the circumstances: We ordered more drinks. The wine that I was drinking got better with each successive glass, lightening my mood, at least. While Tim and Christine got themselves together in the ladies' room, we ordered a few appetizers; once they arrived, we devoured them, leaving only one potato skin and a sad-looking wing on a plate that had once been piled high with food.

Christine apologized when she returned. "It's going to take a while." That's all she said; all talk of a nonsuicide—a murder presumably—was done.

We all murmured that we understood how she felt, even if we didn't, and then undertook the task of ordering a meal that was way overdue if the glasses in front of us were any indication.

Christine smiled. "I would really like to do this again. Soon."

Inwardly, I groaned. Did we have to? Could it be in another six months or so? I had to work out some of the issues in my head, the ones that had no place being in my head, yet there they were, taking up a lot of room. This was perfectly pleasant—albeit seemingly a little too soon after her brother's passing—but instead of rehashing the good old days with my husband's ex-wife, I wanted to go back to Saturday nights spent on the couch with my husband in our pajamas, watching Food Network competition shows and programs about greasy spoons. I looked over at Tim to see what his reaction was, but he looked as impassive as always. If I were Tim, I'd look the same way; before Christine, he had been a chubby widower with a receding hairline and four little kids. As far as he was concerned, he had hit the jackpot with his new wife, an attractive dark-haired woman with a great body, and he wasn't going to rock the boat.

Yes, I saw every facet of that thought process in his unconcerned face. Call it my special gift.

I looked over at Crawford, who was studying what looked like a bullet hole in the banquette; I prayed to God that it wasn't. I guessed it was up to me to respond. I gave it all I had. "That would be great, Christine," I said, much to the bemusement of Max, who had the special gift of being able to read *my* mind, just like I could read Tim's.

Satisfied with that answer, Christine mellowed a bit and finally seemed to enjoy herself. The evening went off without a further hitch, with me deciding to put a lid on the cheap booze or face the dreaded cottonmouth in the morning, and Max deciding that there were worse things than eating good barbecue in a dive joint she would never visit voluntarily.

In the parking lot, poorly lit and not the kind of place that I like to be in by myself, we said good night and went our separate ways. When she hugged me, Max whispered that she would see me the next day at the birthday party and that under no circumstances was I to bring a gift, which is code for "I really liked that bag I sent you the link to," which is exactly what I had gotten her as soon as I'd opened her e-mail.

Once we were in the car, I looked over at Crawford. "We don't have to do that again, do we?"

He pulled out onto the street. "Why? You don't like spending time with my ex-wife and her new husband?" he asked, trying to sound serious but cracking himself up before he got out the last word.

"Seriously," I said. "What is this about? Why does she feel the need to get so close? It's not like she did any due diligence before taking off with Tim for London and leaving us here with the girls."

"Good point," he said. "I don't know. Her own family is just so…" He searched for the right word.

"Bizarre?" I suggested helpfully.

"Dysfunctional," he said. "Gabe is the most normal of all of them, and as you can see, he escaped a long time ago."

"Savannah."

"Yep." He stopped at a light and looked out his window. "I told you what it was like for her growing up with them. Her mother died young, leaving her father with a bunch of kids he had no business raising himself. That any of them turned out okay is a miracle."

"That happens sometimes," I said. "I see it with my students all the time. It's something that has to be inside you. To make you want to get out and make a normal life for yourself. To succeed."

He was quiet, mulling that over. "Do you think she's happy?"

"Who, Christine?"

"Yeah."

"I guess," I said, not really having given the idea any thought. What I really wanted to ask him was "Do you care?" but I stopped myself. I worked through it in my mind. Of course he did. She was the mother of his daughters. He would want her to be happy for a variety of reasons but most likely so his girls could have two happy parents.

By the time we got home, I was beyond exhausted, but Trixie had been neglected for most of the day and needed a walk at least around the block so that we could all get some sleep without hearing her tail thumping energetically on the floor throughout the night.

We entered through the back door, into the kitchen, and waited for Trixie to run to us from whatever corner of the house she had appropriated. We were met with silence. I looked at Crawford, who began calling the dog's name.

Nothing.

I went into the dining room and looked under the table, but she wasn't there. Nor was she on her bed in a corner of the living room, stretched out and snoozing contentedly. I raced upstairs and into the guest room, her other favorite spot because of the sun that streamed in the window overlooking the backyard, but she wasn't there either.

The last place to look was our bedroom, and that's where I found her, prone and panting next to the adjacent bathroom. I crouched down and looked in her eyes, glassy and unfocused, and shouted for Crawford.

The dog could barely lift her head, and I could feel a sob building in my gut. I murmured her name over and over, looking for signs of the dog we'd left behind when we had gone to dinner. Something was seriously wrong, a fact that Crawford could see immediately when he arrived in the bedroom.

"We have to take her to the emergency clinic," I said.

"Where is it?" he asked.

"Ossining," I said. "Can you lift her?"

He could, but barely. She weighed about eighty pounds, and she was dead weight. I held her back legs as he maneuvered her off the floor and into his arms. Somehow he managed to get down the stairs without dropping her.

When we got outside, he asked me to put down the backseat of his wagon, and he lifted her into the space through the hatchback. Never was I so grateful for his dorky, sensible station wagon. I crawled in after her, holding her paw and stroking her head as he sped up Route 9 to the animal hospital, at least ten miles from our house on a road that had a number of stoplights, several of which he blew through once he determined that no one was in the road.

The dog closed her eyes just as we got to the hospital, and I feared the worst, letting out the sob that I had been holding in.

"Is she gone?" he asked, looking at me in the rearview mirror.

"I don't know," I said, gasping as I put my face to her

nose. I felt her wet breath coming out in ragged bursts. "No," I said.

He pulled up to the front door of the hospital and ran out to get help. A white-coated vet tech raced out with a stretcher and helped Crawford lift the dog onto it, pushing the stretcher into the hospital and leaving us in the lobby to fill out a bunch of paperwork about Trixie's history. There was a lot I didn't know; she had been left on my doorstep by a neighbor a few years earlier, and I had taken her in, having loved her from afar for many years before that. I filled the forms out as best I could and hoped that there wasn't something I didn't know that could help them save her.

Crawford paced nervously while I sat in a chair, praying. I didn't think Trixie was that old, maybe six at the most, and I thought that the life expectancy of golden retrievers was a bit higher than that. I fed her the same food every day and didn't let her eat things outside, try as she might, for fear that they would upset her stomach or make her sick. I went over the last several days in my head, trying to reconstruct our time together and figure out if she had ingested something she shouldn't. I couldn't come up with anything. I asked Crawford, but he couldn't either.

"Did you let her out in the back to play without you?" I asked.

He looked at me. "I'm barely home," he reminded me, "and when I am, I take her for her walks and come right back. You know that."

I did know that. I also knew that it was peculiar that a dog that had been perfectly healthy when we left for dinner now looked like she was near death.

After an eternity, the veterinarian came out and introduced herself. "Hi, I'm Dr. Eldard," she said, her calm demeanor a welcome sight.

"Is Trixie okay?" I asked, holding my breath while I waited for her answer.

"She will be," she said. "You got her here just in the nick of time."

I resisted the urge to throw up.

"What's wrong with her?" Crawford asked, putting his arm around me. Whether he was trying to steady himself or keep me on my feet was up for debate.

She looked at both of us, an odd expression crossing her face, as if she didn't quite know how to present the information. "Your dog has been poisoned."

TWELVE

WE LEFT TRIXIE at the animal hospital for observation. Dr. Eldard assured us that with some intravenous fluids and medications to counteract the effects of the poison, Trixie would be as good as new the next afternoon. When we got in the car, the tears started anew.

"Who would do that?" I asked between sobs. The question joined the lingering one that Crawford had expressed immediately following the doctor's news: "How and why would someone do that?" We drove home, not quite as quickly as we had driven to the hospital but not at a leisurely pace either, arriving within a half hour. Before entering the house, Crawford told me to wait on the patio. He leaned down and took the gun from his ankle holster and held it by his side, unlocking the back door and stepping in quietly and gingerly, doing a canvass of the whole house before allowing me to come in.

I sat down heavily in a chair at the kitchen table and put my head in my hands. I had that hollowed-out feeling you get after a prolonged crying jag. Crawford pulled open the refrigerator door and took out a beer, sucking down half of it in one swallow. "Want something?" he asked.

I shook my head. The buzz from the cheap white wine had worn off, and a headache was making its presence known at my temples. "Find anything?" I asked.

"Not a thing," he said, "but someone had to be in here. That dog is by our sides all the time. It just doesn't make any sense."

"Should we call the police?" I asked.

"That was my next step," he said and dialed 911.

I'd love to say that our local police department doesn't have any clue as to who I am or where I live, but that would be a lie. I've been involved in more untoward activity than most almost-middle-aged college professors, and sometimes, the way I get looked at by our local cops, I think that they have a dartboard with my face plastered on it. Having Crawford make the call—professional courtesy and all— would lessen the annoyance of having to come out to the Bergeron homestead again. He hung up, his face still sad.

"She's going to be okay," I said. We had taken turns comforting each other the whole car ride home. If I needed any evidence that he loved that dog as much as I did, here it was.

"I know," he said. "Listen. Stay here. Don't touch anything. I want to look around."

He kept some extra work stuff stashed in a high cabinet in the kitchen that only he could reach. I had no interest in what was in there, but he didn't want anyone else to come across it while looking for a glass or a plate. He opened the door and took out his collection of crime scene stuff: gloves, bags, and a few other odds and ends. Pulling on the gloves, he headed for the bedrooms upstairs.

Someone had been in our house, had broken in to poison our dog. The thought hit me, icy tendrils of fear creeping up my back so real that I shivered. It added up to a very creepy scenario, one that was almost impossible to believe. Who would want to break into our house? Harm our dog? Had either one of us, or even one of the girls, talked about once having a large sum of money in the house, something that would have sparked the curiosity of a criminal? The house seemed to be in exactly the same shape as when we left it, despite the sick dog. Someone had planned this; someone who knew we had a dog. But who? And why?

Crawford came back downstairs just in time for the village police to ring our front doorbell. He let them in, explaining our situation, and let them go to work. There were four cops, all in uniform, and one detective, whom I had never met. For that, I was grateful; hopefully, he wouldn't have any preconceived notions about me, but you never know. His colleagues, Detectives Hardin and Madden, particularly Madden, didn't find me charming or interesting at all. As a matter of fact, they didn't really like me, prone as I was to poking around where I shouldn't. Cops were funny like that; they liked their civilians to stay out of their business, even if said civilians thought they were mucking things up royally.

To kill time, and because she had said I could, I called Dr. Eldard to make sure that Trixie was still doing as well as she had hoped after some fluids and medicine. After I spoke to the vet tech, the vet got on the phone herself.

"She's doing great, Mrs. Crawford," she said. "We ran some more tests and did a full CT scan. The dog ate some tainted food, but fortunately not enough to kill her. It was, however, enough to make her very sick."

"But she'll be okay, right?"

"She'll be fine," the vet said. She sounded pretty confident, and that made me feel better. "She's resting now, but her vitals are better than when you brought her in. It's looking good for Trixie getting out of here tomorrow. Call me in the morning. I leave at eight."

I hung up but remained in the kitchen, trying to stay clear of the cops who had invaded my house. I let Crawford answer their questions and show them where everything was. They weren't going to find anything. Whoever had done this had been prepared and obviously had known what they were doing. This was a professional job, through and through.

I hoped that whoever it was who had found it necessary

to break into my house had fled and was far, far away. Because if I caught up to him, I would kill him. Or her.

Nobody messes with my dog.

THIRTEEN

CRAWFORD WAS RIGHT. Not one thing was out of place in the house. There wasn't a fingerprint, a hair, or any kind of evidence that anyone had been on the premises, aside from the sick dog (and don't think I wasn't still in a rage about her). Crawford's a pretty good investigator but he mostly thinks about the dead; the thought did cross my mind that he might have missed something, and I felt immediately chagrined that I doubted him.

We discussed Max's birthday. We decided that I would go alone, as soon as we had picked up the dog and I was confident that she was well enough for me to leave, if Crawford stayed home. Although we now shared custody, she was my dog all the way, the one living being I had brought into the marriage. I e-mailed Max to let her know what had happened and tell her not to be alarmed if I was late to the party; I would get there as soon as I could. Max's response? "You'd better not be late."

Or what? I wanted to ask. It wouldn't be the first time I was on the receiving end of Max's ire, nor would it be the last. I decided to take my chances.

We picked Trixie up at one thirty, as soon as the doctor called and said it was acceptable to come get her. She was almost as good as new, despite the bandage wound around her front paw where the IV had been. She didn't exactly bound down the hall of the animal hospital toward us, more a slow lope, but the vet assured us that she would be back to normal in a few days. If she wasn't for some reason, we were supposed to call and make an appointment for follow-up. Dr. Eldard didn't think that would be necessary, and that made me feel better. What also made me feel better was the hug she gave me before we left. This was a woman who knew what our animal meant to us and had taken good care to make sure that not only would she survive, she would be just like her old mischievous, rambunctious self.

I was reluctant to go to the party, knowing that the dog was still a little wobbly, but I knew Max would never forgive me if I opted to stay home with an animal rather than go to a party in her honor. She wasn't an "animal person," as she always pointed out, a statement that Trixie, if she could talk, could explain better. The dog loves everyone but my best friend, and nobody is sure why, although we think that maybe Max gives off a vibe that says she's not an animal person and Trixie can sense it. Who knows? All I know is that when Max comes over, Trixie runs for the hills, something she would never do when anyone else entered the premises.

Max's parents live in a town about twenty minutes north of me in a gorgeous contemporary with views of the Hudson River. I hadn't been to the house in years, usually seeing Marty and Gigi Rayfield in the city or at a big family function that required a catering hall to fit everyone. I always felt at home, though; I had spent a lot of time in this house over the years and with them, and they truly had become my surrogate family in the wake of my parents' untimely deaths.

I drove up the long hill that led to the house and parked in the circular driveway, trying to find a space that would allow whoever else was there to leave, but also let me make a quick getaway if necessary. I grabbed the big bag next to me that held the pocketbook that Max had requested and went to the front door.

Having never had siblings or children of my own, I'm

always surprised by gatherings that are loud and boisterous and include a cast of characters; hence, my loss of emotional equilibrium at the twins' birthday party, a day that seemed like a lifetime ago. From inside Marty and Gigi's spectacular manse I could hear the sounds of Max's brothers—four in all—and their various broods engaged in some kind of game. Through the windows on either side of the door I could see that the children were all in stocking feet sliding from one end of the marble-covered floor to the other, stopping short as they approached the sliding glass doors that fronted the balcony that had the views. As I waited, one of the little ones slid straight into the door, but from what I could gather, that was part of the fun.

Until someone put an eye out. Maybe it was thoughts like that, often verbalized, that led Max to christen me the "Ultimate Party Pooper."

Marty finally heard the doorbell and let me in, wrapping his arms around me in a bear hug. At five foot six, he was several inches shorter than me, but that never stopped him from trying to lift me off the ground while embracing me. Now that he was eighty, I got nervous as he attempted to do it again, managing to get my shoes off the floor by about an eighth of an inch. "Alison! It's been too long," he said. "Gigi! It's Alison! I told you she'd get here!"

Max's father was spry and still sported the red hair that he was born with, tinged with only a little gray, which gave him the look of a weathered, wizened elf. Max had inherited her diminutive stature from him; her mother was a statuesque, glamorous woman who claimed to have "dated"—a.k.a. "slept with"—Cliff Robertson while she was a featured player at some Hollywood studio back in the day. Marty and Gigi were an oddly matched couple, not unlike Max and Fred, but devoted to each other and still, at their advanced ages, the life of any party.

Gigi sashayed across the floor, all blond bouffant and

massive diamonds, and grabbed my hand in hers. "So good to see you, darling." She air-kissed both my cheeks, something I never did, but which she seemed to think was de rigueur in deference to my French heritage.

My family had been very reserved, just the three of us coexisting as one little unit, me with my never-ending supply of Nancy Drews, my father with his model airplane collection, and my mother with her ever-present *Vogue* in hand. Visiting the Rayfields always felt like I had landed on another planet where males predominated, females were coiffed, stylish, and a little quirky, and I loomed over the proceedings like a giant, silent dodo bird. It usually took me a few minutes—or a martini or two—to get acclimated, and I was out of practice. At that moment, I wished for the comforting touch of Crawford's hand on my back or just his calming presence. I handed Gigi the big bag and took a deep breath. I did my best to insert myself into the festivities with a minimum of awkwardness. "Where's the birthday girl?" I asked Max's parents.

"Kitchen," Gigi answered, gliding off with the gift.

Marty took my hand. "Come on. I made you a pitcher of martinis, and you're late, so you need to catch up."

Max was in the kitchen, but her back was turned to me when I got there. Fred saw me first and by the look on his face, I knew that we had a problem. I went up behind Max, who was holding what seemed to be a glass of wine that looked like it had come from a Medieval Times restaurant—large, filled to the rim with what appeared to be a full-bodied red, and set upon a metal stem made so elaborately that it almost looked alarming. It was the kind of glass that someone in a horror movie might use to serve poison. The Rayfields were nothing if not a little ostentatious. I put my arm around Max, and she turned.

"So glad you could come!" she exclaimed, but she wasn't sincere.

"I know. I'm late," I said. "You got my e-mail, right?"

"Yes, I got your e-mail," she said. "How's your dog?"

"She's fine, I think."

"Where's Crawford?"

"With the dog."

"Who's fine."

I knew where this was headed, and I looked at Fred for support, but he was staring gloomily out the window and at the spectacular view. "I'm sorry, Max, but I had to make sure the dog was truly better before I left."

She softened a bit, realizing how much Trixie meant to me, but she was still a little terse. "It's four o'clock," she said pointedly.

"I got you that pocketbook you wanted," I said brightly, the only diversionary tactic I had in my arsenal.

She softened even more. "Well, alright then." Marty appeared by my side and handed me a martini. "We held dinner for you, though, and I'm starving." She motioned toward Marty with her giant glass. "He wouldn't hold a meal for me for anything. But for you? That's a different story."

Fred pulled me to the side, down the hall, across from a beautifully appointed bathroom. "What the hell happened?" he asked.

"Not a clue," I said.

"You think it's about Christine's brother? The money?" he asked, but he already knew the answer to that question.

"I would say yes, but I guess we can't be sure. Maybe the local police will turn something up?"

He snorted. "Not likely," he said, his superiority complex regarding suburban law enforcement on full display. "I'll be over. I'll figure it out."

Knock yourself out, I thought as he lumbered away, attacking a plate of pigs in a blanket before throwing himself heavily onto the couch in the family room. I joined him and sipped my martini, knowing that it would be my only drink for the night, since I had to drive home.

Before long, Gigi called us to dinner in the dining room, a grand affair with a table that sat eighteen comfortably. I sat between Max's nephew, Boris, and his sister, Natalia, two children who had been named during the Cold War, or so it would seem. Then I remembered that they had a Russian mother, and I spied her at the end of the table, sitting beside Marty and regaling him with some story that had his complete attention. Boris, ten, broke the ice by asking if my hair was always that frizzy.

"You mean today or just in general?" I asked.

"Your whole life." He speared a butter pat with his steak knife and dangerously slathered it on a piece of bread while I watched, hoping that I wouldn't have to fashion a tourniquet from my linen napkin.

"Kind of."

His face took on a sadness that was profound in its sincerity. "Oh."

"Hey," I said. "It's not so bad. Sometimes I straighten it and it actually looks pretty good."

He wasn't buying it. I turned my attention to Natalia, who was hoarding a bowl of peas. "May I?" I asked.

"When I'm done," she said. I started to notice a very distinct personality gene running through the Rayfield clan: tactless honesty coupled with complete self-absorption.

Max called down from the other end of the table. "Hey, Nancy Drew. How's your latest case coming along?"

"Which one would that be?" I asked.

"The case of the dead brother-in-law."

"Still dead," I said. I wondered what was happening here and why thinly veiled hostility had become the main course. I studied the pattern on my plate.

"Is that why you were so very, very late?" Boris and

Natalia's mother, a woman whose name escaped me, asked. I think. With her heavy accent, I wasn't entirely sure.

I took a shot at an answer. "That and the fact that my dog was sick," I said.

She grabbed her chest in horror. "Then why are you even here?"

Max answered for me. "Because she's my best friend and she wouldn't think of missing this party."

I looked to Fred for some support, but he was eyeing his prime rib with a hunger that looked like it could never be satisfied.

Marty, always a gentleman, changed the subject as I caught Max's eye and mouthed "I'm sorry," even though I thought I had already apologized profusely for a pretty insignificant infraction against the friend code. If she wanted to have a contest about who was a better friend to whom and I trotted out my list of grievances, she would surely lose. Marty raised his glass and in a display of paternal devotion offered a lovely toast to his only daughter, a woman who was turning into a first-class shrew right before my very eyes. Fred then offered his own tribute, but the only words I could make out were "meat" and "love." Everyone else seemed just as mystified, but nobody was classless enough to ask for a repeat performance.

Max had softened to me by dessert. We were on the back deck, the place with the best view of the river, and she looked small and weary. "I just worry about you is all," she said.

"And that's how you show it?" I asked.

She shrugged. "I guess."

"Listen, I'm sorry I was late, and I'm sorry that things—that I—have been so consumed by this whole mess. It's over now, though, and things will go back to normal and you'll have me all to yourself again." *Just the way you like it*, I thought, the implications of that troubling me just a little bit. "I promise that we won't have any more weird dinners with Christine, either." Her reaction to the latest goings-on was strange to me, even for Max, but I chalked it up to her sensitivity over her birthday, stress at work, being married to Fred, and a host of other things that wouldn't bother normal people but that got her emotions all in a jumble.

"No, it's my fault. I'm sorry," she said, grabbing my hand. "It's just that you know how I get around my family."

I did know how she got around her family, but if this was the only way she could apologize, I felt compelled to respect that.

"One of these days, you're going to get in a jam that you can't talk your way out of, and that worries me," she finally admitted. "One of these days, if you don't stop getting involved in things that don't have anything to do with you, you'll be the one getting poisoned." Once that was said, she reverted to her regular personality, the one that could only focus on one thing at a time, that thing usually being herself. "Let's have cake."

I watched her hustle back inside and chewed on what she'd said.

I had to admit that she just might have had something there.

FOURTEEN

CRAWFORD DID SOMETHING completely out of character Monday morning by calling in sick. Technically, he wasn't sick, but he did a good enough impersonation of a sick person that he didn't arouse too much suspicion. He wouldn't leave Trixie alone, and he didn't want me to incur the wrath of Sister Mary by calling in sick myself. I was relieved. I had fretted all night about leaving the dog home by herself, and the thought of something happening while we were both at work filled me with dread. I kissed him and hugged him tight before I left, grateful that I could go through my day secure in the knowledge that he was keeping close watch on my canine child.

Try as I might, the horror of the weekend still lingered in my mind, and apparently on my face. Those who didn't know me well gave me a wide berth, and those who did know me asked if everything was okay. I assured all concerned parties that all was well and that I had just had a stressful weekend, leaving them to make up their own scenarios. With my history, I'm sure there were creative scenarios aplenty, but I didn't have the energy to set the record straight. I kind of slogged through my day, teaching all of my classes and even getting to the cafeteria for a quick lunch with my colleague from the Religious Studies Department, Abe Schneckstein, but even his bonhomie was no match for my sullen mood.

Briggs was working the counter and the grill simultaneously, and he gave me a big smile when I approached the line. "What can I get you, Prof?"

"Surprise me," I said, seeing Abe maneuver to a table by the window so that we would have a beautiful river view as we ate. He kept kosher and always brought his lunch to school; I watched him amble off to the men's room to wash his hands, as he did before every meal we shared, before coming back to carefully unwrap whatever it was that the lovely Mrs. Schneckstein had packed for him.

After a few minutes, Briggs presented me with a panini, mozzarella, roasted red peppers, and pesto between beautifully grilled slices of focaccia. "Thank you," I said. Kid had a knack. Marcus had been wise to hire him.

"Thanks!" he said, obviously pleased with his creation. "Anything else?"

I took a surreptitious look at his left hand, happy when I spotted a bare ring finger. "No, thanks, Briggs." There was no one behind me, so I took a moment to dig. "Where did you learn to cook like this?"

"Culinary Institute," he said.

"And you're cooking here?" I asked. That surprised me more than the beautiful sandwich he had prepared.

"Tough market out there," he said. "Regular hours here, pretty good pay, and Marcus is great to work with."

I took a bite of my sandwich, too hungry to wait. "I didn't take into account the regular hours. Must make your wife happy."

He blushed. "Oh, there's no wife, Professor Bergeron."

Bingo. Next step was to get Meaghan in here. He was tall and gainfully employed, a much better match than Mr. Super Senior, in my book.

I paid for my lunch and met Abe by the window table. He asked me what was going on, and I filled him in, letting him drink in every salacious detail of the past few weeks while he ate a bagel with some kind of spread on it.

"So you're now more involved with Crawford's ex-wife?" he asked.

"I guess you could say that," I said, laughing it off, even though in the back of my mind was this new relationship with Crawford's ex and her contention that her brother had not committed suicide. Was this her way of getting over the grief of losing someone she loved? How in the heck is someone who ingested a bunch of pills not a suicide? It seemed pretty cut and dried, yet the thought of how steadfast she was in her belief was something that stayed with me.

When all was said and done, I concluded that this was her coping mechanism, and Abe agreed with me. As a rabbi, he had seen his fair share of grieving spouses, siblings, and parents and had a good handle on what could be considered a normal response to something so devastating as suicide. He assured me that Christine couldn't possibly have known a man who had been away for almost a quarter of her life and that we needed to keep that in mind even as she asserted that her brother would never take his own life.

I left Abe feeling better. I taught another class, then had stopped by my office just to pick up my things before calling it a day when there was a knock at my door, a sound that made me grimace in frustration. All I wanted to do was get the hell off campus and home to my husband and our dog, have a glass of wine, and relax. The night of worrying about how Trixie would fare all day without us, an unfounded fear after all, had taken its toll, and I was completely spent.

I called out to whoever was on the other side of the door to come in. To make it clear that my departure was imminent, I put my messenger bag on top of my desk and began putting books, folders, and assorted papers into it.

Mary Lou Bannerman poked her head in before coming all the way into the office. "Am I catching you at a bad time?" she asked.

For some reason, I was relieved to see her and not another student, someone who might suck up a good hour of my time asking for help with an assignment or requesting a recommendation for graduate school. Even though I wasn't required to see students outside of my regularly posted office hours, I never turned anyone away, so it was my own fault if I didn't get off campus until after six some nights. "No, please come in," I said, "and have a seat."

"I'm not staying," she said. Her class had ended hours before, so I wondered why she was still on campus; maybe she was taking other courses at St. Thomas? She must have read my mind. "In the library," she said, pointing toward the building just beyond the cemetery that could be seen from my office. "I wanted to work in complete silence, and being as we're remodeling our family room and one of our bathrooms at home, I knew that would be impossible." She looked at me, worry scurrying across her beautiful features. "You didn't seem yourself in class today, so I just wanted to make sure everything was alright."

I was close to cracking, but I managed to hold it together. I don't know what it was about her—her sincerity, her concern, or just her serene demeanor—that made me want to burst out crying and reveal everything, but I had to remind myself that she was a student and I was her professor and that kind of behavior was completely inappropriate. "I had a stressful weekend. I guess I wasn't able to shake it off as quickly as I had hoped."

She stayed in the door of my office, a notebook and the textbook for our class held to her chest. "I'm so sorry. Anything you want to talk about?" she asked. She smiled. "I guess that's a little out of the ordinary, you talking to a student about your stressful weekend?"

I nodded. "You could say that."

She smiled again. "I thought so. Listen, though, if there's anything I can do—"

"Someone poisoned my dog," I blurted out. I put a hand to my mouth. "I'm sorry. That's what happened. Someone poisoned my dog," I said, and as I repeated it, I felt a tear slip down my cheek; I hastily brushed it away, but she saw it.

She dropped the notebook and the textbook on my desk and came over to give me a hug. The scent of her perfume, reminiscent of a fragrance my mother used to wear, was comforting, and I took a deep breath, inhaling it along with the memories it brought forth. I broke the hug quickly. "Thank you," I said.

"Who on earth would poison a dog?" she asked.

I continued putting papers into my bag, not intending to do anything with them when I got home; the action gave me something to do and a way to avoid looking into the kind face of this woman who had seen her own share of heartache. "I don't know," I said, "but I'm going to go home and curl up with her and make sure she's doing better."

"That sounds like a splendid idea," she said. "I hope you have a lovely evening."

"Thank you, Mary Lou."

"I'm glad everything is okay with your dog. What's her name?" she asked.

"Trixie."

"Sounds like a beautiful name for a beautiful retriever," she said.

I had never said what kind of dog she was; I gave Mary Lou a quizzical look.

She pointed to my desk. "That's her, right? With your husband?"

I looked at the picture on my desk in which Trixie was front and center, Crawford kneeling behind her. I had taken it one weekend when in a misguided desire to get some fresh air I had dragged the two of them to a spot about a half hour north of the house that boasted spectacular views.

What it also boasted was a hiking trail that went straight up at a forty-five-degree angle, so when we arrived at the top, we were incapable of looking at the view, thanks to our exhaustion from making the trek. I remember my hands shaking as I aimed the camera at the two of them, managing despite my fatigue to get a great shot, the fall leaves behind them in spectacular array.

What was wrong with me? Here was this nice woman trying to help me get past my horrible state of mind, and all I could think was that she hadn't known the breed of my dog prior to entering my office and having a conversation with me. I needed sleep badly. I was losing it.

She patted my shoulder one more time. "Come on. I'll walk you out."

I threw my bag over my shoulder and locked my office door on the way out, grateful for the company of this lovely lady who wanted to write a novel about a murder.

As I had often thought in the past, St. Thomas University made strange bedfellows. I realized as she walked away in the parking lot, having seen me to my car, that I never asked her why she had come by my office.

FIFTEEN

Max and Fred were at the house when I got home, and I moaned to myself as I drove up the driveway, having spotted their car parked at the curb. It's not that I don't love my best friend; she can be a little *much*, though, and God knows she had been really irritable lately. I wasn't in the mood. Knowing that they were there filled me with dread; I had a date with the luscious Trixie Bergeron-Crawford and her even more luscious owner, Crawford, and a bottle of wine that didn't have "Gallo" written anywhere on the label. I got out of the car and picked my way across the backyard in my heels, thinking that they would be the first item of clothing I removed when I entered the house.

The group was clustered in the kitchen, Chinese takeout containers strewn across the counter. At least they had had the good sense to bring dinner. Drinks were well under way, and I heard Fred's booming voice bouncing around my small Cape Cod. Everyone fell silent when I walked in.

"What's wrong?" I asked.

"Nothing," Crawford said quickly. "Everything's fine. Trixie's doing great."

"Where is she?" I asked.

"She's upstairs next to our bed." He pointed toward the stairs. "Go see for yourself."

I took my shoes off and held them in my hands as I went up the stairs. Trixie was in her favorite spot on the throw rug next to Crawford's side of the bed, stretched out and sleeping peacefully. When she sensed my presence, her eyes flew open and she got up, lumbering over to me for some love. I got on the floor in my work clothes and kissed and hugged her, ruffling her ears. Her nose was wet and shiny, just as it should have been, and her eyes looked clear. I let out a sigh of relief, my breath still redolent from my lunch with Abe, the panini having been followed by an espresso chaser.

After she was satisfied that I had given her enough love, Trixie drifted off and went back to her spot next to the bed, where she fell heavily to the ground, her back legs tucked underneath her, her front paws under her chin. The dressing from her intravenous puncture was still wrapped around her leg, but she didn't seem troubled by it, so I left it on. I pulled off my skirt and sweater and threw on a pair of baggy pajama pants and a St. Thomas T-shirt; Fred and Max weren't what I would consider "company," so I made the decision to go with comfort over style. After I washed up, I went downstairs to partake of the Chinese feast that awaited me.

Not being the types to stand on ceremony, they had eaten before I had gotten home. I resisted the urge to tweak Crawford about it, but when the guy needs to eat, the guy needs to eat, and the alternative was a testy and weak man who wasn't a lot of fun to be around. I heaped a pile of lo mein and General Tso's chicken onto my plate and put it into the microwave for thirty seconds, hoping that that would land me somewhere between lukewarm and nuclear, heatwise. Crawford had already made me a martini—three olives, a little dirty—which was waiting for me on a place mat on the kitchen table. I carried my plate over and sat down, digging into the lo mein first.

I didn't wait until I had finished chewing my first bite before pointing my fork at Fred and saying, "If I find out who poisoned my dog, I will kill them."

He put his hands up in surrender. "I believe you."

Crawford pulled open the refrigerator and handed Fred a beer, grabbing one for himself as well. "I have to call the detective tomorrow, but nobody seems to be able to figure out how someone got in here." He opened his beer and tossed the cap into the sink. "Including me."

Fred gave him a hard stare. "You're better than that."

"Don't think I don't know that," Crawford said. "It's driving me crazy, but I can't find where they got in."

Fred downed his beer and banged the bottle onto the countertop, so hard that it was a miracle that it didn't shatter. "Let's look."

"I'm telling you, Fred," Crawford protested, "we were all over this place."

"Yeah, but I wasn't all over this place, and that's what you need."

Max nodded vigorously. "That's exactly what you need."

"That and an alarm system," Fred said before he started canvassing the downstairs. "I don't know what's wrong with you people."

"You people?" I asked.

"Yeah, you people. Suburbanites. The kind that think nothing bad will ever happen to them."

As he exited the kitchen, I called after him. "Hey! I once saw a body with no hands and feet! Check that! *Two* bodies with no hands and feet. Don't lecture me on what we suburbanites think about safety." Too bad he was gone. Although even if he had stuck around to hear my tirade, he wouldn't have cared. That's how Fred rolls.

Max looked at me. "Think they'll find anything?" I shrugged.

"It'll make them feel better one way or the other," she said.

I hadn't really looked at her when I walked in, just having given her a cursory glance. "Are you wearing a Lambda Pi Eta sweatshirt?" LPH was the Department of Communications honor society at St. Thomas and elsewhere, and Max had been a member in good standing back when Bill Clinton was in his first term, before he'd even met Monica Lewinsky. That item of clothing was soon to have its twentieth birthday, but what was more amazing was that it was still in such good shape; certainly it had seen its fair share of barroom floors, Max having been a bit of klutz back in the day.

"Still fits," she said proudly, puffing out her chest.

"Why wouldn't it?" I asked. "You've been a hundred pounds since the day I met you." I forked in another heap of lo mein. "And it's an extra large." I put my fork down. "What's going on with you? Is it your birthday? The big four-oh?"

The sound she made was a cross between a Bronx cheer and something much more dismissive. "No," she said, but it didn't sound convincing.

"Then why are you dressing like a teenager again?" I asked. "I miss the Jimmy Choos and the Prada coats and the Diane von Furstenberg wrap dresses. I miss you," I said, pointing at her.

"I'm still here," she said.

"Then why are you dressing like you did when we were in college? The Ramones T-shirt? The ripped leggings?"

"Hey," she said, jumping off her perch on the counter. "Do I criticize you for dressing like Leave It to Beaver's mother? Huh? Do I?"

"That would be June Cleaver," I said.

"Right. Her." She leaned in and picked a piece of chicken off my plate. "The pearls, the pumps, the sweater sets. Do I criticize you?"

"As a matter of fact, you do. All the time. Sometimes I feel really bad about myself because when I think I'm looking good, you dispel that notion with one word."

She let out a little puff of air. "You make it sound like I'm not nice to you."

"Sometimes, you're not."

"You don't respect what I do," she said.

"Yes, I do."

"You're always making fun of the shows on my channel," she said.

"*Hooters: PIs*? Come on, Max. That's funny," I said. Why she couldn't see that eluded me. We had had this discussion a hundred times; I would never not see the humor behind the show.

"I'll have you know that that show is making people a ton of money."

As if that were proof of its legitimacy. "It's funny, Max. Women running around in tank tops and short shorts solving crimes?" I asked. She wasn't having any of it.

She gave me a hard look. "Do you really want to do this?"

I was tired. My dog had been poisoned. My husband looked like he had shell shock. No, I did not want to do this.

"Stop making fun of what I do," she said.

"Okay, and you just think about what you say to me. That's all I ask."

As she often does when confronted with the truth, Max changed the subject. "How's Trixie?"

I decided to ride her wave of denial. "She's fine." I put my napkin on top of my lo mein and chicken. "I would tell you to go up and see her, but as we both know, she hates you."

Max snorted. "Dog has no taste." We heard Fred and Crawford banging around above us. She looked up at the kitchen ceiling. "God, I hope they find something. Fred will be in a funk for days if they can't solve this locked room mystery."

"Good point." I stood and rinsed my dish off in the sink. "Speaking of your birthday, what are we doing?"

"Nothing," she said quickly. "I just want to forget that it's happening. The party at my parents' was enough for me."

I knew it. She was having a major issue with turning forty. "But we need to celebrate together," I said, not content with leaving well enough alone. Above me, I heard Fred grunt and then let out a triumphant cry. "I guess they found something."

I hadn't really focused on the fact that someone had broken in, concerned as I was about Trixie's health first and foremost, but hearing the effort that they were putting into solving the mystery of how someone had gotten into our hermetically sealed house made me realize that I should be paying closer attention. I went to the bottom of the stairs and called up. "Success?"

More Fred grunting followed by Crawford swearing convinced me that I should wait until they revealed their discovery on their own. Max jumped back up on the counter, and I returned to the table. They came down five minutes later, sweating but happy.

"We found it," Crawford said.

"Who found it?" Fred asked.

"Fred found it," Crawford said, giving credit where credit was due. "In the lingo of Nancy Drew, it was a second-story job. A cat burglar."

He was making light of it, but I could tell that he was confounded.

"Fred looked out the window and saw a crushed bush beneath the guest room window. It was against the house. We all missed it." Crawford washed his hands at the sink. "There was just the slightest dent in the screen, too." He ripped off a paper towel and dried his hands. "I can't believe we missed that. Of course, they repaired it pretty well."

Fred frowned. "You're losing your edge, brother. It must

have been the worry about the dog." He downed his beer. "Although I could see how you missed the broken hedge. You two aren't known for your landscaping skills. Half the hedges in your yard are broken."

We both ignored him. "Really?" I asked. "That was pretty brazen, climbing up the side of our house and breaking in."

Fred shrugged. "It was dark. You've got those high shrubs at the back of the house. I'm not surprised—whoever it was—that they figured out a way to get in." Fred's jacket, a giant piece of fabric with intricate stitching, was draped over the counter, and he pulled it on. "So you'll be back tomorrow?" he asked Crawford.

Crawford looked at me for approval. "I think she'll be fine, Crawford. Yes, go back to work." The sooner we got our lives back to normal, the better.

"I'll call the village PD tomorrow and see if anything has turned up." Crawford looked at Fred and shook his head. "You never cease to amaze me."

Fred made a face that was the closest thing to a smile I had ever seen him attempt.

Max leapt off the counter and grabbed Fred's hand. "Let's go. I have to plan for a production meeting tomorrow." She leaned over me and kissed the top of my head. "See you later. I'm glad the dog's okay," she said in that hurried way that made me think that after all these years, she still had a hard time showing me any kind of affection in any kind of overt way. We were probably still a little at odds because of our conversation earlier and the fact that she was being a complete weirdo about her birthday.

After they left, Crawford joined me at the table. "You have enough to eat?" he asked.

"Plenty," I said. "I'm going to hit the sack."

"I have to ask you something," he said.

I waited.

"Christine called today. She's still insisting that Chick's death wasn't a suicide."

I sighed. "Sure looked like a suicide to me," I said, desperately trying to wipe from my mind the image of Christine's brother slumped over a vomit-stained suicide letter.

Crawford ran his hands over his face. He had had it with Christine's talk of nonsuicide, too. "Do you think you could ask Mac McVeigh if he would talk to her? Assure her that it was suicide?"

I was exasperated, probably more so because I was exhausted. I mulled over his request, coming to the conclusion, finally, that if we were going to get any peace at all when it came to the death of Chick Stepkowski, using my relationship with the medical examiner was a small price to pay.

SIXTEEN

MAC MCVEIGH JUST happened to be the sort of medical examiner who wasn't averse to talking to someone like Christine. He even went so far as to invite us to his office in White Plains to chat. I had been embarrassed even making the call, but I saw that Crawford was in a bit of a pickle and that this wasn't going to go away until Christine had some kind of closure—and at this point, I wanted Christine to have closure just so she would go away. The phone calls, the drop-ins, the e-mails…they had to stop. I was as sorry as anyone that her brother had left, come back, and then left for good, but I had my own problems, and they were related to figuring out who broke into my house and poisoned my dog.

If it wasn't suicide, I was leaning more toward accidental death. Maybe Chick had chronic pain. Why else would he have had all that Vicodin in his apartment? Maybe it was left over from a recent surgery that Christine didn't know about. Let's face it: There was a lot she didn't know about her incredibly eccentric, and up until recently absentee, brother. All I knew was that the guy had offed himself, and coming to terms with it was very difficult for her.

When Christine arrived in my office the day of our meeting with Mac, however, I immediately regretted all of the bad feelings I had had and the impatience I had felt. The usually perky, pixie-faced woman had been replaced by someone drawn and pale, someone defeated. She had lost weight, and on her little frame, every lost pound showed, not like on us big gals who can hide a five-pound loss or gain with the greatest of ease. I held back a gasp, but she could tell that I was surprised by her appearance.

"I know," she said. "I look like hell."

"Sit down," I said, closing the office door behind her. "What's going on?" I asked.

She started crying. "I am just so sad. All the time. I can't do anything except cry and cry and cry," she said, tears rolling down her pale cheeks.

I sat down beside her and put an arm around her. I don't think I could have felt worse about having lost patience with her; she was in so much pain that it was radiating from her in waves. "Maybe after we talk to Mac you'll feel better."

"He's just going to tell me what everyone else thinks and that's that Chick killed himself." She rustled around in her big purse and came up with an old wrinkled tissue with a lollipop stuck to it. She held it up for me to see. It was green and had a piece missing. "I am way too old to be raising four little kids," she said, going from crying to laughing in mere seconds.

I handed her the tissue box that was on my desk. After she had wiped her eyes and blown her nose, I asked her the question we had all been thinking. "What makes you believe that Chick was incapable of killing himself?" I asked as gently as I could. There were other questions I would have loved the answers to, like where he had been all those years and why he had so much money stashed away in a tenement, but I left those for another time. Or even, who would have killed him?

Her eyes, a vivid blue normally, were the color of sapphires after her crying jag, sapphires rimmed by red. "He was happy to be back. He wanted to be in our lives. Never once did he say anything about being sad, or depressed." She blew her nose again. "It was more like he had put whatever had happened behind him and wanted to start fresh."

In a sleazy tenement apartment in Mount Vernon? It was a little hard to swallow.

"Where did he get the money?" I asked.

She got defensive. "Chick did very well for himself for a very long time."

It didn't jibe with the hovel he was living in, and I told her so.

"It was temporary. He was going to move."

The housing market in the past several years had been glutted with places that had been foreclosed on; in my own village alone, I could think of ten places that he could have seen that would have been a thousand times better than the apartment he had chosen.

Maybe it was temporary. It was probably also a hiding place. That seemed obvious to everyone but Christine.

I'm not above talking myself into and out of things, but all of the signs were pointing toward a brother who was probably involved in something nefarious. Who knew what that was? Who cared, besides his heartbroken sister?

I looked at the clock over the door. "We have to go. I don't want to be late."

The drive took a little under a half hour, and we were knocking on the ME's office door a few minutes after scoring a gem of a parking spot right in front. Mac was sitting behind his desk doing the *New York Times* crossword puzzle, his glasses pushed up on top of his balding head.

"Ladies," he said, standing. "Before we commence, I'll need some help."

I was used to Mac and his crazy non sequiturs, but Christine was a novice. She looked confused.

"Where is Pago Pago?" he asked, tapping his pencil on top of his puzzle.

"Samoa," I said. How do I know this? Because Fred is half Samoan and has told me everything there is to know about Samoa.

Mac filled in the answer. "Thank you, my friend." He sat back down and took his glasses off the top of his head. "So, Ms...."

"Please. Call me Christine."

"Christine. I hear you don't agree with my ruling on your brother's cause of death?" he asked, his tone kind. He offered her a half smile to tell her that he didn't mind being questioned or doubted. He was friends with me, after all.

Christine sank down in her chair, deflated. "I don't know why we're here."

Mac got up from behind his desk and came around to where we were sitting, perching on the edge. "Can I get you some water? Coffee?"

We both declined.

He looked at Christine. "I can't imagine the pain you're feeling over the death of your brother."

She started crying again. I had been hoping we could avoid that.

"For what it's worth, I can tell you with certainty that your brother ingested enough pills to kill himself twice over. To me, it seems that he was intent on making sure that he went to sleep and didn't wake up."

She nodded, her head bowed.

Mac leaned in and took her hand. "I also can tell you that he didn't suffer. There was no pain. Not at all."

Her weeping grew louder, and I took her other hand. My mind flashed on the vomit on the desk, and I wondered if that was normal or if Chick had had a change of heart at the last minute and tried to undo the damage that he had inflicted on his body. Now wasn't the time to explore that possibility. Or ever.

"Please believe me, Christine," Mac said. "I've been doing this job since, oh, Lincoln was president." He smiled when Christine laughed through her tears. "I'm so sorry, but your brother took his own life."

"What about the gash on his head?" she asked, grasping at straws.

"He hit it on the desk when he passed out."

We sat in silence for a few minutes while Christine attempted to digest the news, news she already knew but had been reluctant to take to heart.

When she didn't respond, he continued. "Let's think about this logically. How could he have been murdered," he asked, "because I know that's what you're thinking, if he swallowed pills?"

"Maybe somebody made him take them?" she asked.

Mac nodded slowly. "Maybe." He crossed his arms. "Did you know of anyone who wanted to kill him?"

She smiled sadly. "I didn't even really know my brother anymore, when it comes right down to it." It was the first time I heard her make this admission. Maybe the truth was finally dawning on her.

"I know you've spoken to the same detectives I have. No one, based on the surveillance camera mounted on the corner, came in or out of that building who didn't belong there. They have verified every last person on that tape." Mac touched her arm. "I'm sorry, Christine."

"Maybe it was someone in the building?" she asked.

"Do you really think that someone in the building killed him?" Mac asked.

We let that sink in for a while. The silence told me that she didn't think a resident of that sad and depressing place had killed her brother.

She stood suddenly. "I don't know why I'm asking you this, but I have to."

Mac and I both braced for another, more pointed question about Chick.

She surprised us both by asking something completely unrelated. "Can I give you a hug?"

Mac stood and threw his arms out. "I thought you'd

never ask." He wrapped his arms around her while she cried a little more.

"Thank you," she said. "You're a very nice man."

"Thank you for saying that," he said. "My 'customers' usually don't send me thank-you notes for my services."

Typical Mac gallows humor, but it made Christine laugh, regardless of the fact that her brother had been one of Mac's "customers."

We walked outside into the crisp autumn air and stood on the sidewalk in front of the low government building.

"Lunch?" Christine asked hopefully. She looked at her watch. "Albeit a late one?"

I didn't really feel like eating after having been in an office adjacent to the morgue, but more than that, I needed to get some work done. "I'm sorry, but I really need to go back to school, Christine," I said.

She looked disappointed. "That's fine. I have a babysitter meeting the kids after school, so I thought I'd take advantage of that." She laughed. "Funny how I thought that once the girls were over eighteen, I'd get my life back. Now look at me."

"Tim's kids seem great," I lied. Thoughts of one of them hiding Trixie's tennis ball popped into my mind, but I pushed them aside.

"They're a little…rambunctious? Yes, that's a good way to describe them. But we're working on that."

I went around to the driver's side of the car and unlocked the doors. "Are you better now that we talked to Mac?" I asked.

She looked at me across the top of the car. "Honestly?" she asked. "I don't think I'll ever be better."

Ask a stupid question, get a tragic answer.

SEVENTEEN

THE NEXT DAY, I invited Meaghan to go to lunch, away from school and the hullabaloo of the cafeteria where quarters were close and a private conversation was nearly impossible. She's not stupid; she knew if I was spiriting her off campus, there was something serious we needed to discuss.

When we sat down at Merryweather's on the avenue, my new go-to place for an off-campus lunch, we ordered drinks and chatted about the upcoming basketball season, her practice schedule, and the new coach. Through no fault of my own, I had been the interim basketball coach for a spell when Meaghan was a freshman, and as Fred, my volunteer assistant coach, had once said, it didn't really suit my skill set. That was an understatement. I had never been so happy to go back to teaching, even if I missed interacting with the girls on the team.

Meaghan knew something was up, but she wasn't going to be the one to break the conversational ice, as it were. She kept the chatter light, asking me questions about how my semester was going, if her father and I had any plans to travel during winter break, that sort of stuff. The sort of stuff that would keep me talking and avoid the real purpose of our visit. The sort of stuff she would never ask about under normal circumstances.

After I felt like I had answered every question she could throw my way, I got down to business. We had ordered our food and were awaiting its arrival. "So, how are things going with...?" It was at that point that I realized I didn't know Mr. Super Senior's name.

"Alex."

"Right. Alex."

Her face lit up. "Great! He's a great guy. We're having a great time." She took a long drag on her soda straw. "It's so great."

"So, things are great?" I asked.

She nodded vigorously.

How to do this, how to do this...I mulled over the segue from Alex, the oldest senior on the planet, to Joanne Larkin, the cranky psych teacher, to Forensic Psych, once Meaghan's hardest class and now her avocation, to her most recent test. "Professor Larkin is thrilled that you're doing so well in class."

"Alex is a great, I mean excellent, tutor."

"Must be."

Something in my tone tipped her off. She narrowed her eyes. The jig was up. "What does that mean?"

I poked around the breadbasket, stalling. "It's just that you had a remarkable turnaround. First you were practically failing, and then you got a near perfect score on your test."

Meaghan's the more mature of the twins, but even she turned petulant every now and again. "That's because I studied." She fell silent as the waitress placed a sandwich and fries in front of her. Once she was gone, Meaghan looked at me again. "And I was tutored. What are you trying to say?"

I looked at my spinach salad and then at Meaghan's turkey club, bacon hanging out from between three slices of perfectly toasted bread, and instantly had order envy. I tried not to focus on that, preferring to think up a good rebuttal. "What I'm trying to say is that I wonder if Alex had any sample tests that he used to help you study."

Meaghan, who had been using her knife to dislodge

some ketchup from the bottle, dropped it noisily onto her plate. In my opinion, she came to her conclusion pretty quickly, that yes, I was accusing her of cheating, leading me to believe I had hit a nerve. "You think I cheated," she said, her face a combination of incredulity, anger, and hurt, all rolled into one expression. Slowly, she took her napkin off her lap and placed it next to her untouched food. She stood. "I'm going to go back to school," she said.

"Wait!" I said, grabbing her arm, but it was too late. Her mind was made up.

She looked down at me, her eyes filled with tears. "I can't believe you think I'd do something like that."

"Not you! Not intentionally!" I said, trying to explain my thought process. To her back, I called, "But maybe Mr. Super...I mean, Adam?" Wrong again. "Alex! Alex!" Too late. She was out the door of the restaurant, intent on making the six-block trek back to school on her own.

Brilliant, I thought. *Well done, Bergeron.* I sat at the table for a few minutes until the waitress came over. "Is there a problem?" she asked.

Yes, but not one that you can help me solve unless you have a time machine. "No," I said, handing her the salad, "but could you please wrap this up to go?" After she walked away with the salad, I pulled Meaghan's sandwich and fries in front of me. *Be careful what you wish for; you just might get it,* I thought, taking a huge bite of turkey club, its bacony goodness tasting like the nectar of the gods but with a soupçon of guilt.

My cell phone rang just as I was finishing up the last fry and my second soda; I was sure to be buzzing on a caffeine high all afternoon after two huge Diet Cokes. Crawford. "How you doin', pally?" I asked.

"Did you accuse Meaghan of cheating?"

That didn't take long. "Not in so many words."

"She's really upset." His voice was flat. For normal folks,

that signifies things like disinterest or boredom; in Crawford, it signifies something a little more complex. This time, it was anger.

"I know. I'll make it right."

"What is this about? Do I even want to know?"

"Where are you?"

"The precinct."

"Then let's talk about this later. In the meantime, I'll make sure to work it out with her."

"Please." He sounded exasperated. "Did she cheat?"

"I don't know."

"Maybe we should get all the facts before we try to figure this out?"

"Are you mad at me?" I asked.

"Do you really think she cheated?"

"Not on purpose."

He let out a groan. "Okay, let's talk about this later. I don't think I can handle it right now."

"Work bad?" I asked.

"Alison, I'm a homicide detective. Work is never really good," he said. He had a talent for stating the obvious.

"I meant worse than usual."

"Yes, worse than usual."

Must have been a banner day for murders in our little corner of the Bronx. That was concerning.

"It's Christine," he blurted out.

Hmmm.

"She won't let this go," he said. He blathered on, and believe me, Crawford is not a blatherer. "I remember this from when we were married. Once she got something in her head, she just wouldn't let it go. Now she wants to see the surveillance tape that tracked the people going in and out of the apartment building. How did she find out about that?"

If he didn't know, I wasn't going to tell him; he was the smarty-pants detective after all. "No clue."

"How do you tell someone that their brother was a complete loon?" he asked.

"I think you just tell them," I said helpfully.

"See, that's what separates us," he said. "You and me, that is," he added, as if there were any doubt.

"What's that supposed to mean?" I asked.

"Nothing." He sighed into the phone again. I wasn't looking forward to our evening together, if indeed we were going to have one. "I should have retired when I had the chance."

Oh, that again. "You still can." Somehow, his not retiring was turning into my fault, and I wasn't going to be left holding that bag.

The noise he made let me know that he didn't think I understood just how hard it would be to undo the decision that he had made all those months earlier. Regardless, it was his choice. This time, I wasn't getting involved.

We hung up, the issue unresolved. I can't say I wasn't a little happy that he was finally as fed up with his ex-wife and her mysterious murder theory as I was; I'd thought she'd come back from London and we'd peacefully coexist, twenty miles between us. Neither of us had banked on the fact that we'd have to deal with her crazy family and the fallout from her brother's eventual suicide.

I thought back fondly to the time when I was an adult orphan, divorced, with only myself to take care of; it was a time before poisoned dogs, and break-ins, and stepchildren, and ex-wives. Then I remembered the crippling loneliness, and the feeling of coming home to an empty house night after night. The weekend stretches where I only used my voice once, and that was to order a coffee and a bagel at the local deli. The time B.C.: before Crawford.

I finished my soda and threw some money down on the

table. The way things were now was the "new normal," and I was going to have to learn how to deal.

I vowed to myself that I would be the best second wife and stepmother on the planet, even if it killed me.

EIGHTEEN

ALTHOUGH MY INTENTIONS weren't the purest—I needed re-
assurance and he's as reassuring as they come—I felt good
picking up the phone to call Kevin McManus, my good
friend the former priest. If anyone knew how to talk me
into a better mental place, it was my old buddy.

Thinking about Kevin, I realized we hadn't spoken in
a while. I didn't know his work schedule, but I was fortu-
nate to find him at home, with a few free minutes before
reporting to the catering hall where he was banquet manager. I called him from my office. I didn't ask for absolu-
tion about some of the less-than-generous thoughts I was
having about my husband's ex, but I filled him in on the
situation with Christine and asked if he had any advice.

A heavy sigh filled the space between us. "Oh, Alison.
This is a tough one. I think you just have to ride it out."

That wasn't what I was hoping to hear, but I wasn't entirely sure what I had wanted him to say.

"Is she religious? Would talking to a priest help?"

"Why? You know someone who could talk her off the
ledge?"

"I'm just wondering if the stigma attached to suicide,
for her as a Catholic, is the reason she's holding on to this
idea that Chick may have been murdered."

"Maybe." I grabbed a pen. "If you have someone in
mind, tell me." I jotted down the name of someone Kevin
knew in the archdiocese, thinking I would broach the subject with Christine if it came up again.

"Do you think it is possible that he *was* murdered?" he asked.

"Who knows?" I said. "I met the guy that one time and he was a wacko. I guess anything is possible. I was there, though, and it looked like he'd taken a lot of pills. I can't imagine how someone could have been forced to do that."

Kevin seemed to agree. "Hey, let me know if there is anything else I can do, okay? Counseling brides and their insane mothers is a bit different than doing the Lord's work and helping someone deal with grief."

I was surprised to hear him say that. Up until this point, he had never expressed any regrets about having left the Church. I let it go. "We need to get together," I said.

"Let me get through the fall weddings and the two bar mitzvahs on the schedule and we'll talk."

Sounded like a plan. Who was I to get in the way of extravagant wedding planning and religious rites of passage?

I left my office to get some lunch, running the gauntlet of students during the change of class, and ran smack into Sister Mary at the bottom of the stairs. She was wearing what appeared to be a smile—an expression I rarely, if ever, saw her attempt. First a smile out of Fred and now one from Mary. Things were definitely going my way.

"How is it going with Mrs. Bannerman?" she asked, her arms crossed over her starched, short-sleeved navy blue blouse. I wanted to tell her that it was after Labor Day and her seersucker skirt should be put to rest for a few months, but wisely kept my mouth shut.

"Wonderful," I said. "She's an apt pupil. Very enthusiastic about the class."

"Excellent," Sister Mary said, and she was off, her pumps sounding like a team of Clydesdales marching across the tiled student union floor.

"Excellent," I murmured to myself in my Mary voice, the one that I use when Crawford has left a load of laundry in the washer overnight or has left me without gas in my car. "Did you know that 'seersucker' derives from both the Hindi and Urdu languages?" I continued in my best Sister Mary voice, cracking myself up. How I knew that arcane piece of seersucker lore was beyond me, but I did. I continued talking to myself in Mary's voice, finding myself funnier than usual.

My euphoria was short-lived. Back at my office, my lunch in a brown paper bag and just begging to be eaten, I had a little surprise waiting. Mr. Super Senior, whose name escaped me even though Meaghan and I had been talking about him only a day earlier, was standing in front of my office.

Dare I say, he did not look happy.

NINETEEN

"WHAT CAN I do for you, Andrew?" I asked, giving it a shot at his name. I knew it began with *A*, but that was it.

"It's Alex," he said, following me into the office and throwing himself into one of my chairs, his backpack crashing to the floor.

"Okay, Alex." I sat behind my desk and tried to affect my "Alison Bergeron, Serious Academic," position by folding my hands together on top of a stack of files that for all I knew were completely empty. I wasn't very good at keeping my desk clean. "How can I help you?"

"Did you accuse Meaghan of cheating?" he asked, skirting the line between true curiosity and blatant insubordination.

How much to let on here? "Alex, this is between me, Professor Larkin, and Meaghan."

"And me!" he protested.

"Not really," I said, even though it was. If he had fed her a test, even without her knowing, he was indeed involved, but for right now, I was keeping it in the family. And Joanne Larkin. "I just want to make sure that Meaghan is using typical, and legal, study habits to do well in her classes."

"Yeah, but I'm her tutor," he said. "You see why…"

I let that hang out there for a while, letting Alex come to the conclusion that anything else he said might indict him, either justifiably or not. I raised an eyebrow. "Are you sure you want to pursue this with me?" I asked.

He stayed silent.

I went in for the kill. "Did you give my stepdaughter a test from a previous semester of Professor Larkin's class?" I asked.

He stood and worked his tongue around in his mouth, searching for an appropriate response. He went with indignation. "Did it ever occur to you that I might just be a great tutor?" he asked, invoking Meaghan's favorite adjective.

I thought for a moment. "No, it never did."

He didn't have a response for that. He picked up his backpack, laden with books and a laptop, and started for the door. "You don't even know me. Why do you hate me?" he asked.

Good question. I didn't have an answer. You really can't hate someone for not finishing school on time, and I had probably already convicted him in the court of my personal opinion, but that wasn't enough of an answer. "I'm trying to protect my Stepdaughter. That's all."

He left in a huff, and I didn't care. I picked up the phone and did what I should have done the last time Joanne Larkin was in my office: I asked her if she reused tests from previous semesters in her current classes.

"Now why would you ask that?" she wanted to know.

I decided that going with the whole "there might be a cheating scandal afoot" wasn't the best idea, so I made an answer up on the fly, something I was able to do lately with alarming alacrity. "Just wondering. I belong to a Listserv that discusses the merits of using the same test from year to year."

"Well, that's an awfully irresponsible Listserv if you ask me."

I took umbrage at her disdain for the imaginary Listserv and the hardworking professors who subscribed to it, even though they didn't really exist. "So you don't? Reuse tests?"

"No, I don't reuse tests," she said, and I could imagine her readjusting her unflattering glasses on her face.

"These kids will take any advantage that they can, Alison. You have to be vigilant," she said. "Are we still talking about Meaghan and her remarkable recovery from her failing grade?"

I remained quiet.

"Because, frankly, I have been thinking about that myself."

"You have?" I asked. I didn't like where this was going.

"You see, I have had a little experience with these incredible turnarounds, and I've found that they are usually the result of less-than-stellar study habits."

"What are they the result of?" I asked, steeling myself for the answer.

"You know what I'm talking about, Alison," she said. "Now. Why don't we end this talk of tests being reused and just be grateful for your stepdaughter's good fortune?" She hung up.

So maybe I had been wrong about Mr. Super Senior. Maybe he was a good tutor, and she had studied hard. I had been wrong about Meaghan, obviously. So here was another situation I had to make right. I texted Meaghan and waited, eating my sandwich while I did, but she never texted me back. I still wasn't convinced that Mr. Super Senior was completely blameless in this whole thing; after all, he had been among the throngs that I had seen when I was hiding on the convent stairs, and his academic record didn't support his contention that he was a "great tutor." As a boyfriend? Who knew? This wasn't something I was going to forget even though my limited snooping to date had led to a dead end.

The day passed quickly, much to my delight, and I headed home to spend time with Trixie, who was back to her old tricks after her near-death experience. When I walked in the back door, she had a pair of suede flats in her mouth, chewing away noisily and happily. When she saw me, she dropped the one shoe that was in her mouth and pushed it away with her paw as if she hadn't been engaged in footwear foul play.

I put my messenger bag on the counter and bent down to assess the damage. Besides some extreme wetness from her saliva, she hadn't done too much harm. I looked into her doleful face. "I thought we were done with this?" I asked, expecting an answer.

She put her head down on her paws and closed her eyes, pretending that she was asleep. I guessed that she was exhausted after an afternoon of shoe play. I picked up the shoes and put them in the sink, wondering what the effect of more water would be on suede.

I was contemplating that when Crawford walked in with a bag from my favorite sandwich place in the Bronx, the one that doesn't pretend that its sandwiches are healthy, and that prides itself on marinating its roasted red peppers longer than should be considered safe. I clapped my hands together.

"Rota's for dinner?" I asked, holding my breath.

"Yep," he said, putting the sack onto the counter next to my bag. He gave me a kiss; if the way he smelled was any indication, it had been a very bad day indeed. I backed away, wrinkling my nose.

"Don't ask," he said.

"I didn't plan to."

"Let me take a shower and then we'll eat, okay?" he asked, already on his way upstairs. "Don't touch the bag!" he called back over his shoulder.

I told him I wouldn't, but it was the first thing I did. The sandwiches were wrapped in white paper, so I couldn't see what was inside, but the greasy spots that made the paper translucent were a very promising sign. Something in there had lots of oil and vinegar on it, and that made me very happy.

I was halfway through the *Times* crossword puzzle when he came back down, his hair still wet from the shower, sporting a T-shirt and jeans. He ripped open the bag, which I'd cleverly reclosed after my snooping. "Chicken cutlet with mozzarella and roasted red peppers or eggplant parm?" he asked, sliding the sandwiches out of the remains of the bag.

"Half of each," I said, grabbing plates from the cabinet. "Beer or wine?"

"Beer," he said, pulling out a container of pasta salad as well.

We made plates, took them to the kitchen table, and dug in. He asked me how my day was.

"It was fine," I said, leaving out the details of my meeting with Meaghan's boyfriend and my conversation with the ever-cranky Joanne Larkin. Unfortunately, the way I averted my eyes, looking anywhere but at him, gave him an indication that I was skirting around the truth. If anyone can figure out when the details are missing, it's him. I took a healthy bite of my sandwich and let out a sound that indicated that he had done well in choosing.

"Are you leaving anything out?" he asked. "Do I need to frisk you?"

"What would frisking do to get me to talk?" I asked, pushing my chair back, ready to make a quick getaway even while the idea of being frisked by Crawford gave me a thrill. "Great sandwiches, by the way."

He dropped his onto his plate. "Spill it," he said. "I know you. You only talk about food when you're hungry and when you're avoiding talking about something else."

"There's nothing to spill," I protested. "Normal, ordinary, lovely day at school."

"Now I know you're lying. You always have something to complain about. Something to tell."

He had a point.

"What gives?" he asked.

I didn't have to answer because the phone rang; I looked at the caller ID and held back a groan. "Christine," I said, trying to look as impassive as possible.

He dropped his sandwich onto his plate, deciding what to do. "Don't answer it," he said.

The phone kept ringing and ringing, and it was starting to annoy us. Finally, after the tenth ring, the call went to the answering machine, the volume turned so loud that we could hear everything she was saying, even though the machine was in the living room. Crawford looked down at his sandwiches, his enthusiasm for them lost.

Christine's voice had its usual nervous timbre; I hadn't heard her sound any other way in the past several weeks. She hemmed and hawed, not wanting to bother us, before blurting out the detail that brought our dinner to its unfortunate and untimely end.

"Um, Bobby? Someone has broken into my house."

We waited a beat, looking at each other.

"But it's weird. Nothing's missing."

TWENTY

SO RATHER THAN spend the evening with my dog, the shoe vandal, and my husband, I was on my way to Connecticut with him to offer support to the shaken Christine.

His ex and her extended family were really starting to get on my last nerve.

They were also getting under my skin and cramping my style and every other hackneyed expression one could use to express annoyance. Rather than burden Crawford with my dissertation on separating from her and her brood and all of their troubles, I stewed in edgy silence all the way up 95.

We had ascertained over the phone that everyone was fine and that the house was free of intruders before I allowed myself to arrive in this frustrated state, but the fact that I wasn't talking was a dead giveaway to my husband that I had had enough. We didn't need to talk; our telepathy was finely honed and in good working order. As we pulled off at her exit, he told me that he understood completely what I was feeling.

"You do?" I asked. "How so? My ex-husband is dead, conveniently, so you don't have to deal with him and his peccadilloes. Your ex, however…"

"I know," he said, sounding as exasperated as I was.

We let it go for a few minutes as he wound his way through the streets of downtown Greenwich, looking for the street that Christine and Tim lived on. "Do you think that her break-in is related to our break-in?" I asked.

"I guess anything's possible."

"It seems odd. First us, then them." I knew he had already thought of it, but I thought it bore repeating. "And nothing missing from either house."

"Bingo."

We pulled into a lovely tree-lined street in the very affluent suburb. Christine's house was an old, restored Colonial, the kind of house that I would love to live in but could never afford, even with our combined salaries. Old Tim must be raking it in, because with a bad economy, not many people I knew were making the kind of scratch, as Max would say, that would allow them to live comfortably, old-money fashion.

The police had come and gone, by the looks of things; the house was locked up tight, a few lights blazing in the windows on both the first and second floors. We knocked on the front door, Crawford using the heavy brass knocker. Christine opened it, her eyes puffy and red.

"Come in," she said. "It's so nice of you to come."

Well, you asked us to, I wanted to say, but instead I leaned in and gave her a kiss. "You okay?"

"I'm fine," she said, stepping aside to let us into the beautiful large foyer. *I want one of these*, I wanted to cry. When you walked in the front door of my house, you were in the house. No ante-room, no place to hang your coat, just a quick step through the front door and you were in. I took a minute to look around, noting a large formal living room on the right and an even larger, more beautifully decorated family room on the left, obviously the place where the family spent most of their time. Behind the stairs that emptied into the foyer was the kitchen, a room that was sure to be leaps and bounds over my little cooking area, what with its four-burner stove and smaller-than-normal refrigerator. Despite the fact that they hadn't moved in that long ago, there was not a box in sight. Everything had been unpacked and put away. Heck, I still had unpacked boxes in my basement, and I had lived in my house a long time.

We followed her into the kitchen, and it didn't disappoint. Everything was either white or stainless steel and immaculate. I didn't know how this was possible with four little kids, but she seemed to have figured out how to do it. Tim was sitting at the kitchen table, a big slab of wood that was suspended on thick wrought iron, nursing a beer. He looked up wearily, unaccustomed as he was to the world of crime. *You'll get used to it*, I wanted to say, even though I didn't think that was what he wanted to hear.

"Hi," he said. "Anyone want a sandwich?"

I always wanted a sandwich, but I decided that asking for one now would be in bad taste. Crawford and I demurred, but all I could think of was my sandwich back home. In my house. With my dog. I wondered if it would still be there when we returned.

Tim was clearly agitated. "You up to speed on what happened?"

We sat down at the table with him while Christine got drinks, water for Crawford, a glass of wine for me. (What? It was late. I was in Connecticut. I deserved a glass of wine if I wasn't getting a sandwich.) "No, we don't know what happened beyond what Christine told us over the phone," Crawford said.

"There's really not much more to tell," Christine said, handing me a glass of cabernet with some serious legs. This wasn't something she'd be drinking if she was still married to a cop, I'll tell you that much. "Someone broke in while we were at Liam's soccer game and seemed to be looking for something, but left when they couldn't find it."

"How did you know someone had gotten in?" Crawford asked. "Did they trip the alarm?"

Christine looked over at Tim, sheepish. She opened her mouth to talk, but Tim cut her off.

"She doesn't set the alarm," he said, his voice tense. "Doesn't see the need. Thinks we live in a safe community. I try to tell her that this is where they come to break into people's houses."

I didn't know who "they" were, but I assumed he meant "the bad guys." I didn't want to let my mind wander to whom else "they" might be.

"Now do you believe me?" he asked, giving her a hard look. Wow, when Tim meant business, he really meant business. Maybe I should have taken the sandwich; the process of assembling it might have had a soothing effect on him. I had never seen him this worked up, or even this alive. "They got in through the front door. Which, I bet, wasn't even locked."

I kicked Crawford under the table. Up until this point, Tim had been a bland, boring guy, one that we couldn't get a read on. Give him a good break-in and suddenly he developed a personality. Crawford kicked me back—judging from the look on his face, not to tell me that he understood why I was kicking him, but to tell me to stop.

Christine looked on the verge of tears, so I offered up helpfully that we had been broken into as well. Crawford broke his "no kicking" rule and kicked my shin.

"You were?" she asked, grabbing a napkin from a ceramic holder in the middle of the impressive kitchen table.

"Yes," I said, "and they didn't take anything from us either. Not that we have anything to take."

Tim exploded. "This is your brother's fault! We didn't have problems like this before he came back into your life."

That opened the floodgates. Christine started crying, Crawford looked at me as if we had just stepped into a lion's den, and suddenly, my cabernet tasted like cough syrup. Nothing like a good meltdown to ruin a perfectly good post-break-in mood and a delightful red wine. I could see Crawford's mind working, trying to decide whether he should come to his ex-wife's defense, risking a tongue-lashing from her current husband and a withholding of sexual favors from his current wife. He decided, after much thought, smoke from the process practically coming out of his ears, to keep his mouth shut.

Christine was having one of those crying jags accompanied by hiccupping and loss of breath. She tried to state her case to Tim, but she was too far gone. He responded by stomping off, after politely saying "excuse me," like a good WASP would, making haste for the front stairs and the second floor of the house.

Something hit me. It was quiet, and nobody was trying to burn the house down. "Where are the kids, Christine?" I asked.

"The little ones are already asleep, and the two older ones are sleeping at friends' houses. It was prearranged, so that worked out well. We dropped them off after the game," she hiccupped between sobs. She looked at Crawford. "Do you really think this has something to do with Chick?"

I kicked Crawford again. "Don't speak" was the message I was sending. This woman was already on the verge of a nervous breakdown; the thought of her dead brother having something to do with this might send her over the edge. To find out that he might have been involved in something untoward would break her in two.

"I don't know," he said, his voice cracking a bit, a telltale sign for me that he was lying. I wondered if she had picked up on that little character flaw when they had been married.

Nature called, and while it couldn't have been a worse time to exit, what with Crawford now playing the lying game, I had to go. "A restroom?" I asked.

Christine pointed toward the front stairs. "Go upstairs. The powder room is a bit of a mess. If I find out who stuffed a Power Ranger down the toilet, there will be hell to pay," she said, something I found hilarious even if she didn't. I stifled a chuckle as I exited the kitchen.

I headed upstairs, thrilled that I would have a chance to survey the second floor of this incredible home. The wide-planked floor was a shimmering, dull gold under my feet, and I was grateful that I had changed into my rubber-soled clogs so they didn't make much of a sound as I traversed the hardwoods in search of the bathroom. I stayed on my tiptoes, keeping the squeak as rubber hit wood to a minimum. The bathroom was adjacent to what seemed to be a bedroom, but a quick look through the crack in the door revealed that it was an office. Tim was sitting in a high-backed leather chair, facing away from the door and looking out to the backyard, pitch black save for a spotlight shining on the pool. The office was all dark wood and gleaming brass, a giant laptop sitting open on the desk.

"I think the money is ours," he said, and not that quietly.

I couldn't help myself. I stopped a few inches past the barely open door.

"Crawford and his new wife are here." He paused, listening to what the person on the other end was saying. "She's a bit of a busybody, from what I gather. Gets involved in other people's business far too often. But Christine seems to have taken a real shine to her." He paused while listening. "I guess. She seems fine. Just always poking around."

Like now. The harrumph that was building in my chest stayed lodged there because I knew that what he said was true.

"As big a stiff as ever," he said, and I bristled. Crawford. Couldn't be anyone else. Everyone in Christine's family was the opposite of "stiff." For the life of me, I couldn't think of an adjective that would adequately describe them. I also wanted to tell Tim that if you looked up "stiff" in the dictionary, a picture of his tense, unsmiling face was right beside it.

"It's with the public administrator. As soon as that is settled, it should be ours. Sit tight." I heard the squeal of the chair's springs as he turned around to face the door. I hustled toward the bathroom, which I found without trouble, and I locked myself inside.

I turned toward the toilet and was confronted by a little child who looked suspiciously like a troll. I did the only thing that someone in that situation could do. I screamed.

The child's face melted slowly into a mask of tragedy and horror, a shriek trapped at the back of her own throat waiting to be expelled. I held my breath. "Shhhh…shhhh…shhhh!" I said, thinking that I would put my hand over her mouth before she could let the noise out, thought better of it, and put my hands over my own mouth, pantomiming silence.

It was all for naught. The scream came out in one stunning and mighty roar, at a pitch that I was sure most humans, besides myself, couldn't hear. I was wrong. Tim emerged from his office, banging on the bathroom door, probably thinking that an intruder was still in the house. I opened the door, the sounds of little—what was her name, anyway?—whatever-her-name-was obliterating any explanation I could give the husband of my husband's ex-wife. He raced past me and scooped her up, covering her head with kisses while she screamed into his ear about the lady who scared her.

Seriously? I scared you? I wanted to ask. Try looking into the face of a troll when your bladder's protesting. That will scare the life out of you; I guarantee it. I did a quick inventory. A mental excursion to my nether regions confirmed that no, I had not wet my pants.

Tim finally exited with the aforementioned troll, and I took care of business. She was still outside wailing in the hallway when I emerged, and I tried to look concerned, but really, her reaction was way over the top. I gave her a look that said that we were never going to be friends and started for the stairs. I returned to the first floor, where Christine must have missed the trauma of her troll/child, because she was deep in conversation with Crawford, a.k.a. "the stiff."

Takes one to know one, Tim.

He didn't look too stiff at the moment. Au contraire, he and Christine were laughing and joking, and she didn't look traumatized at all, considering her house had been broken into and her downstairs powder room was out of service for the time being.

"Sorry for scaring the…little one," I said.

"Oh, that," Christine said. "I heard her crying. Tim was up there, right?"

"Yes," I said.

"She sleepwalks. It's crazy. We run into her at all hours of the night. It's like seeing one of those undead kids in *The Shining*." She laughed.

That was an apt description, come to think of it.

Christine stood. "Thanks so much for coming. I know it's been weird since the girls' birthday. I promise not to bother you anymore."

"Really?" I asked. It wasn't until Crawford threw me a look that I realized I had said it out loud.

She must have thought I was kidding, because she didn't seem upset at all. "Really. Thanks. You two have been amazing."

"That's us," I said. "The amazing duo."

She showed us out, and I could barely wait until the doors were closed to tell Crawford what I had heard. Well, everything except the part about him being a stiff. He didn't need to hear that. He kind of already knew it.

"Did you hear that before or after you scared the living daylights out of the kid?" he asked. "It sounded as if she were being stabbed to death."

"Christine didn't seem too concerned," I said.

"She knew Tim was up there. They prefer him anyway," he said. "Even after all this time, they still don't consider Christine their mother, and she's still adapting to raising someone else's children."

I let that sink in. I hadn't had the luxury of "adapting"; shortly after our marriage, Christine had taken off for London with Tim, leaving me with Meaghan and Erin and everything that came with being their stepmother. "So she doesn't care that the kid was screaming bloody murder?"

He didn't respond.

"I'm not criticizing her—"

He cut me off. "Yes, you are."

Well, if I was? What did that mean? I decided to change the subject, because if I knew anything, it was when a fight was brewing, just waiting to break out. "It sounds to me like Tim is banking on getting Chick's money," I said.

Crawford took a minute to decide whether or not he wanted to respond. "They probably will. Christine is the sole beneficiary in Chick's will."

"How did you find that out?"

"She told me," he said, merging into the right lane on 95. Slowly, he moved over to the left lane. Crawford is a left-laner all the way; years of driving a police car at top speeds had conditioned him to speed even when there was no need.

"Did Tim know that?"

"How could he not?" he asked. "They're married."

I didn't say anything, my mind working out the details of that little admission.

He put a hand up in my direction. "Stop. Right now. I know what you're thinking."

"And what's that?"

"That he was murdered. That Tim had something to do with it. That Christine may have been right all along."

Maybe. But not in that order. I think I may have come

to the conclusion that Christine may have been right all along first.

He continued, perturbed. "Chick was crazy. Always was, ever since the day I met him. Who knows where he got the money? Who cares?"

"Are Christine and Tim having money problems?" I asked, first out of curiosity and then because I wanted to know exactly how much my husband's ex-wife had been telling him about her personal life.

His answer made me happy. "How would I know?" He passed a slower-moving car on the right and returned to the left lane. "All I know is that I think it's weird that there were two break-ins at two separate but related locations, and that nothing was taken." He looked over at me. "Yes, I think it's weird," he admitted, which he hadn't done prior to this moment.

At least we agreed on something.

TWENTY-ONE

WHY IT HAD never occurred to me before I don't know—maybe because I hadn't cared?—but I threw the name Jaroslav Stepkowski into the search engine on my school computer and waited to see what I might find out about our dearly departed Chick. Up until now, I hadn't really cared to investigate Chick's backstory, but with the situation becoming less clear and the details of his death becoming more suspect—in my mind and Christine's, anyway—I thought that doing a little background check, the kind that an average citizen like myself could do with a computer and a little spare time, would be in order.

Tim's overheard conversation led my mind in several different directions: Ponzi scheme, bankruptcy, maxed-out credit cards. Why else would he want or need the money so badly? Was he playing it fast and loose at work with clients' money and so needed to hedge his bets, so to speak? Or did he just want to buy a new speedboat or something equally ridiculous, in the throes of a midlife crisis? Pondering all of this and coming up empty, I turned my attention back to my search on Chick.

Searching yielded little in terms of information. Chick's wedding announcement from years before had been in the *Times*. Fancy. I noted that he had gotten married on exactly the same day in exactly the same year that I had married my ex. (We were not in the *Times*, but we were in the local paper and in my parents' church's bulletin. That's as fancy as we got.) Chick's ex-wife was a blowzy-looking blonde in a really tight strapless wedding gown that managed to make her look both slutty and gone-to-seed. Chick was slimmer than when I had met him and had a full head of black hair that he had styled in a modified mullet.

How they had ended up in the *Times* was beyond me until I noticed that his frowzy bride, the aptly named Sassy Du Pris (which I suspected was a stage name; the type of stage I could only venture a guess at), came from a wealthy, albeit louche, family from the South who had made their fortunes in porta-potties. It was all right there in black and white, but not in so many words. Farther down in the article, Chick was identified as having been the director of marketing for Sans-a-Flush. Why Mrs. Stepkowski, née Du Pris, needed to be onstage was something I would have to figure out later, but that gal had "stripper" written all over her, from her tacky weave down to her Lucite-heeled wedding shoes.

The thing that caught my eye was her hair, a mountain of blond spun sugar, piled high atop her head and slung over her right shoulder in a modified Martha Washington kind of 'do that doesn't look good on too many people, Sassy included. I flashed back to Chick's funeral and the woman standing by the archangel gravestone, studying her manioure. Had Sassy Du Pris, long out of the picture, made a brief appearance at Chick's burial? If so, why hadn't she made herself known? More importantly, did I really care to find out?

I decided that rather than ruminate on the boring subject of Chick's ex-wife visiting the cemetery where he was laid to rest, I would find out more about the bride's family's company. Who doesn't want to learn everything they possibly could about porta-potties? I went to the company Web site, which boasted, "You'll feel like a king when you sit on our throne!" I wondered if Chick had come up with that witticism. What a wordsmith.

After the wedding announcement, there was nothing of note in the search engine. Just your basic annual report links and details of the company's win in an intercompany softball league. Apparently, Chick could throw some heat and had led Sans-a-Flush to the regional championship. Before I could go any further, there was a knock at the door, and Meaghan stuck her head in.

"Hi. Do you have a minute?" she asked.

I pushed away from the computer. "Sure. Come on in." I didn't know what this was going to be about, but I hoped we could clear the air. She looked a little sheepish and not at all agitated, and I took that as a good sign.

She sat down, her backpack hanging down between her long legs. "I'm sorry," she said.

"For what?"

"For getting so mad at you," she said.

"It's okay, Meg," I said. "I hope I didn't upset you. I just don't want you to be in a position of having to explain yourself to the university judiciary if something comes up."

She hemmed and hawed for a minute before blurting out the truth. "He did give me a test. As a sample." Her cheeks turned red. "But you have to believe me. I had no idea. I didn't ask him to do it."

I let that sink in. "Okay." I thought about the next question and how I really didn't want to hear the answer. "How close was it to the test you took?"

That's when she started crying. "It was identical."

Oh, boy. The face of cranky Joanne Larkin swam in front of me, the same Joanne Larkin who had chastised me for subscribing to a fake Listserv where fake professors gave the identical fake exams every semester. Was she cutting corners and just not brave enough to admit it? I had certainly been guilty of a few corner-cutting measures myself, like not having homework or papers due on Friday or giving a multiple-choice test when an essay or short answer test would have been better. It wasn't often, but it had happened, and the secret code among professors is that we don't judge one another when one of our minor cheats comes to light. I realized that I was hashing all of this out in my brain while staring at Meaghan, who was still stricken at the thought of her malfeasance.

"Listen," I said. "First things first. Aaron—"

"Alex."

"Right. Alex. You need to stop having him tutor you." She waited. "And?"

"I wouldn't be upset if you broke up."

"But I love him!" she cried, a bit more melodramatically than the circumstances called for, but I was in no position to judge. I've been known to dabble in a little melodrama myself every now and again.

"Fine," I said, if only to get her to keep her dramatics to a minimum while she was in my office. "Just stop having him tutor you. Tell him that I'll do it, or that you're doing better, or that you don't think you need his help anymore."

She sniffled loudly into a lank tissue that she pulled from her pocket. "Which one?"

"Which one what?"

"Which excuse should I use?"

I enunciated, speaking slowly and clearly. "I. Don't. Care." I put my head in my hands. "Any one of them is fine."

"Are you going to tell my father?" she asked, standing and slinging her heavy bag over her shoulder.

I thought about that one. "For now? I don't think so. But I'm warning you, Meaghan. Stay away from that kid," I said, not wanting to screw up his name again. I thought back to the night before and how Crawford surely would have asked about the situation with Meaghan had Christine not called with the news of the break-in. Her mother's bad luck had helped Meaghan luck out. "I know you love him, but he can't love you if he would put you in this position."

"You hate him," she said.

We were back to that old accusation. I decided to come clean. "Right now, yes, I do."

She looked crestfallen. "He's really nice."

"I'm sure he is," I said. *He's also closer to thirty than he should be while still in college*, I wanted to say but didn't. "In my opinion, though, he's been at this school way too long, and if he's involved in a cheating scandal? Well, let's just say that however nice he is, he's going to get in big trouble."

She understood. Before she left my office, she squinted at my computer. "Why are you looking at porta-potty companies?" she asked.

I had forgotten that I had left Sans-a-Flush's Web site open. I clicked back to the school's home page as quickly as I could. "Oh, nothing. Sister Mary asked me to look into rental toilets for the next Spring Fling." The lie was so flimsy that even Meaghan didn't believe it. I stopped her before she could question me further about the location of the toilets since there were clearly enough commodes in the building to accommodate the Spring Fling attendees. I told her to take off, keep her nose clean, never accept wooden nickels, and make lemons out of lemonade before she left.

She slunk off, her six-foot frame slumped over and defeated. I felt bad for a minute and then turned my internal rage to that dopey boyfriend of hers. It was Erin's boyfriend we thought we were supposed to hate, what with his assorted piercings and body art, but the kid turned out to be a gem who not only put up with Crawford's bitchy little offspring but did well in school and kept her on the straight and narrow. I always thought that Meaghan would have better taste in men than this bore she was besotted with, but I had been wrong on that account.

I swung my chair around and stared out the windows, looking out toward the sisters' cemetery. A lot of women, many of whom had taught me and had been my colleagues, were buried in that cemetery, and sometimes, when my head was clouded, I strolled through and looked at the headstones, looking for wisdom and a little clarity. Sometimes, I actually found it. I decided that today was one of those days when a little stroll might be necessary.

As I straightened up my office, I thought about my conundrum. I was conflicted. Did I tell Joanne and risk her wrath at my accusation, thereby jeopardizing Meaghan's standing at school? Or did I say nothing? Nobody knew what was up unless you counted me, Meaghan, and Alex, and to be honest, I wasn't even positive what his role was. Did he buy the paper or had he kept it from years past? Was it possible he just wanted her to use it for practice? How was I going to approach this?

I strolled past Dottie, the worst receptionist known to receptioning, without letting her know where I was going. Even a quick conversational interlude with Dottie could take a wrong turn with just one misused word, and we would be heading down a road neither of us wanted to travel. We preferred, instead, to respectfully ignore each other. I get under her skin, for some reason, and she really bugs the crap out of me, so after all these years of my teaching at St. Thomas and working alongside her, we decided that pretending that the other didn't exist was the best policy. Today I couldn't tell if she assiduously avoided me, or if she was so engrossed in her latest tome, *Love's Fertile Splendor*, that she really didn't notice me. I tiptoed past her desk and made my way outside, using the back staircase that I had a great view of from my office.

My conversation with Meaghan weighed heavy on me. Although I'd never go so far as to say that Meaghan and Erin were like my own children, they were as close as you could get. Crawford and I skimmed and skittered around the child conversation a lot; I was no spring chicken—but had not reached middle age—and he had his hands full with raising two teenagers. If I looked deep into my heart, though, a place I rarely went, I had to admit that I did think about it. What did it say about me that I had been much surer of my desire to be a mother when I was married to my first husband, a man I really didn't love, than I was with the love of my life, Crawford? Maybe a baby would have provided a distraction to Ray, while I wanted Crawford all to myself. I didn't know the real answer and, as was my custom, I didn't want to give it much thought. Scratching off layer after layer of emotion wasn't something I enjoyed. I preferred, as it were, to let nature take its course.

The first gravesite I visited wasn't terribly old; Sister Alphonse had died less than a year ago. She once told me that she had prayed for my happiness and that soon after, Crawford had appeared. Granted, he was investigating a murder and I was a person of interest, but I guess Alphonse hadn't been specific about what kind of man she wanted me to find. Or when. Nevertheless, Alphonse's power of prayer, obviously finely honed after over eighty years in the convent, made my future husband appear and bring me more happiness than I ever could have imagined. I pulled a sugar packet from my pocket—Alphonse's sweet tooth was something that I would remember for the rest of my life—and placed it on top of her grave marker, something I did every time I visited. There were ten packets altogether on the cool stone, a few less than there should have been, but with the bird population in the vicinity of the cemetery, that wasn't surprising. I talked to Alphonse more since she had died than when she had been alive, and while she didn't talk back, she let her spirit be known in ways that would mystify others but were obvious to me. A fluttering leaf, a sudden gust of wind, a sliver of light that fixated on a particular word on another grave marker—"peace," "love," "charity," words that let me know where she wanted my heart to go.

Today, I asked her what I should do about Meaghan's situation, and I waited. I stood staring at her grave marker for a long time, wondering what she would do in a similar instance, but Alphonse had been a bit of an enigma so I wasn't entirely sure. After a few minutes, I reached down and drew my fingers across her name, etched in the stone.

"Nothing to say today?" I asked. When it was clear that Alphonse didn't have an answer for me, I started back toward the building, a little clearer of mind, but not much. I still wasn't sure what to do, and that troubled me. Usually, I went with my heart and did the first thing that came into my head, not always a winning combination, but one that eventually worked out in the long run.

Just as I was leaving the cemetery, picking my way across the gravel at the entrance, I stumbled backward, landing at the base of a great and majestic gravestone. Obviously, Sister Irene Mary Stanislaus had come from money, because her family had erected a great and soaring angel in her honor, a marker that towered above the rest of the sisters' stones. I stood and dusted myself off, my skirt marked with a little slash of mud across the hem; I cursed lightly under my breath and looked at Sister Irene Mary's epitaph:

Great is truth and mighty above all things.

I guess I had my answer.

TWENTY-TWO

As I MADE my way back to my office, I decided that I wasn't going to seek out Joanne Larkin today but later in the week. I had to wrap my brain around this situation and figure out the best way to approach it. I have never been officially diagnosed, but I suspect I have a terminal case of foot-in-mouth disease, one that gets worse when I have to deal with a sensitive situation or topic. Rather than blurt out the first thing that would inevitably come into my head, I was going to jot down a script, one designed to counter any objections Joanne might have to my accusation and that would keep Meaghan in school and in good standing both academically and athletically. Meaghan would probably handle getting expelled better than she would handle getting bounced from the basketball team, but neither scenario was a good one, and they went hand in hand.

Members of the cross-country team went by in a blur of purple, our predominant school color, and a blast of chilly air kissed my face. I thought about Meaghan and her bad taste in men, something that up until recently we had in common. Both of us had great fathers yet had exhibited incredibly poor judgment when it came to the opposite sex. I hoped that she would see the light, as I had, and move on from Mr. Super Senior, someone who I hoped graduated at the end of the year, joined the Peace Corps, and headed to a far-off land where cell service and texting were still a decade away from being a reality. It didn't seem like my fervent hope of them breaking up was in the cards, though, so I had to think about Plan B, which was finding a way to make him look unsuitable to her without pushing her farther into his warm embrace, kind of like the polar opposite of playing Cupid.

I had too much on my mind, the least of which was school, and I had to get my focus back when it came to teaching. I was carrying my usual load, but with all of the family drama taking center stage, I was behind on a variety of tasks, including the grading of some creative writing exercises that I had given my class the week before. It was funny how that worked: Students waited until the last possible minute to hand in assignments, yet didn't give an inch when it came to when I got things back to them. It had become obvious to me over the years that most of my students thought I was some kind of professorial eunuch, laboring solely for their pleasure at the temple of St. Thomas University. The fact that I had a husband, a dog, some stepchildren, and a social life of sorts never entered their minds, so focused were they on their own pursuits of education, sex, and booze. Most of the time it made me laugh, but this week, after break-ins and dog poisonings and cheating scandals, I was ready to tell each and every one who asked where their test was or why their paper wasn't graded to "stick it."

After a calming visit to the cemetery, I had managed to think myself right into a black mood, a mood that would surely persist until I got some perspective on my work and hunkered down. As I rounded the corner to the stairs that would take me back to my office, Mary Lou Bannerman appeared, a paper bag in her hand.

"Hi!" she called in that ever-cheerful way that she had. I didn't know what she took to stay in this state of perpetual bliss, but I wanted some. "Did you have lunch?" she asked.

I thought about the peanut butter sandwich on wheat bread that I had packed that morning and that resided at the bottom of my messenger bag, probably as flat as a pancake by now and more than a little odiferous. "No," I said.

She thrust the bag toward me. "Fresh mozzarella with sun-dried tomato and pesto."

My mouth watered at the thought. "You don't have a glass of a witty yet serious Chianti in there, too, do you?"

She smiled wider. "No, but that surely could be arranged."

I took the bag. "It's like you can read my mind," I said. "I was just thinking that I was going to go back to my office and eat lunch before my next class. I was also thinking that the lunch I packed was completely unappetizing." I opened the bag and saw that in addition to the sandwich, there was a bag of gourmet chips, the kind that are made from a variety of root vegetables but are still loaded with calories and sodium, just the way I like my chips.

She turned and looked toward my office, waving a hand in that direction. "Well, bon appétit," she said. "I'm off to the library. I'll see you tomorrow in class."

"Yes, that," I said. "I was hoping to get your assignments back, but it's not looking good."

She waved a hand dismissively. "No worries. Whenever."

"If only all of my students were like you. Sandwiches and patience. My life would be perfect," I said, starting down the stairs toward the door. Looking into the hallway, I spied the back of someone leaving my office, pulling the door shut behind him or her, which was odd, because the note that I'd left on my door asked students to either e-mail me or put a note in my mail slot if they wanted an appointment outside office hours. The sun glinted off the double-paned leaded glass, so I couldn't make out if it was a man or a woman. By the time I got there, the only people on the floor were Dottie and a number of my colleagues all either leaving or going back to their own offices.

Dottie was actually working when I got to her desk, a spreadsheet open on her computer. "Hi, Dottie," I said, checking the mail slot behind her for a note from a student.

She raised a penciled-in eyebrow, no thicker than a toothpick, at my greeting. Today's getup was a flowered tunic paired with purple leggings, eye shadow to match, natch.

When it was clear that was her greeting, I asked her if she had seen anyone go in or out of my office, or if anyone had left me a message. She continued working on the spreadsheet, giving me a curt shake of her head to indicate that she hadn't seen anyone nor had anyone left me a message. At least that's what I deduced.

My door was closed, just as it had been when I left, and when I went inside, nothing was out of place. I walked back out to Dottie's desk and asked her again. "Dottie, no one?"

"I didn't see anyone," she said, turning to face me, "and nobody left you a message." She swiveled back around. "I have work to do," she said.

Well, that's a first, I thought, hurrying back to my office to eat my sandwich. I was sensitive to the fact that I might have missed a student; students were quick to report to Sister Mary if their needs weren't met by any of the professors under her charge, and I had been lectured more than once about my commitment to making sure that students were well cared for and that my office hours made their visits the most convenient for them, even if they cut into time I should have had to do my own work. I took the sandwich out of the bag and dove in, turning to look at my computer while I ate.

I was pretty sure I had left the browser on the school's home page, but when I touched the mouse and the screen lit up, that wasn't the case. The browser was back on the Sans-a-Flush page.

That's funny, I thought.

TWENTY-THREE

"WHAT ARE YOU eating?" Max asked after I picked up the phone.

"Fresh mozzarella and tomato."

"I just had a burger from Shake Shack."

"Good for you," I said. "We don't have gourmet food on every corner here in the Bronx, Max. Fortunately, I have a student who is kind enough to bring me a sandwich every now and again."

"Ass kisser."

"No, just a nice lady," I said.

"Lady?"

"Yes," I said, then described Mary Lou Bannerman and her reason for being at St. Thomas. "She's really lovely. I was less than enthusiastic when I found out she was going to be in my class, but she really has been a ray of sunshine."

"Well, that's nice. You have someone your own age to pal around with," she said.

I was quick to point out that Mary Lou was older than me. As was Max.

"Well, whatever. Better than having to spend time with teenagers who don't get your humor." She dropped her voice to a whisper. "Listen, I have some bad news."

A line like that always makes my blood run cold. "What?"

A little sob escaped, and since Max isn't a crier, I knew that this was serious. "It's my dad."

I don't know why she didn't lead with that news, but

she's Max and she doesn't usually follow normal conversational or social conventions.

"He had a stroke. It's not serious, we don't think, but he's in Westchester Medical Center and he's being observed."

"What happened?"

"Mom found him at the kitchen table, dribbling coffee out of the side of his mouth. She said that he was having trouble talking and that his right hand wasn't working either."

"What can I do, Max?" I asked.

Her voice was a little hoarse, from crying, I expected. "Just pray."

"Of course," I said, "and if you need anything, or they need me to do anything, just call. I'm only twenty minutes away from the medical center."

"I know," she said. "He may get transferred to a rehab facility in Tarrytown and get back up to speed. That's what we're hoping, anyway."

"And that's exactly what will happen," I said.

"You think?"

"With your father?" I made a dismissive noise. "Of course. That old guy is stronger than Fred."

I could hear the smile in her voice. "You're right. He's in good shape, right?"

"The best."

"So he'll get through this," she said, trying to make it more of a statement than a question.

"I have no doubt."

"Thanks." She changed the subject as she is wont to do when things get too intense. "So this Bannerman lady. Is she a good writer?"

"Too early to tell," I said. "If she takes the second semester of this course, she'll probably finish her novel and then we'll see."

"What's her novel about?"

"Her husband's murder."

"Ooohhh," Max said. "That oughta be interesting." I heard the other line ringing on her office phone. She said something unintelligible, her voice muffled.

"What?" I asked, not sure that I had heard her correctly, but she was gone, as was her custom, without saying goodbye. I finished my sandwich and cleaned off my desk, preparing to head upstairs for my freshman composition class, the one with the kids who wouldn't know a past participle if it hit them in the face. Thank God for Mary Lou Bannerman and her offering of sustenance; it would help me get through the next fifty minutes or so.

I was thinking about how I could skip out after class and head up to the medical center as I arrived at my classroom, preoccupied with the thought of an ailing Marty and concerned for Max. Still in the hallway, I texted Crawford about Max's father, letting him know that I would be visiting the hospital after school. After that, I took a deep breath and went into the room, where I was pleased to see I had full attendance. *Will wonders never cease*, I thought.

After class, I raced back to my office to get things in order. I hadn't heard back from Crawford, so I didn't know if he had read my text, but I figured he would have found out from Fred by now what was happening. I wasn't worried about him not knowing where I was for the time being. As I was putting some files and papers into my bag, I was suddenly racked by the pain of knowing that sooner rather than later, most likely, Max would be losing a parent, someone who also had been something of a surrogate parent to me. Up until this point, Max had led a pretty charmed life in terms of what she had had to deal with; in her family, no one had had a major illness, everyone was settled and happy, and her parents were healthy, living on their own now that their children were grown. In my own experience with losing my parents, Max had been supportive, yet held me at arm's length during that time, preferring to give over the lion's share of bereavement duties to her mother and father, who had supported and nurtured me during two hellacious periods in my life. What would this do to her? I wondered. Max doesn't like things that are not tidy and neat, and my life throughout the years had been decidedly messy. She had done what she could to be there for me, but now that she was entering the time when her own parents were past elderly and into the realm of the "old-old," as they are now called, how would she deal? Sure, I had talked a good game, letting her know that I thought her father would be fine, and maybe he would be. Realistically, though, how many eighty-year-olds, despite good health, make it back to 100 percent after a stroke?

I was glad Fred was in her life. Although the guy didn't speak much, he was her rock, and that might be all she would need to not go off the deep end should something terrible happen as a result of Marty's stroke.

Just as I was about to take off, my office phone rang. To answer or not to answer, that was the question. I thought of Sister Mary's lack of affection for me and decided answering it would be in my best interest, just in case she had called to chat about one of my myriad shortcomings as a teacher.

I wished I hadn't answered. It was Christine.

"Alison, I'm sorry to bother you, but I can't get ahold of Bobby," she said.

Neither can I, I thought, but held back on that observation. "What can I do for you, Christine?" I asked, sounding a little cool to my own ears.

My frigid tone didn't seem to have any effect on her. "I'm a little shaken, Alison."

I let out an exhale and resisted the urge to ask, "What now?" Instead, I asked her what was wrong in the most sympathetic tone I could muster.

"It's Sassy. Sassy Du Pris? Chick's ex-wife?"

I knew who Du Pris was, but I didn't let on. Whatever she already thought of me, I would hate for Christine to think I was cyberstalking her family, even if all I was doing was a little research. "What about her?"

"She called me," she said, "and she said that she wants the money."

"Well, she doesn't have any claim to it," I said.

"I know, but she said that she would do whatever it takes to get it." Christine sobbed into the phone. "I know this woman. She means it."

TWENTY-FOUR

FOR THE SECOND time that week, I found myself driving to Connecticut to calm a frazzled and upset Christine Stepkowski Crawford Morin, and this time, if she offered me wine, I would only be able to have a half glass at most, given that I had to drive back to Westchester. I was furious that I was doing this and that it might interfere with my visit to Marty, but I hoped that talking Christine off the ledge wouldn't take that long and I could squeeze in a visit before hours were over. I was a one-woman counselor and self-appointed designated driver, and those two things made me ill-tempered. I pulled up in front of her impressive manse and got out of the car, slamming the door so hard that I'm surprised the windows didn't shatter.

So why was I there? Despite everything, I liked Christine. Did I resent that she had had an excellent adventure abroad while I stayed home, making sure *her* kids had everything they needed and then some? You betcha. Was I a little perturbed, maybe even jealous, over her easy familiarity with Crawford, such that it wasn't unusual to see her touch his arm or put her arm around his waist? More than you'll ever know. Even so, would I wish that brood of little troll-like rug rats on anyone, even my worst enemy? No, and that's why I was there. She had her own share of troubles, not the least of which was that she was raising little kids all over again, little kids who had sprung from someone else's womb and who had a host of unformed ideas about what it was to have a stepmother. It made my time with Meaghan and Erin seem like a walk in the park, and trust me, it wasn't.

While I waited for Christine to answer the door, my phone buzzed in my bag. A text from Max read *Call me*, a message I had had from her several hundred times over the past few years. I texted her back that I had to do something and then would be all hers.

Christine answered the door looking exactly the same as the last few times I had seen her, her eyes red, her cheeks flushed, her body language jittery. She pulled me into the house. "Thank you for coming, Alison."

I know she would have preferred Bobby, but she got me instead. I wasn't sure why we couldn't do this over the phone, but she had sounded so completely unnerved that having someone who was acquainted with the situation— that would be me—to relate the latest developments to in person seemed to be the only way she was going to get off the proverbial ledge. At least she had had the good manners to realize that it had been an imposition, I thought, as I spied a coffee urn on the table alongside some of the most delicious-looking chocolate chip cookies I had ever seen. I prayed silently that they were for us and not the troll-children.

I took a seat at the giant kitchen table, which was more of a casual dining set than a standard breakfast nook kind of table. Her kitchen, as it had been before, was gleaming and spotless. I thought guiltily of the dingy rug at my back door, the one that I wiped my feet on when I came in the house but that Crawford seemed to think was invisible, preferring instead to track his mud throughout the first floor until I screamed at him to take his shoes off. How did she keep this place so clean with six people in residence, four of whom used to live under a bridge somewhere? I thought about this as she scurried about, pouring me coffee, handing me milk, and freshening up her own cup. Her racing around the kitchen led me to believe that she had already had a few more cups than her tiny frame could safely absorb. I pulled her cup away from her.

"Maybe you should switch to decaf," I said.

She laughed, but as always, at least lately, the laughter turned to tears.

"What happened?" I asked.

"Is it weird that I called you?" she asked, before launching into the story of Sassy's call.

I employed my old trick of counting to ten before speaking, but my silence spoke volumes. She looked crestfallen.

"It was weird. I knew it. I'm sorry," she said.

"It's fine," I said. "I'm here now, and I want to hear what happened." I reached down for my messenger bag on the floor and came face-to-face with one of the midget children, a different one from the sleepwalker. I gasped. "Oh, hello, honey," I said.

The child, of indeterminate gender, just pointed at me. "Her," it said.

"That's Alison, Devon," Christine said, scooping the toddler up in her arms and handing him a cookie that was as big as his pretty impressively sized head; I wondered what the late Mrs. Morin had looked like. "You remember her, don't you?"

"Her," he mouthed around a big chunk of cookie.

I stared back at him, determined not to be spooked. How scary could he be? He was wearing one of those patterned diapers that promised that he would be a "big kid" any day now. Clock was ticking, Devon. Kindergarten appeared to be right around the corner, and he was still crapping in his pants.

"Go find your sister and put on a show," Christine said, watching him run off. She dropped her head into her hands. "I'm too old for this."

I had to agree with that. I was tired just watching her

try to take care of the kids, never mind actually interacting with them.

She took a big bite of the cookie in front of her, half eaten and on a paper napkin. "I don't know why I'm eating," she said, seeming to lose her train of thought.

"Sassy," I reminded her. If she didn't focus, Devon would be potty trained before I heard even one detail from this tale.

"Right." She took another bite of cookie. "Sassy was Chick's wife. They divorced right before he vanished."

I knew that already, but again I kept my mouth shut.

"Ask Bobby," she said, invoking my husband's name in that familiar way that made the hair on my neck stand up. "We weren't crazy about her, but I'm sure her family didn't know what to make of Chick either. He was kind of a character."

You think?

"Anyway, when it came to the divorce, we never did hear Sassy's side of the story, but Chick's side was pretty horrible. Cheating, abuse, drinking…you name it."

Having seen Ms. Du Pris's wedding announcement, none of this came as a surprise. She had tattoos over her tattoos, and that was back in the day when only women of ill repute had "ink."

"The weird thing was that her family was really wealthy." Christine shook her head. "I think she was kind of the black sheep. The rest of the family seemed quite lovely. Genteel, in fact."

That didn't surprise me as much as it surprised Christine. The Stepkowskis were a study in skewed family dynamics, but only in reverse: Christine was the only genteel one among a group of Neanderthals. Sassy should have fit right in. Christine was the Marilyn in the family of Munsters.

"How did she find you?" I asked.

"How does anyone find anyone these days?" she asked. "She found me online. Through my Facebook page. My cell phone number is listed in my info section."

Which is precisely why I don't have a Facebook page, but I saved that conversation for another time. The last thing I needed was my students or my colleagues scanning my wall for personal information or insights into my personality or habits. I was already suspect among many people on campus; why give them more ammunition? "Hmmm," I said, sounding more thoughtful than judgmental, I hoped. "So what does she want?"

"She wants money. All of it, whatever that means. I don't know if she means the ten thousand he gave the girls or the quarter million he had stashed in his mattress."

"I didn't know you could actually get that much money into a mattress." That was one of several pieces of this puzzle that still amazed me. I thought the old stuffing-money-in-the-mattress scheme was an urban legend.

"I told her that it was with the public administrator and that we didn't know who would get it." She looked at me. "It sure won't be her, if I have anything to say about it."

"How could it be? They've been divorced for ten years."

"Yes, but that's where it gets complicated. Apparently, Chick owes her back alimony, and she said she's going to fight for it."

"So pay her off and keep the rest." Sounded simple to me. This still didn't sound like something that would push Christine over the edge. Christine didn't need the money. Or did she? I thought back to the conversation I had overheard the last time I was here, the one where Tim was talking about getting the money. I waited for the piece of the story that would reveal all.

"She said she would burn my house down if I did anything to stand in her way." She looked at me. "She would do it, too. That's what she tried the day Chick filed for divorce. She tried to burn their house down." She shook her head in disbelief. "She came from such a nice family. A lovely sister and brother, and her parents were just so…" She looked for the word. "Genteel."

On second thought, Sassy Du Pris sounded like a real charmer—definitely someone not to be trifled with.

"Wait," I said. Something occurred to me. "Back up. How did she know about the money?"

Christine blew her nose on the napkin that had previously held her cookie. "That's the weird part," she said. "She said Chick called her right before he died."

TWENTY-FIVE

CRAWFORD WENT WHITE when I mentioned her name.

"So you remember her?"

"Remember her? I've been trying to forget her for ten years," he said. He pulled off his gun and his badge and stowed them in the uppermost cabinet in the kitchen, the one that no one, myself included, could reach. He shuddered. "She was scary."

"You were scared of her?" I asked, resisting the urge to laugh.

"She was scary," he repeated. "Really scary."

"Scary enough to kill someone?" I asked, thinking back to Christine's contention that Chick had been murdered.

"Everyone, at one time or another, could probably kill someone," he said rather cryptically.

"That's a nonanswer."

"Yes, she could kill someone," he said, grabbing a beer from the refrigerator. "Hell, she tried to burn the guy's house down. With him inside. What does that tell you?" he asked. "Want a glass of wine?"

"And that's a nonquestion," I said.

He busied himself opening a bottle of red from the wine rack. He shuddered again. "I had hoped I would never hear about her ever again."

"I think I saw her at the cemetery," I said. He went even whiter. "Really?"

I told him about the big blond lady, the one with the hat that obscured her face but didn't do anything to hide the cascade of yellow hair, looking into the distance at Chick's family, gathered graveside.

"Sounds like her." He wiped a hand across his face. "So she's back."

"That bad?" I asked.

"The worst," he said, pouring a generous amount of wine into a large goblet and handing it to me. "Did I ever tell you about their wedding?"

"Up until a few weeks ago, I didn't even know Christine had a brother named Chick. Why would you have told me about their wedding?"

"Good point," he said, draining his beer. Obviously, the telling of this story required liquid courage. "They had it at Tavern on the Green. Really swanky. Her parents looked shell-shocked the whole time; whether it was because of her or him, it was hard to tell. The bridal party consisted of Chick's neighborhood buddies and her 'friends from work,'"—he finger quoted—"and me." He laughed. "In case I wasn't clear, her friends from work were strippers, just like her."

"Oh, I'm so sorry, Crawford." I couldn't help but let out a chuckle. Next to that crowd, he *was* a stiff.

He grabbed another beer and pulled out a container of left-over pasta. "Can I eat this?" he asked.

"Be my guest," I said, looking forward to the rest of the story.

"Anyway," he said between forkfuls of cold pasta, "you can only imagine the bachelor party. Chick wanted us to rent a party bus and spend the night trolling the city for strip clubs. I went to the dinner beforehand and then begged off."

"Wise move."

"Anyway, the wedding. So you've got her family, the strippers, the hoodlums from the West Side, me and Christine, and Christine's family."

I got a mental picture.

"So it's time to cut the cake, and everyone is singing and watching what the two of them will do. Will they gently feed each other a piece of cake or will it get messy?"

"Messy!" I called, getting in on the fun of the retelling of the most bizarre wedding reception in history.

"Bingo. She takes the cake and pretends that she's going to feed him and then picks it up and shoves it in his mouth, breaking his two front teeth and giving him a bloody nose."

"You're making this up," I said.

"I wish I was."

Now I knew why Christine had been so upset. Sassy sounded like a complete loon.

"Her family was mortified, and Chick was taken out of his own wedding reception in an ambulance."

I thought back to my own staid first wedding and the fact that Chick and Sassy had gotten married on exactly the same day. All signs were pointing toward that particular day as being a bad-luck day to tie the knot, even if I had only married your run-of-the-mill philanderer and not a dancer from an all-male nudie revue.

"Speaking of her family," I said, "where do they fit in? How did they get a kid like her?"

"Apparently, she was adopted as a teenager by the Du Pris family. She was orphaned after her parents died in a car accident. So she was well on her way to being a hell raiser before the Du Pris family got their hands on her." He shook his head and forked in another mouthful of pasta. "She had a nice sister and very sweet little brother who were her adoptive parents' biological children. They all seemed close even if Sassy stood out from the rest. Those poor people. I can still see the look on her father's face when she broke Chick's teeth." He came over and gave me a hug, kissing me lightly on the forehead. "Before I forget, thank you."

"For what?"

"For going to see Christine. She must have been a wreck."

"You could say that."

"She was terrified of Sassy and her temper. Sassy would flare up at the drop of a hat, and she and Chick would go at it." He went back to his pasta. "I'm used to that kind of marital pyrotechnics, having been on a number of domestic abuse calls, but Christine? She just couldn't handle it."

"Is that why they got divorced?" I asked.

He shrugged. "Who knows. It was acrimonious. I can tell you that. That's why when Chick called her his 'sweet Sassy' or something like that, I was surprised." He shook his head. "That wedding never should have happened."

I got up and opened the refrigerator, rooting around for something to eat. I spied a hunk of Manchego cheese in one of the drawers and a pear that had inexplicably landed at the back of one of the shelves but still looked edible. "Having never met this Sassy person, I can't imagine why she is so frightening, but I'm getting a picture. She told Christine that she would burn her house down if she didn't get the money."

"Sounds about right."

"Should Christine call the police?" I asked.

He finished off the pasta while standing, never sitting down at the kitchen table to eat like a civilized human being. "I'll take care of it in the morning. I'll make a call to Greenwich PD to keep an eye out for her." He chuckled. "She's not hard to miss, what with the hair and the boobs."

I was busy looking for some crackers and was glad I was facing away from him; this way, he wouldn't be able to see my face as I grimaced at the thought of him riding to the rescue of his ex. Again.

He came up behind me and wrapped me in a tight embrace, and I forgot, momentarily, that I was on the verge of exasperation. I leaned back into him and let my head rest against his chest, his heart beating next to my ear.

"She always was such a worrywart," he said, and to

me, he sounded almost wistful, as if her worry habits were something that he had once cherished and treasured.

I stiffened. "Okay," I said, pulling away. "That's it. Can we get through the rest of this night without talking about Christine, or her crazy family, or her sociopathic former sister-in-law, or Chick's money and where it came from?"

He stepped back and leaned against the sink. "What's going on?"

I sounded as irrational as I felt. I knew Crawford didn't have any romantic feelings for Christine anymore—he hadn't in over a decade—but I wasn't secure enough to have her so enmeshed in our lives and constantly needing support. That's why she had Tim, in my opinion. He was her husband and he needed to support her. Just because he worked long hours at whatever he did and left her alone a good portion of her waking hours wasn't my concern. Or Crawford's. I told him all this in a tear-filled rant that left me thinking that maybe I was losing my mind and perhaps got him to think that might be the case, too.

"Besides, those little kids are weird," I said between sobs.

He put his arms around me. "I know," he sighed. "The weirdest. They all look like trolls."

Something about the way he said it, acknowledging that Tim's brood was a strange little assortment of midget demons, made me laugh until I was gasping for air. It was just the sort of release I needed after thinking much too hard about Christine, Chick, and the oddly named Sassy.

TWENTY-SIX

I'D LIKE TO be able to say that my first reaction the next day, upon seeing Christine coming down the back steps of the building, was joy, but it wasn't. It was a very unattractive curse word that had two parts, one of them being "mother," and shouldn't have entered the mind of—never mind be uttered by—a cultured, supposedly intellectual college professor. There she was, though, jauntily skipping down the steps toward my office, I assumed, a spring in her step that I hadn't seen in a long, long time.

I realized I had forgotten to call Max back. I tried her office, but her assistant said she hadn't come to work. A call to her cell went straight to voice mail. A text was unreturned, something that had never happened; Max can text faster than anyone else I've ever met. Seriously, she should be in some world texting competition. She'd clean up.

When Christine got to my office, I made a great show of how busy I was, pulling my hair up into a messy ponytail and wiping imaginary sweat from my brow as I toiled over a stack of papers that I had already graded. After a perfunctory knock, she plopped into a chair across from my desk. I guessed she was staying for a while.

"Hi, Christine. What's up?" I asked, circling a red *A* on the top of some kid's paper whose face I couldn't connect with the name.

"I need a favor."

Great. Another favor. I couldn't think of one favor I would be able to give her, especially if it included babysitting the troll children. I tried to look neutral on the subject of favors requested by my husband's ex-wife.

She elaborated. "I can get back into Chick's apartment today. The detective who responded said I could meet him there at four o'clock."

It was three, and I was done for the day. I saw where this was headed.

"Please?" she asked. "But you can't tell Bobby."

I dropped my head onto the stack of papers. "Why did you have to say that?"

"What?"

"'Don't tell Bobby.'" I groaned. "Don't you know that's a surefire way to entice me into doing something I shouldn't?"

She giggled. "That's what I was banking on."

I grabbed my bag, in its usual spot under my desk, and pulled out my phone. "Listen, I don't have a lot of time. I want to get over to the medical center to see Max's father. I haven't been to visit him yet." I texted Max to let her know that I would be there later; I was still feeling bad that a day had passed and I still hadn't seen Marty.

"I don't think this is going to take very long," she said.

Famous last words.

I found myself following Christine's minivan across the Bronx and into Mount Vernon to meet Detective Andre Minor, a guy who looked so much like a young Sidney Poitier—the Sidney Poitier from *Guess Who's Coming to Dinner*—that I wondered why it hadn't hit me before when I had seen him at Chick's funeral.

Maybe I *am* middle-aged.

He was waiting on the steps of the decrepit tenement, his hands shoved deep into the pockets of a beautifully tailored trench coat. His sartorial sense put Crawford's colleagues to shame; most of them wore ties that were too short and shirts that had seen better days.

"Mrs. Morin?" he asked, looking at me.

I pointed at Christine. "That would be her."

He looked at me, waiting for an explanation of whom I was and why I had accompanied Christine. I left it at "friend of the family."

"I'm terribly sorry for your loss," he said to Christine. He motioned toward the front door of the building. "Shall we?"

Sexy with manners, too. That was a winning combination. We followed him inside, and I took mental inventory of all of my single friends, noticing that Detective Minor was not wearing a wedding ring and wondering which frustrated colleague I could set him up with and how. I knew Joanne Larkin was single, but she just wasn't deserving enough. Anyway, Minor looked like he wouldn't appreciate the witty insouciance of Joanne's cat sweater collection. As we made the trek up to Chick's apartment, my mind was on fix-ups rather than what possibly awaited us behind his dented door.

Chick's apartment looked pretty much as we had left it a few weeks earlier. The bed that had contained the big stash had been slashed open, the springs visible. The dirty comforter that had once been laid across it was on the floor; I picked it up, folded it, and placed it at the end of the bed. Water dripped in the sink, but that was a problem we weren't going to solve in this neglected building. The three of us stood, listening to the dripping of the faucet and the wind rattling against the single thin pane of glass in the solitary window at the end of the apartment, right next to where Chick had taken his last breath. The blood had been wiped away, unsurprisingly; if the Mount Vernon police hadn't done that, Crawford probably had, making sure Christine never saw the collateral damage from her brother's suicide, the blood that had leaked from his brain while his organs shut down after ingesting so many opioids.

Detective Minor stripped away the remaining crime

scene tape and then handed Christine the keys to the place. "Here you go," he said. "They're all yours."

I could tell she was trying not to cry. This was the first time she had been in the apartment, and although I had tried to warn her earlier what it looked like, nothing prepared her for the dark, depressing space where her brother had spent his last weeks. I wondered if she still thought that everything about Chick's reappearance was completely normal. His living situation—with that much money in his possession—certainly didn't speak to someone who was "normal" on any spectrum.

Detective Minor made a discreet exit, leaving Christine and me to figure out what was in the apartment and what she might possibly want. I looked in the one closet and found that it held a suitcase and a few clothing items. The bright red pants that Chick had worn to my house for the birthday party were hanging neatly on a trouser hanger, a sharp crease evident in the legs. A quick review of the kitchen cupboards revealed only one plate and a water glass. There was no silverware, aside from a bent fork. The bathroom had few toiletries, the bare minimum of supplies one would need: deodorant, shaving items, a bottle of shampoo.

Christine had come prepared with a few large black plastic bags; she handed me one and asked that I throw everything from the bathroom into it, a task that took me all of thirty seconds. I went back out into the one room that served as living room, dining room, office, and bedroom and helped her put the clothes that didn't fit in the suitcase into the rest of the bags she had brought. She was taking her time, shaking everything out and gazing at it longingly: a checkered shirt that had metal snap buttons, a cardigan sweater that had seen better days. I pulled the red pants off the hanger and handed them to her; she seemed to want to handle every garment, as if searching for the solution to the mystery that was Chick.

She took the pants from me. "He was wearing these at the party."

. I nodded, careful not to make a judgment about the vivid hue of the pants and how ridiculous they had looked on a stocky man. She shook them out, just as she had every other piece of clothing, and then laid them on the bed to fold them neatly. I didn't understand why she was taking such care; the items were ending up in plastic garbage bags, but it was some kind of ritual that she needed to perform, and I certainly wasn't going to get in the way of that.

I turned and looked out the window to see what the view might be from a fifth-floor walk-up in a bad part of town. Just as I expected, it was a view that was even more depressing than the interior of the apartment in which I was standing. I turned back around and looked at Christine, still standing by the bed but now holding a slim envelope. She looked at me, her eyes wide.

"What is it?" I asked. Something told me that the plot, as they say, was about to thicken.

She held it out toward me, but with the distance between us, I couldn't see what was written on the front even though it was scrawled in thick, dark marker.

"Now do you believe he committed suicide?" she asked.

I came closer, the words coming into sharp focus.

Open this in the event of my death.

TWENTY-SEVEN

LADIES AND GENTLEMEN, we had ourselves a crime scene.

Although I didn't think that finding an envelope that implored its finder to open it in the event of the writer's death was an indication of murder, Christine seemed to think it was. I tried to gently say that perhaps this was suicide note #1 or suicide note #2, depending on how you viewed the original suicide note in the chain of events. For all I knew, it was a xeroxed copy of the original suicide note, the first one so damaged by vomit splatter and stain that nobody could really decipher what Chick had been thinking when he wrote it.

Christine was furious at me for not immediately jumping on the bandwagon, so I decided that staying silent until I could make a hasty getaway would be my best course of action.

Detective Minor smelled as good as he looked, I had come to discover. He was comforting a distraught Christine, wailing in a corner of the kitchen, the note having been removed from her hands and now in a Ziploc bag in Minor's trench coat pocket. Turns out he had been waiting for us to exit the building, not sure how safe it was to leave two unarmed women to roam the streets of the neighborhood with dusk approaching, and had come back to tell us that he was still in the vicinity just after we had discovered the note, not giving us enough time to read it or form any opinion on the fact that written on its yellowed pages was an indictment of one Sassy Du Pris, someone Chick felt sure was going to take his life someday. Minor told us this after extracting the note carefully from its worn envelope.

All I could think was *oh*, *jeez*, over and over, when I wasn't thinking about what Crawford would have to say about this once he arrived. Minor had called him, since he was involved with both me and Christine in some way and the only person Minor would trust to get us out of there without touching anything further.

Christine's sobs turned into sniffles about five minutes before Crawford joined us.

When he walked through the door, I looked at him and said, "Fancy meeting you here."

He stiffened a little, and I could tell he didn't think it was a time to joke. Maybe it wasn't, but this situation was getting more surreal by the day, and all I had left in my coping arsenal was a good dose of black humor. Really— was there anything left to say that hadn't been said on the subject of Chick Stepkowski, supposed suicide and now possible murder victim, if his sister's conviction was any indication of that fact? I guess so, and we were going to have to figure out what that was. In the back of my mind, I thought of how devastated Mac McVeigh was going to be if he found out that he might have been wrong a second time in as many years. Poor guy would leave town and no forwarding address.

Crawford got a rundown from Minor on what was happening. The detective was suitably circumspect, which made me love him even more, good taste and fabulous cologne notwithstanding. "Could be nothing. Could be something."

Crawford nodded, crossing his arms over his chest. "I hear you."

God knows what that meant.

Christine was sitting on the bed, clearly exhausted by our discovery. "She killed him. She killed him when he wouldn't tell her where the money was or how to find it. She killed him just like she tried to that time she burned the house down."

"This Sassy person?" Minor asked.

Crawford blanched at the utterance of her name. "Yes."

"So the relationship ended on bad terms?" Minor asked.

"You could say that," Crawford answered.

"So how do I find this Sassy person?"

Crawford crossed over to the kitchen and looked out the window; I wasn't sure what he was looking for unless it was Sassy and her whirlwind of terror. "Nobody knows. I ran her through DMV and came up short."

He did? He was more worried than I thought.

"I checked a few other databases, and there's no record of her anywhere beyond her stint in a minimum-security prison in Virginia about ten years back."

Right around the time Chick left. I wondered if there was a connection there and voiced it aloud.

"They were already divorced," Christine said.

"What was she in for?" I asked, wondering why no one else was curious about the timing.

"B&E," Crawford said, a little dismissively. I pressed him for some more information. "Her own family had her arrested for breaking and entering a Sans-a-Flush facility near Roanoke."

"Any idea what she was looking for?" Minor asked. At least someone was interested besides me.

Crawford shrugged. "No idea. Maybe money? Sassy never did seem to have enough money to satisfy her. She always thought she deserved more." He looked at Christine. "Does that seem to cover it?"

"That's putting it nicely," she said.

That put a different spin on things. That lump sum of money had always been baffling, so to know that Sassy was looking for it and hell-bent on finding it did lend a little credence to Christine's assertion that Chick had been murdered. She said aloud what I and anyone else with half a brain cell had to be thinking. "She killed Chick for the money. When he wouldn't tell her where it was or what he had done with it, she killed him."

I repeated what I told Crawford about the woman I saw at the funeral, standing apart from the rest of the mourners at the cemetery. "Big, blond, slutty looking," I said.

Crawford and Christine answered in unison. "That's her."

Minor's mind was elsewhere. "Where did the quarter mil come from?"

I waited to see how Christine explained this one. She was always protesting how successful Chick had been, King of the porta-potties and all, but obviously, there was more to this story. She stayed true to form, though, and carried on with her story about Chick's success in a business no one else wanted to touch.

Minor arched an eyebrow. "With all due respect, Mrs. Morin—"

She held up a hand. "I know. It's a lot of money. My brother wasn't the most traditional character in the world, but he wasn't bad. He wasn't dishonest."

I looked over at Crawford, who was dutifully studying the ground.

Christine caught the look and protested further. "Alison, he wasn't. Chick was a good man, he just…he just," she said, searching for the right words, "lost his way." She looked at me, satisfied with that explanation.

Whatever she wanted to tell herself was fine with me. "Lost his way?" I asked incredulously. "More like beat it out of town."

"That's not true!" she said. "He just needed to find himself. He needed to get away from Sassy. He suffered after losing his job. Losing his wife. He needed a fresh start."

Whatever. She could delude herself all she wanted, but the guy was a crackpot, and the fact that he had that much cash was suspicious. There was no way around it. I changed the subject, addressing my question to Minor. "Does anyone think it's weird that you've been all over this apartment and yet we," I said, pointing to myself and Christine, "find a note that indicts the crazy ex-wife of the deceased?"

Minor wore the same expression that Crawford usually did when I pointed out the obvious, bored disinterest. "Perhaps."

"I mean, you seem pretty sharp, Detective Minor," I said. "I can't imagine that someone in your department, under your tutelage, would miss something so obvious."

He could do nothing but agree.

The doubt cast, I looked at Minor. "Can I leave?" I asked. "I drove my own car."

He thought about that. "I guess you can," he said. "Where can I reach you if I have any further questions about this...situation?"

I gave him my extension at St. Thomas, my cell phone number, and our home number. Satisfied that he could reach me either day or night, I bid Christine goodbye, but I could see that our relationship had chilled slightly since the questioning about Chick and my obvious suspicion about his largesse. She wouldn't look at me as I took my leave.

Crawford walked me to the stairwell. "You were a little hard on her in there."

I arched an eyebrow in response.

"We all know that he was nuts, and that the origin of that money is suspicious, but she's really grieving," he said. "I don't want to press her too hard right now."

"So we're supposed to lie to her and pretend everything is hunky-dory?"

His silence told me that we should even if his expression was ambivalent.

"Well, count me out, then," I said. "I'm going to the hospital to see Max's dad. I'm way overdue for a visit."

He leaned down and gave me a kiss. "I'll walk you out. It's getting dark."

I held up a hand. "I'm fine. My car is right in front. Stay with her," I said, hooking a thumb in the direction of the apartment.

I made my way down the culinary minefield that was the stairwell in the building, the smell of curry still as strong as it was the first time I had been here. When I got to the bottom of the stairs, I realized that while I had been waiting for Crawford to follow me, he had stayed behind; knowing that the suggestion had come from me didn't make it any easier to swallow.

I got to the hospital a few minutes before visiting hours were to end, but it didn't matter anyway. Marty Rayfield had died an hour before, and I never had a chance to say goodbye.

TWENTY-EIGHT

I TOOK MY anger out on Crawford, which wasn't fair, but I wasn't thinking straight.

He walked in about an hour after I got home from the hospital. By the time I arrived, Max's family was gone, and I wasn't able to reach her on her cell. I had finally gotten through to Fred just a few minutes before Crawford came home, and he filled me in on what had happened. Seems that Marty had decided that he was well enough to go home and, despite Max's best efforts at getting him back into bed, commenced putting his things together. Whether it was the disagreement with his daughter or something entirely un-related, nobody knew, but he had suffered a massive stroke that had killed him instantly, all in front of Max. Fred said she was taking it about as well as could be expected, in that she was in bed and not wanting to talk to anyone. I couldn't help feeling that if I hadn't been so involved with Chris-tine and the mystery involving her brother and a big wad of cash, I could have been there to help Max as she went through the most painful thing she had ever experienced.

I also couldn't help feeling that Max felt exactly the same way.

Different emotions kept coming to the fore, but my anger definitely made its presence known. Crawford could practically feel it in the air when he walked into the house, calling my name with a question in his tone that let me know that he knew I hadn't been happy when we had last been together.

"I know," he said before I could utter a word.

"You know what?"

"I know about Max's father. I know that you didn't get to see him. I know that if you hadn't gone with Christine to Chick's apartment, you would have been there for Max," he said, taking off his jacket and draping it on the back of a kitchen chair. "I know about how annoying this whole situation is and how you didn't plan on being so immersed in the life of my ex-wife and her family. I know that my kids can be a pain in the ass. I know that my shoes are giant and sometimes you trip over them. And I know that I'm messy and that sometimes I don't replace the toilet paper," he said, gravely even though that last admission was designed to lessen the blows of the other ones. "I know it all."

I couldn't stay mad at him after that litany of admissions, so I stood and let him take me in his arms, where I let out the sadness and anger that I had been holding in not only this night but since Christine had reappeared, bringing her wacky brothers along for the ride.

"Hey, did you like how Minor kept referring to Chick's ex as 'this Sassy person'?" he asked, doing a passable imitation of Minor's deep voice. "I didn't think it was a good time to tell him, and you, that her full name is Sassafras."

I pulled back. "You're making that up."

"I wish I was," he said. "Sassafras Tiffany Du Pris."

"So it's not a stage name?" I asked. "Sounds made up what with the French pronunciation and all. *Du Pree*," I said, affecting my best French accent. "Yep. Made up."

"Not a stage name, not made up," he said. "Makes it easy to keep track of her movements in and out of the penal system."

"Should I care that she's on the loose and looking for Chick's money? Maybe she's the one who poisoned Trixie. Whoever broke in was pretty good—like someone who's already done time for breaking and entering."

He thought about that for a minute. "I don't think so. I doubt she'd come sniffing around here. She's smart enough to know that we don't have any claim to the money. Besides, she knows I'm a cop."

Your point? I wanted to ask. Having a cop husband hadn't helped me all that much in the past, but if he wanted to tell himself that his law enforcement background was a deterrent to the wiles of Sassy Du Pris, I had to believe him.

He walked over to the refrigerator and pulled out a beer. "On the other hand, if you see a gal, say, six feet and one fifty, wandering around the village in stripper heels, I would say that you should be alert to her movements."

I saluted him. "Gotcha. Good advice."

He elaborated. "If I know Sassy, and she wasn't exactly what I'd call complicated, she's looking for Christine mostly. Christine's the one with the money. Or so Sassy thinks."

I wondered how that made him feel, a question he obviously anticipated, judging by his response.

"Which is why I've got Greenwich PD on alert and I've let Tim know that he should impress upon his wife to set the alarm, keep the doors locked, and just be aware of her surroundings."

"Do you think Sassy is capable of murder?" I asked again.

Crawford shrugged. "She knocked out her husband's teeth on their wedding day. That, to me, speaks of a certain propensity for violence, don't you think?"

"Propensity for violence?" I asked. "Stop getting fancy with vocabulary. It makes me think you've been drinking."

"How about 'she's crazy as catshit and I wouldn't put anything past her'?"

"Better," I said. "So if she's that crazy, how come no one is looking for her?"

He raised an eyebrow in my direction.

"They are?"

"What do you think?" he asked.

"That I should never doubt you," I said.

"Everyone in a fifty-mile radius has a picture of Sassy Du Pris."

"That's Sassafras to you."

"She won't get within ten feet of anyone we know. Trust me."

"I will." I had a thought. "Your professional opinion, please. Did Chick commit suicide or get murdered?"

He crossed his arms over his chest and looked up at the ceiling. I thought I was going to get something really profound but all he said was "Suicide."

That's what I thought.

The weight of Max's loss suddenly fell on me again. "I have to see Max tomorrow. What does your day look like?"

"What do any of my days look like? Why?"

"I figure I'll teach and then get over to her apartment or her mother's house, wherever she is. I just need to know if I should call the dog sitter for an extra walk in the evening."

"Probably not a bad idea." He drained his beer and put the bottle next to the sink. "You hungry?"

"More tired than hungry." I knew the question meant that he was hungry, though. "What do you want to eat?" I pulled my shoes off, holding them above my head lest Trixie get any ideas. "Just don't say Indian. I can't stomach the thought of it after being in Chick's building again."

He looked at me quizzically, but I didn't elaborate. I headed upstairs and changed out of my work clothes into a pair of jeans and a T-shirt. I hoped that by the time I emerged, he would have a plan for dinner and I wouldn't have to think any more about it. I stifled a little sob when I thought about a man who had taken such good care of me, a man I never got to say goodbye to. I decided that I would try Max's apartment one more time to see if she felt like talking. Fred answered.

"I know I just called, but…"

"She's sleeping."

"Really?"

"Valium."

That explained it. "Did you tell her that I called?" I asked.

His grunt indicated to me that he had.

"I'll call tomorrow," I said, feeling dejected. I found it strange that she didn't want to talk to me, but as I had learned over the years, Max's reaction to things was never what I expected or considered normal.

Fred's phone manners were as decorous as Max's. He hung up without saying goodbye, leaving me to stare at the phone in my hand.

My inclination was to strip off my clothes and climb under the covers, but downstairs was a very handsome and very hungry man, someone who recognized and freely admitted his own foibles and emotional baggage. Who was I to deny him a chicken parm wedge at his favorite Italian place now that he had come clean? I knew that if push came to shove, he would always help Christine, but getting him to admit that the situation was becoming a needless pain in the butt was a step in the right direction. I would never leave her stranded either, but I needed to vent, and thankfully, he didn't think me a rotten person for doing so.

He had already walked Trixie when I came down to the kitchen, and she was gnawing happily on a giant bone under the dining room table, her favorite place in the house.

"Ready?" I asked.

We took his car. The backseat was still down, a reminder of when we had taken our very sick dog to the veterinary hospital a few weeks earlier. On top of it lay the bag that Crawford kept in the car to hold a change of clothes and some toiletries—and maybe a framed picture of me? I could only hope. I resisted my natural urge to peek inside.

"So the village PD really has nothing on our break-in?" I asked as we made our way through the darkened streets of our little village. Since he hadn't mentioned any progress on the case, that seemed like a safe assumption. Still, it never hurts to ask. "Are they actually investigating it?"

"Not a thing," he said, angling into a parking spot behind the restaurant, "and now they're dealing with those loons who have occupied the park in the center of the village, so they have their hands full." He was referring to a group of protesters who had taken umbrage at the pipeline that might come through the village at some point in the not-too-distant future.

"You mean the people exercising their right to assembly? Free speech?" I asked, getting out of the car. The night was cloudless, the stars twinkling over the Hudson River, the moon almost full.

"Don't go all ACLU on me. I agree with what they're doing, but I'd like a little more manpower on our case. I'd love to know who poisoned our dog so I could hit them over the head, accidentally of course, with my radio."

We went into the restaurant, a knotty-pine paneled affair that smelled like garlic after years of the kind of old-school Italian cooking that went on in the kitchen. Crawford and I took a booth toward the back of the place, me ordering what was sure to be a really crappy Chianti and him sticking with the safer beer choice. Once we ordered, he reached across and squeezed my hand.

"Thanks for being so patient."

"I haven't been patient. Trust me."

"Well, there are few women who would do what you're doing with my ex-wife. I know that."

"You're already getting laid tonight, Crawford. Don't lay it on so thick," I said.

"Too much?" he asked.

"Way."

The topic of Christine and anything related to the Step-kowskis off the conversational menu, he asked about Max's father. I immediately welled up. "He was a doll. You know that."

"I only met him at the wedding and one other time, I think."

"He was very good to me after my parents died."

"I know," he said, his own eyes getting misty at some thought, maybe me at a young age with no siblings and no parents, doing my best to make a broken and irreparable marriage work. Although he was a stiff, according to his former in-laws, he had compassion to spare. He looked down.

"Did Fred like him?" I asked. I knew that Fred talked to Crawford more than to anyone else, Max included, some-times.

"Loved him."

"This is going to be hard all around, then," I said.

We were way overdue for a quiet evening like this, and I felt like we were turning the corner on the amount of ac-tivity we were going to be required to be involved in. Just as Crawford signed his name to the credit card slip, some-one turned on the jukebox. "Your Cheatin' Heart" blasted through the speakers, and Crawford got a look on his face that let me know that he had just remembered something.

"Hey," he started.

"All taken care of," I lied, thinking that Meaghan's in-volvement in Joanne Larkin's midterm debacle still needed to be dealt with. Keeping Crawford in the dark was part of my master plan; if I could make the whole thing go away without bothering him with it, my transformation to "Ali-son Bergeron, Redeemed Stepmother" would be complete.

Before we got outside, the sound of a car alarm broke

through the sound of Conway Twitty's warbling serenade. Crawford hustled me out of the restaurant only to find the lights of his sensible station wagon blinking on and off, the horn blaring. All of the doors were closed, but the car locks had definitely been tampered with. Crawford hit the keypad and stopped the cacophony, much to the delight of an older couple exiting the car next to his.

"You should tell your girlfriend not to pull so hard on the doors if she doesn't have the keys," the man said, his face a study in consternation.

I looked at Crawford. "Girlfriend?"

The woman, a rotund meatball as round as she was tall, chimed in. "Yes. The big blonde."

Crawford and I looked at each other, realization dawning on us simultaneously. "Which way did she go?" he asked.

The woman had a flare for the dramatic, obviously. Her hands fluttered as she described the woman's exit. "It was like she vanished into the wind, never to be seen again."

TWENTY-NINE

NOW WE WERE sure that Sassy Du Pris was back in town, looking for something that none of us had—money. As we lay in bed that night, I voiced a thought that had been nagging at the back of my brain for a few days now.

"Do you think she's involved with Tim?"

From under his bent arm, Crawford let out a sigh. "Now what would make you say that?"

"I don't know," I said, and I didn't, really.

Crawford did. "You overheard a conversation that you had no context for about a guy who was hoping to get two hundred and fifty thousand dollars. To draw a line from him to Sassy is really a stretch," he said, his voice muffled. "Go to sleep."

I couldn't. There was too much going on. Between the afternoon at Chick's and then a lovely dinner that turned ugly with the thwarted attempt to break in to our car, my mind was awhirl with theories and loose ends and a host of other things. Then there was Max's father's death. That was sad enough in itself, but it also nagged at me because I had been too busy—make that preoccupied—with life as I knew it to go visit a man who had done just about everything he could to help me even though he wasn't a blood relation. I felt sick not that he was dead, but that he had died attempting a breakout from the medical center, still convinced of his own immortality and ability to move on like nothing had ever happened.

Come to think of it, Max was a chip off the old block.

Crawford was asleep, deep breaths coming from between his parted lips. The guy was a study in extremes; wide awake one minute, sound asleep the next. I envied his ability to turn off the dialogue that was surely in his head, the same one that was in mine. What had happened, what did Sassy have to do with it, and what could we do to figure it out? Those were the questions that were circulating in the card carousel of my mind.

Crawford stopped breathing for a second, as he often did when he was in a really deep sleep, and I nudged him to make him turn on his side so that he wouldn't suffocate. He changed position grudgingly, as if I were being completely unreasonable. After another half hour of listening to him snore, stop breathing, and then choke back to life, I made a mental note to call a sleep clinic to get him straight so that I didn't have small heart attacks every night, thinking that he wouldn't wake up. I finally got out of bed and padded down to the kitchen, Trixie on my heels, not content to let me rustle around in the refrigerator by myself.

I don't know what I was expecting to find, but a peek into the refrigerator confirmed what I should have already known: There was nothing in there. Crawford's schedule is hectic, and I could exist solely on vodka and pretzels, so grocery shopping is the one chore that often gets tossed to the side in favor of takeout food or dining out. Looking into the barren refrigerator made me sad. I vowed then and there to start watching Food Network all the time and figuring out this thing that they called "cooking."

Trixie was placid one minute and on alert the next, her ears up and the hair on the back of her neck standing at attention. A low growl started deep in her gut and traveled up to her mouth, coming out as a warning bark that startled even me. The only light in the kitchen came from the open refrigerator, and my hand on the appliance handle felt like it had turned to stone. To turn around or not to turn around; that was the stupid question. My hand dropped from the handle, and slowly I turned toward the kitchen window over the sink. It looked out into the backyard, the one where Christine's stepchildren, nieces, and nephews had attempted to start a bonfire what seemed like a hundred years ago. I don't know what I expected to see in the window, but I was surprised when I saw nothing at all, just the blackness of the vacant backyard and a light in the distance coming from someone's porch light on another block.

I looked down at Trixie. "Just a raccoon, my friend. Nothing to worry about."

My dog was smarter than I was. I learned that the hard way when I heard the sound of something sharp hitting glass, a violent and sudden noise, breaking the silence of what should have been a dull evening in a sleepy suburban town. For the second time that evening, I heard the wail of Crawford's car alarm, a sound that I hoped never to hear again. It sounded like a banshee screaming, and I'm not even entirely sure what a banshee is.

I opened the back door without thinking and took off across the backyard, my feet bare, the dog nipping at my heels. I reached the driveway, where Crawford's car alarm was singing a sad, sad song, one that kept time with the flashing lights illuminating the tacky weave that belonged to none other than the elusive Sassy Du Pris.

Girl could move. She was tearing down my driveway, in her hand Crawford's bag of extra clothes—the one that possibly contained the framed picture of me, though I wasn't holding my breath—as she took a hard left and started down the street, running on impossibly high heels.

"Sassy!" I screamed. "Sassafras!" I fumbled around in Crawford's car, trying to figure out how to turn off the alarm before the whole neighborhood woke up and realized that I really was the giant pain in the ass that about 40 percent of the neighbors already thought I was.

Although Crawford falls asleep with no trouble, waking up is another story. He appeared in the back door, clad in a pair of boxer shorts and dress shoes, a gun in his hand. "What's going on?" he asked as he made his way across the backyard, the gun dangling in his limp hand.

"It's Sassy," I said, pointing down the street.

He was still half asleep. "Should I chase her?"

"Of course you should," I said, pushing him in the direction of her departure. "What the hell is wrong with you?"

"I took an Advil PM. Maybe three. Things are kind of cloudy." He slumped against the car. "She broke my windshield."

I sighed. He couldn't chase her now even if he wanted to. Judging from the haste with which she had beat it down our driveway, only a racehorse on speed would have been able to catch her.

It was cold. I pulled my arms into my T-shirt. "She's fast."

He looked at me, his senses dulled by the sleep aid.

"Maybe we should call 911?" I suggested. He lumbered back into the house, and I followed him. I found him staring at the phone, wondering what he had come in to do. "I'll call 911," I said, "and make some coffee. You go put on some pants and a shirt." He started off down the hallway. "Leave the gun!" I called after him. He walked back and placed it on the counter.

The 911 operator—who either hadn't heard of me or was professional enough not to have a reaction when I said my name and gave my address—promised to send someone right over. I said a silent prayer that it was none of the cops who had already been here. Then I wondered if my home-owner's insurance would go up. My propensity for using public servants so freely might put me into a new category.

Crawford came back looking like the old Crawford—the

one who could string a few words together well enough to form a sentence and/or dial 911—dressed in jeans and an NYPD T-shirt, I suppose to let the village PD know who was boss. On the law enforcement food chain, NYPDers consider themselves higher than all others, and since peeing in public, even to mark one's territory, is considered a "public nuisance" misdemeanor, they opt instead to flash their badges, wear their police-issue clothing, or brandish their big guns in the presence of other cops.

"You look better," I said.

"Cold shower," he said.

"That was a little drastic, don't you think?"

"Not if you felt like your head was filled with cotton candy."

It was only a few minutes later that our driveway was filled with local police, who regarded Crawford's car as if it were a hunk of kryptonite. I helpfully offered that the car had been broken into by a woman named Sassafras Du Pris and she was on the loose.

One of the responding officers, a woman who looked young enough to be my daughter, asked me how I knew the woman's name.

"Long story." I looked at Crawford. "Can you explain?"

He could. With his usual economy of words, he described Sassy and her relationship to our family and explained why, possibly, she would want to break in to our car and steal a bag of giant man clothes that would fit only a small percentage of the population. "She's looking for money," he finished. "Money we don't have."

"Why does she think you have this money?" the officer asked. Her name was Prynne, as in Hester. Curiouser and curiouser.

Crawford gave her a look. "I can only guess that she thinks we know of its whereabouts, given our connection to the deceased."

It was like a lightbulb went off over her head. "Ahhh," she said, jotting down a few notes in her leather-bound notebook.

Crawford pulled me to the side. "Are you sure it was Sassy?" he whispered.

"Big blonde in stripper heels? It wasn't Snow White as far as I could tell."

"She ran away in stripper heels?" he asked, not really able to get a mental picture of what that looked like.

I nodded. "I know. Hard to fathom." It was cold, so I started for the house. "By the way, I'm getting in my time machine and going back to a time when I could change the course of history and make this day never happen."

"Sounds like a plan," he called after me.

The dog was hiding under the coffee table in the living room, a space that was way too small for her voluptuous frame. The lights and sounds of a police invasion had left her shaking, her tail between her legs. I lured her out with a piece of cheese that I found in an otherwise empty drawer in the refrigerator. As I sat on the couch, petting her silken fur, I wondered how Sassafras would feel once she found out that she had absconded with a pair of large trousers, a 46 long blazer, and a tie that had probably seen better days. Was breaking and entering worth the reward on this one? Probably not.

I hoped that none of us were around when she figured out that she was on the hook for this felony and had gotten no closer to finding the money she so desperately wanted.

THIRTY

I WAS EXHAUSTED, but relieved to go back to work. The same couldn't be said for Crawford, who was still dealing with the aftereffects of having taken one too many Advil PMs, thinking that his large size necessitated a near overdose. He had no answer as to why he had taken one, never mind three, of the pills; I reminded him that in all the time I had known him, he had never had insomnia, let alone had trouble falling asleep, especially after a day spent at work and then in a dead man's apartment.

"Don't lecture me," he said, crankily.

If he thought that was a lecture, he definitely still had drugs in his system.

I didn't feel as bad as I thought I would, even though I was bone tired. The sun was out and the campus was alive, as it always is in the middle of a semester, particularly before winter has hit and everyone gets really ornery. I went into my office and tossed my bag onto my desk, nearly spilling the large cup of coffee that I had purchased in the cafeteria. I righted the coffee cup, pulled a few folders out of my bag, turned on my computer, and got to work, figuring out what needed to be done immediately and what could wait until the end of the day.

I still hadn't heard from Max. I dialed her number first; it went straight to voice mail. Same for Fred. I wondered what was up. Was she so distraught that she couldn't talk, or was there something going on that had completely missed my radar? Or, as I knew deep in my heart, was she angry because I had never seen Marty in the hospital? I texted Crawford to ask Fred what was up, if indeed Fred even showed up for work that day. The guy had a work ethic like no other, but losing his father-in-law might have encouraged him to break his streak of ten years in homicide with the fewest absences of anyone in the squad.

So now that we had two Sassy Du Pris sightings, albeit brief ones, there was an all-points bulletin out for her arrest. Finally, someone was taking this woman's reappearance seriously; I knew Christine would be happy about that. The police were tracking down the old couple from the restaurant to see if they could ID this mystical creature, a violent stripper with a checkered past beyond her marriage to Chick. Crawford had called Minor to let him know that he should consider a recanvass of the building to see if anyone had seen the big, buxom, and blond ex of the man who had died in 5D. To me, she was like a unicorn—fabled, storied, and hard to find. That is, of course, if unicorns wore high heels and could run like the wind in them. I had only seen Max's Hooters PIs run in high heels, and trust me, they had nothing on Sassy.

My fatigue led me to make a decision that I thought, after the fact, might come back to bite me in the ass, but I went for it anyway. Going to see Joanne Larkin would probably end up being a bad idea, but I was tired of pussyfooting around the likelihood that she was reusing tests; we needed to get to the bottom of this, if only to clear Meaghan's conscience on the whole subject. I had only seen my step-daughter briefly in the hallways, but every time she saw me, she avoided me like the plague, even though it was clear that I believed her. She was ashamed of something, and I could only hope it was the fact that she was involved with the oldest college student at the school, if not in the world, and nothing else.

Joanne was drinking a mug of hot tea when I entered,

the limp string from her tea bag hanging off the side of her mug, which had a witty saying about cats and dogs, in which cats came out superior, stamped on the side. She had on a bright orange sweater with a head-sized pumpkin fastened to each shoulder. Really, Joanne? Holiday sweaters and cat mugs? Maybe I should go easy on her; this was clearly a woman who had few joys in her life.

"May I sit?" I asked.

She looked reluctant to give me a chair but finally relented.

"Listen," I started, using one of the oldest, most tension-inducing openings in the history of conversation as a starter. When someone tells me to "listen," my first reaction is to bristle, not pay attention. I saw that my opener had the same effect on Joanne. "You and I both know that my stepdaughter is a good student, a little lazy maybe, but not a cheater as you intimated during our last phone call."

"Really? And how would we know that?" Joanne asked, making a show of swirling her tea bag around in her cat mug.

"Come on, Joanne," I said. "You know as well as I do that Meaghan is a good student who wouldn't stoop so low as to cheat on your exam."

I waited for her reaction; she had none.

I went for broke, leaning in so I could whisper. I didn't want anyone to overhear the next thing I had to say. "I know you reused that test, Joanne. It's not a problem. I just don't want Meaghan to be penalized in any way for doing something she had no idea she was doing if, for some reason, this whole thing comes to light."

Her face turned hard. "Prove it. Prove that I reused that test."

How to do this without getting Meaghan in more hot water with her teacher was proving difficult. I didn't think I'd get the cooperation of Mr. Super Senior either, so my hands were tied. "You're right. I can't." I stood. "I'm just protecting my stepdaughter."

"There shouldn't be a problem, Alison, as long as you stop talking," she said.

"Really, Joanne? That's how you want to play this?"

"Really, Alison. Leave it alone. No one is implicating your stepdaughter in anything, and as long as she keeps her nose clean, this whole thing will go away." She took a sip of her tea, and I was somewhat happy to see—judging from her grimace—that she had burned her sharp tongue.

"Maybe she could take another exam?"

That suggestion didn't seem to please Joanne. She had no other exam to offer, and that was a problem. "No."

"What about if we tossed the grade and she made it up some other way?"

She stared at me.

"Joanne, if you didn't reuse the exam, then it was stolen from you, before the test." I stared back at her. "Don't you see that we have a major problem here?"

"Alison, you're the only one with a problem." That pretty much summed it up. "Now, if you will excuse me? I have work to do," she said pointedly, as if I didn't work at all.

I bit my lip. *"Work" like xeroxing tests from years gone by so you don't have to break a sweat?* I wanted to ask but didn't. Before I got out into the hall, she called to me to come back in. "Alison? If something compels you to reveal any of this information to anyone else, then consider Meaghan's record permanently sullied."

"Meaning what?" I asked.

"Meaning that I will turn her in."

Shit. That didn't go the way I wanted it to.

I left her office, passing by the chapel and President Etheridge's office before taking the back staircase to the Humanities floor. Waiting for me in front of the closed door was Mary Lou Bannerman.

Never was I so glad to see a student. Particularly a middle-aged one who always seemed to travel with gourmet goodies.

"Good morning," she said as I got closer, the small paper bag in her hand leading me to believe this was a social call. The Baked by Susan logo on the side boasted of something from a small bakery north of me that had gotten rave reviews in both local and regional papers. She proffered the bag. "Fresh scone?"

Fresh scone? Was I human? And did this woman know me or what? I grabbed the bag from her hand, unlocked my office door, and shepherded Mary Lou in, trailing behind her, thoughts of eating the scone in two bites swirling around in my addled, exhausted brain. Hopefully the coffee on my desk was still hot. "Did you have one?" I asked.

She patted her nonexistent midsection. "Trying to lay off the treats for a while. At least until Thanksgiving is over."

I wish I could exhibit such restraint, but I can't. I ripped open the bag and found a lovely chocolate chip scone, sugary goodness dusting the top, waiting for me. I took a big bite. "This is good," I said, chasing it with a slurp of coffee. Yes, still hot, if the numb spot on my tongue was any indication; restraint is not my strong suit, particularly when it comes to food and drink. "Thank you." At that moment, I might have fallen in love with her just a little bit. Today, she was wearing a gorgeous cashmere sweater over a crisp white oxford and skinny jeans, a pair of leopard-print Tory Burch flats on her feet. The woman was the epitome of class and style, even if her latest short story needed a little work. I tried not to think about the moth hole I had discovered in the sweater I had donned that morning; it was under my right arm and wouldn't be visible to anyone I encountered during the day. Probably.

"What did you think of my latest short story?" she asked.

Dang. I thought we were going to avoid that until I had

finished my scone at least. I took a bite out of the middle of the pastry and chewed for a while. "Okay, well, it's…"

"Not good," she finished.

"No!" I said. "Not not good, but not your best work either."

"What do I need to do, do you think?" she asked, looking far more worried than I thought she should.

I attempted to reassure her. "It's fine. Just a little…ponderous?" I suggested. "More dramatic than it needs to be?"

She exhaled, relieved. "Oh, I thought you were going to tell me to start over."

"Never," I said. "In my experience, it's the rare story that needs to be scrapped completely." That wasn't entirely true, but it was in this case.

She put a hand over her heart. "That is so good to hear."

I put the scone down. "Why does this mean so much to you, Mary Lou?" I asked. She seemed to have an unnatural devotion to the class and to becoming a better writer; I wanted to know what was at the heart of that.

She pursed her lips together. "Well, let me see. I guess I've been doing things for everyone else for so long that I wanted to have something to call my own?" She appeared to be trying that reason on for size, but it didn't seem to satisfy her as a complete explanation.

I think I understood it even though I had never felt that way.

"And maybe because I've never really been good at anything, so I wanted to see if I could get better at something that I loved doing? To have something that set me apart from the other wives and moms that I know? I've been doing those things for so long, being a wife and a mother, that I'm not sure I know how to do anything else. I guess I'm not really sure who I am and need to find out." She let out a little laugh, but it was tinged with sadness. "Does that sound too…ponderous?"

My heart almost broke. To me, she seemed together, strong, and confident, but inside, it would seem, she was insecure and unsure of herself, a feeling not uncommon to women who spent their lives raising children and helping a man succeed, I supposed. It was foreign to me, having been on my own for a lot of my adult life in spite of two marriages, but I could see how a woman could feel that way if she had never left the house long enough to do anything besides shuttle a kid to an activity or do the grocery shopping, things that Mary Lou seemed to have been doing for a long, long time.

"Finish your scone," she said.

I realized I had been staring at her, trying to figure out how to boost the spirits of this incredibly kind woman by telling her something good about her story. "You write great characters," I said finally.

"I come from a family of great characters, so that makes it easy," she said.

"You?"

"Yes, me." She got up. "Someday, I'll write a story about my family and you'll see what I mean." She went to the door. "This class means a lot to me. Thank you for being so kind."

Once again, my mind went back to my initial consternation at her auditing the class. I'm nothing if not a practiced self-flagellator, returning often to thoughts of my spiritual and emotional shortcomings. "It's wonderful having you in class. Thank you for joining us." As she exited, I called after her. "And thank you for the scone!"

Talking to Mary Lou and eating the scone had been the perfect antidote to my meeting with Joanne Larkin, whose inability to admit that she had screwed the pooch, so to speak, on her midterm was baffling, to say the least. I was getting nowhere with her, and short of having Meaghan drop the class, a thought that had crossed my mind more than once, I guessed I would just have to wait and see what, if anything at all, was going to happen.

I supposed I could ask Crawford, too, but having tried so hard to keep him out of this situation, it didn't make a whole lot of sense to drag him in now. That's what I told myself, anyway. In all honesty, I still thought that either this would go away or I would figure out how to handle it if the poop hit the fan. Although the truth would set us all free, only some of us were interested in it, and Joanne Larkin certainly wasn't what I would call an interested party.

When the phone rang, I prayed that it was Max and my prayer was answered. She sounded tired, frail, and sadder than I'd ever heard her sound, except for the one time she couldn't score Duran Duran tickets for their first farewell concert. "How are you doing?"

"I'm okay." She was lying. She was far from okay.

"What can I do?"

She sighed. "I don't know. I'll let you know when we have everything set up." Then she was gone.

I stared at the receiver in my hand and hoping I could blame Max's reaction to my call on the emotional vagaries of grief and not on something more broken in our relationship. The last few times we had spoken, things had been tense; even I, with everything else going on in my life, could see that.

Who knew why any of us acted the way we did when we lost someone we loved? The day my mother died, I got in her car and drove to Cold Spring, a river town about thirty miles north of where I lived, and sat on Main Street in front of her favorite French restaurant. I cried until a woman passing by knocked on the window and asked if I needed help, her kindness making me even sadder in the face of my loss. No, I didn't need her help, I remember telling her; I needed my mother. No one else. Just my mother. The woman tried to console me, but it did no good. My despair was immeasurable, and finally, after questioning me about who she could call, someone who would come and get me, she got Marty Rayfield's number out of me, and he was there in a flash. Instead of driving me to our empty house, he had taken me back to his home in a village not far from mine and put me up in Max's old room, taking care of every single detail related to my mother's funeral while I rested there, getting myself together enough to escort my mother's casket down the center aisle of the church where she had worshipped with a devotion that was unfathomable to me.

I turned and looked out the window toward the cemetery, the sun casting a burnished glow on the polished marble headstones and grave markers. The giant angel, the one that had implored me to follow the truth a few days earlier, was somewhere in the midst of all the other markers, rising majestically off in the distance. Closer in, I took notice of a figure leaning against another massive headstone, the hair blond, the clothes black, the cigarette dangling menacingly from red, red lips.

Well, by Jove, I thought, *if it isn't the lovely and talented Sassy Du Pris.*

I didn't know if she could see me, but I suspected she could—why else would she be there?—so I tried to pretend that I hadn't seen her and that I wasn't dialing Crawford's cell number as she slouched against the headstone that I recognized as Sister Alphonse's.

"Hey!" he said, far too enthusiastic for the occasion.

"Hey," I whispered.

"Why are you whispering?" he asked.

I didn't know. I cleared my throat. "Listen to me carefully. Sassy Du Pris is in the St. Thomas cemetery leaning against Sister Alphonse's gravestone."

"I'm on it," he said, adding before he hung up, "Stay wherever you are and do not attempt to catch her."

I was all set to listen to him and not do anything stupid. After all, this woman might have murdered Chick. She had tried to burn his house down. She had been in jail for breaking and entering. She might have broken into my house and poisoned my dog. She had certainly vandalized Crawford's car and stolen his giant man clothes. She was not a woman to be trifled with, that was for sure.

Until she did the one thing that pushed me over the edge and had me tearing out of my office as if I were being chased by a nest of hornets: She put her cigarette out on Alphonse's gravestone.

That was the one thing she wasn't going to get away with. If I caught her, and that was unlikely with her ability to sprint in stilettos, I was going to wring her neck.

THIRTY-ONE

I RAN CROSS-COUNTRY one year at my all-girls Catholic high school. I even have the sweatshirt to prove it. Every once in a while, if only to prove Crawford wrong when he insinuates that I'm not athletic or, worse, that I'm out of shape, I put it on to show him that once upon a time, Alison Bergeron was someone. She ran cross-country.

Technically, that's not entirely true. When the coach got a look at me, wowed by the length of my legs and my seemingly unbridled enthusiasm for running, she was overjoyed. That is, until she found out that I was incredibly uncoordinated, verged on asthmatic, and had the stamina of a postmenopausal woman with osteoporosis. In other words, I stunk. However, long arms guaranteed that I could at least be considered for shot put, and since no other girl was willing to give it a try, I took one for the team, hoisting a metal ball behind my neck five days a week and sometimes on Saturday, attempting to put my high school on the map for the "field" part of track and field. My mother, French Canadian, gorgeous, and stylish, was horrified and blamed the genetic mutation—as she saw my freakishly long arms— on my father, who found his own freakishly long arms well suited to his job as a UPS man.

Too bad I didn't have a shot put handy. I would have thrown it farther than I had ever managed while in high school and nailed Sassy in the head. I was irate that she had desecrated my dear Alphonse's gravestone, and she would pay. If it turned out that she was also the one who poisoned my dog, well, she was dead meat. No pun intended.

By the time I arrived at the cemetery, of course she was gone. I stood at Alphonse's grave, my hands on the stone, panting. I hadn't run that fast in...well, forever, and at my age—decidedly not middle-aged—it was not a good idea to go from eating scones and drinking coffee into a full sprint. Someone could get hurt. Or something could rupture. I now knew where my gallbladder resided, and it was right under the last rib on the right of my rib cage. In other words, no good could come of physical activity at my age.

Crawford arrived less than ten minutes after I had called him, no Fred in tow. With him was his colleague of many years Carmen Montoya, she of the tight pants and even tighter backside. She sidled over to the gravestone and sized up the situation.

"You need an *ambulancia*, *chica*?" she asked.

"No, I don't need an *ambulancia*," I said, struggling mightily to catch my breath. "Some oxygen might be nice, though."

"Didn't I tell you to stay in your office?" Crawford asked, squinting in the morning sun.

I lifted my head just long enough to give him a withering look.

"My boyfriend here filled me in on who this Sassy person is on our way over." Carmen lifted her heel to check how much dirt she had accumulated on her black leather boots. "Sounds like a charmer."

"She is," I said. "She may have poisoned our dog, and she threatened his ex, Christine."

Carmen's face lit up at Christine's name. "So Christine is well? Haven't seen that girl in a dog's age. Always fond of her."

I narrowed my eyes at her.

"Not as fond as I am of you," she said, realizing she had innocently stepped in it, so to speak.

"She'd be better if we could find Sassy and get her locked up," Crawford said through gritted teeth.

"We're sure it's her making all of this mayhem?" Carmen asked, pulling large black sunglasses from her purse and donning them.

"Pretty sure," he said as I chimed in, "Positive."

"So let's get her," Carmen said.

I pulled a tissue that had seen better days out of my pocket and went to work on the cigarette butt scar on Alphonse's gravestone, getting all but the last bit of it up.

"Are you cleaning that grave?" Carmen asked.

"Yes," I said, wetting my finger and working on the black stain. "She was a friend."

I saw her exchange a look with Crawford, but I didn't care.

"Did this Sassy person leave all of this sugar around? Is this some kind of clue that I just can't understand?" she asked. "A satanic ritual maybe?"

"No," I said. "I put it here. It's a private message."

"A message to a dead nun?" she asked. Although I couldn't see her eyes, I suspected that she was raising an eyebrow in my direction.

"Yes." I dared her to make another comment.

She didn't, preferring to address Crawford next. "What you want to do, handsome? You're in charge."

"Let's take a walk around and see if there's anything else that turns up." He put his hands in his pockets and started loping around the cemetery.

"Wish I had worn better shoes for this," Carmen faux-complained. She always wore high-heeled boots, no matter what she was doing. "Wait up, gorgeous! As much as I like your backside, I like your frontside even more." Although Crawford's back was turned to me, I knew that he had flushed deep red, and that is why, after all these years together, Carmen continues to sexually harass my husband. She was very happily married and had four kids, so I had nothing to worry about, even though she didn't think twice about telling Crawford how handsome she thought he was whenever she had the chance. Fred would tell her where to stick it, but Crawford was too much of a gentleman, or so I had told myself. Maybe he secretly loved being told how attractive he was by a tough-talking Latina with a back-side that defied gravity.

They did a canvass of the cemetery and came back a few minutes later, Carmen huffing and puffing as she made her way along the gravel path that linked the upper area to the lower, which I had the best view of from my office.

"No sign of her," she said, leaning over and putting her hands on her knees to catch her breath.

"I didn't think there would be," I said. I looked at Crawford. "So now can we put out an all-points bulletin on her?"

"For putting a cigarette out on a grave?" he asked.

I shot him a look. "No. The break-ins, the harassing of Christine, stuff like that."

"Alison," he said, and I knew that he was about to patronize me; he always does when he starts a sentence with my name. "We're already looking for her. Just because I don't talk about it all day long doesn't mean that we don't have this under control."

Carmen held her breath as she awaited my response, which was sure to be a good one, from the look on her face.

I didn't take the bait. If they had it under control, I wanted to ask, why was a six-foot-tall stripper running rampant through two counties? Why was she so elusive that the greatest minds of several agencies of Westchester County law enforcement and the New York City Police Department were having such a hard time finding her? I left all that unsaid, though, because lashing out with Carmen as an audience would lead to further hurt feelings and re-criminations later on. Holding my tongue, while not my usual inclination, was the best thing I could do to maintain marital peace and harmony.

He looked at me, waiting for my response, but I had none. I smiled. "You know what? I trust you. Carry on," I said.

Carmen let out a long breath.

"By the way, what do you want for dinner tonight?" I asked.

It was not a question he was expecting, because it was one he rarely heard so many hours before the meal would be prepared—or purchased—and eaten. "Um, hamburgers?" he suggested, blurting out the first thing that came into his head.

"Then hamburgers it is," I said. "Do I need to give you any more information for a report or anything?" I asked.

He shook his head. "No. We've got everything we need."

Carmen gave me a peck on the cheek and started for the car. "Catch you later, *chica*," she said as she meandered down the path, her boots crunching the stones beneath her feet.

Crawford bent down and gave me a quick kiss, too. "See you tonight."

As he walked away, I called after him. "Any advice for avoiding a pissed-off stripper?"

He shrugged. "If she zigs, you should zag."

"Seriously?" I asked. "Aren't you concerned at all?"

He stopped walking and turned back around. "I'm very concerned, but whatever I tell you will do no good. I've learned that when it comes to you and situations like this, you'll do whatever it is you want anyway." He put his hands in his pockets. "I can already tell that instead of avoiding Sassy, you're going to try to find her, and then you're going to try to tell her that we don't have the money and get her to leave everyone alone."

This guy was a regular Kreskin.

"Am not," I said.

"Are, too."

"Well, I wouldn't know the first thing about trying to find her," I said, and that was the truth.

"I'm sure you'll figure something out," he said. Then he walked back to the car and to a woman who thought he was gorgeous, smart, and sensible and, in spite of sexually harassing him at every turn, probably didn't give him half the headaches that I, his devoted wife, did.

THIRTY-TWO

HONESTLY, UNTIL Crawford had made the astute observation that I might look for her, I hadn't given a second thought to searching for Sassy Du Pris, but now that it was out there, I figured what the heck. The first thing I did when I returned to my office was a Yellow Pages search online, but as I expected, Sassy didn't leave a forwarding address after she got out of the pen on her breaking-and-entering jag. Then I searched for her on Google and found out that back in the day, Sassy Du Pris had had quite the storied career in the annals of exotic dancing. She was a featured dancer who traveled around the country and seemed to have a substantial fan club. I pushed back in my chair and studied the screen, letting my mind wander as I reviewed the events of the past several weeks. Suddenly one word popped into my head and made me sit up straight.

Facebook.

I don't know why it didn't occur to me sooner. Christine had mentioned that Sassy had found her through Facebook, which meant that Sassy had a page or a profile or whatever they called it. I went to the site and tried to log on, but the school server shut me down, saying that Facebook was a restricted site. I tapped my fingers lightly on the keys, trying to think of someone besides Max, who was obviously preoccupied, who might have a Facebook page. It took me all of ten seconds.

He picked up after a few rings, a little out of breath. Exercising, maybe? Since he had left St. Thomas and the priesthood, he hadn't been getting as much exercise, his life in the apartment below his mother not being so great for his waistline. "Hello?"

"Kev, it's me."

"Hey," he said, his tone transmitting some kind of portent. "I'm so sorry about Max's dad."

"You know?"

"Yeah," he said. "She called me from the hospital, right after it happened."

I felt a little tingle of something run up my spine, knowing that something was amiss. With Kevin getting a call before me about Marty's passing, I knew that what I was chalking up to Max's grief was something more. I let that go for the time being, thinking that I would have to hash it out with Max, not Kevin.

"Do you have a Facebook page?" I asked.

"Is the pope Catholic?"

"Last time I checked."

"What do you need?"

I explained the story of Sassy, realizing that I hadn't kept him involved with the ongoing saga of Christine and her estranged sister-in-law.

"You're kidding," he said. "Her name is actually Sassy Du Pris?"

"I believe Sassafras is her Christian name."

"There's no Saint Sassafras."

"Details, Kev. Details." I swung my chair around so that I was staring out the window, hoping, I guess, to catch a glimpse of her again. "Are you near your computer? Can you look her up on Facebook?"

"I can, but depending on how stringent her privacy settings are, we may not learn anything." I waited while he accessed his account. "Oh, my."

He had found her.

"What does it say?" I asked.

"Give me a minute." I heard him typing away. "What do you want to know?"

"Does it say where she lives?"

I heard him exhale. "It says 'around.'" Not helpful.

"What else does it say? Can you see anything at all?"

"She has a fan page."

Of course she does.

"She seems to be in some kind of dance revue."

I laughed. "That's one way of putting it."

"And she's performing at a place called the Elegant Majestic tonight."

"Where is that?"

"Yonkers," he said. "Oh, wait. That's an old listing. Apparently, any future gigs have been canceled."

Even so, I wondered if we could get some information from the people who worked there about our friend Sassy.

Before I could get the words out of my mouth, the ones that told him where we were going later and why, he started protesting. "I have to work. And then clean my apartment. I'm having dinner with my mother. And then I'm going out."

"Don't worry, Kevin," I said. "I wasn't going to ask you to go to a strip club with me." Knowing that Kevin was prideful, as well as a supreme gadfly, I went with the old reverse psychology. "I know you couldn't handle it, what with what you've been through in the past year."

"Are you screwing with me?" he asked. I could almost see his furrowed countenance, the phone pressed tightly against his head.

"No," I said. "I just know you're not up for it."

A heavy sigh came through the phone lines. "Fine. I'll go," he said, "but I can't be out late. I have to work in the morning."

After we discussed the specifics of where we would

meet and when, I hung up the phone. Like taking candy from a baby.

I gathered my books and papers and shoved them into my messenger bag, my next class starting in a few minutes. What to do about Crawford? That was my only question. We had made plans to have hamburgers together, and he was expecting me to cook them. How would I explain that I was going to be out half the night? The "show" didn't begin until ten o'clock if the Elegant Majestic's Web site was accurate. I decided not to worry about it; Crawford's schedule was arbitrary and could change at a moment's notice, a blessing for me in a situation like this. I wouldn't even have to have someone in his precinct killed so that he could investigate; there were plenty of angry people out there who could do that for me. I didn't go so far as to pray for another murder, but a court date, maybe? That would solve all of my problems.

That, and maybe three sleep aids.

I wondered when Sassy had decided that it was too hot to dance so close to the center of the action. According to Kevin, she had been scheduled for a one-week stint at the club, but it was listed as canceled with no explanation, and many fans had written on her Facebook page in protest.

I went off to class, putting the thought of all the questions I wanted to ask her—and the little conundrum of how I would ditch Crawford—out of my mind. When I got back to my office, starving and not at all interested in the sandwich in my bag, there was a text from Crawford.

So sorry. No fred = lots of work. Court later. Hamburgers tomorrow?

Jackpot.

When the day ended, I raced home to change. What did one wear to a strip club? This is the kind of question that Max always has the answer to, but she wasn't available.

I decided ultimately that all black would be the ticket;

I didn't want to stand out among the patrons of an exotic dancing lounge and figured that in the darkness, people would be less likely to pick out the uncomfortable college professor if she were dressed in dark colors. I'd just have to hope Kevin didn't decide to wear a colorful Hawaiian shirt, a fashion "trend"—and I use that word loosely— that he had embraced wholeheartedly. I pulled my hair up under a black baseball cap that belonged to Crawford and took off my earrings, diamond studs that had been a gift from my first husband after an early infidelity. I had a few hours to kill, so I gave Trixie the walk of her life, complete with splashing in a shallow pond at a nearby park. Then the two of us dined on a burger that I picked up from a local take-out place. After I puttered around in the house, doing a few loads of laundry and straightening up the bedroom, I donned a pair of gorgeous high-heeled black leather boots that went with my outfit, got in the car, and headed toward the middle of the Bronx and a diner that Kevin and I had eaten at over the years. It had a parking lot and was not too far from Kevin's house at the other end of the Bronx, so it made a good meeting point. While I waited for him to arrive, I programmed the address of the Elegant Majestic into the GPS.

Kevin showed up five minutes after I had finished, jumping into the passenger seat of the car, again out of breath.

"Why are you always out of breath?" I asked.

He looked at me, his eyes wide behind his very thick glasses. "Because I'm fat! That's why!" he said. "Isn't that what you want me to say?"

I was taken aback. "Um…no." He was fat, but it wasn't my place to tell him that. He seemed to be acutely aware of it already.

He ran his hands along the legs of his dark jeans. "I'm sorry. It's just that living with my mother hasn't been good for my weight. She is constantly feeding me. And when she's not feeding me, she's asking me when I'm going back to the priesthood. That just makes me want to eat more." He turned and looked out the passenger-side window. "I eat my feelings."

I put a hand on his shoulder. "Who doesn't, Kevin?" I took note of the fact that he had gone with the all-black look as well, old habits dying hard. I also noticed that his jacket was a Members Only piece that had to be close to thirty years old, but I held my tongue. He was already hurting, it would seem, so laying it on regarding his sartorial choices would probably push him over the edge. I also had to remember that the poor guy hadn't really had much of a choice in what he wore for most of his adult life, so a clothing misstep was to be expected every now and again. I thought back to the Birkenstock sandals, board shorts, and hipster T-shirts that he used to wear around campus; his attempts at hip had come off as just a bit misguided.

We headed off to the club where Sassafras had been scheduled to shake her moneymaker, literally. I had always wanted to use that expression, and now was my chance. I asked Kevin if he had ever been to a strip club.

He raised an eyebrow in response.

"Well, then, it's a first for both of us," I said, navigating with the help of my GPS into the heart of Yonkers, a place that I didn't think I'd ever been or that I'd ever want to go to again. A low building, the Elegant Majestic sat in the middle of a vast parking lot that held cars both expensive and those in desperate need of repair, its klieg lights beckoning all comers from the easy-on, easy-off highway exit. A sign that boasted girls like you've never seen!—I didn't even want to know what that meant—hung from the marquee adjacent to the street. The most concerning feature, however, was the blacked-out windows. I knew we weren't in Kansas anymore.

"Holy cow," he said, the worst Kevin would say. He gripped his door handle as if his life depended on it. His mother, "the widow McManus" as I liked to call her, had eyes in the back of her head and her ear to the ground, so he would surely be reprimanded for swearing even thirty miles away from her. Let's not even get into the fact that he was at a strip club.

I parked the car and looked at him. "So here's what we're going to do: We're going to try to talk to a few people and find out if they have seen her. I don't know what time this place closes down, but we'll try to get this done as efficiently as possible."

"I have to work in the morning," he reminded me weakly.

"Yeah, me, too. What's your point?" I asked as I took only what I needed—money in the form of a bunch of singles and a wad of twenties that I had withdrawn from the university's ATM earlier—and locked the rest up in my glove box; I told him to do the same. It didn't seem like taking valuables beyond some cold, hard cash into a seedy nightclub was the best plan. I thought Kevin agreed. "Ready?" I asked as we walked toward the front of the club, Kevin a trembling mess beside me. I wondered why he had agreed to come along if he was so terrified. He obviously didn't have the chops for ill-conceived and poorly executed capers which were my stock in trade.

I didn't know how this worked. Did you pay a cover charge and then have access to the entire "show"? Or did you spend your money at the bar and with the girls? We got to the front door, and a burly guy, a tattoo snaking around his neck, put up a meaty hand. "Twenty bucks," he said.

I forked over forty dollars; it was the least I could do for Kevin, since he was just along for the ride. He looked at me, not sure whether to thank me or not. I told him he could buy the first round if he wanted.

We walked through floor-to-ceiling hanging beads into

the first den of iniquity I had ever been in. I was sure the same was true for Kevin, though judging from the look on his face, he was enjoying it far more than someone who had recently put his Roman collar to rest should. I nudged him in the ribs. "Let's sit over there," I said, pointing to a two-top in a dark corner. Moments after we were seated, a leggy brunette approached us and bent over, giving us a good look at some very large, and very expensive, breasts, the kind that looked like two beach balls had been inflated over the chest wall.

"Get you guys a drink?" she asked.

I'd tried to tone it down and not display the gorgeousness that I knew resided under my baseball cap, but "guys"? I tried to give her my order above the din of a bass-heavy song, but all that came out was a throaty croak, my ability to speak seeming to have left me. Behind her, a woman was flipping around with wild abandon on a brightly lit stage, body parts that I hadn't even seen on myself in full view of the enraptured audience, mostly men in their forties and fifties. I focused my attention on our waitress and her beach ball boobs. "Diet Coke," I said.

"You might as well get a drink-drink. It's going to cost the same," she said helpfully.

I looked at Kevin. "Do you want a drink-drink?"

Kevin went with his usual Chardonnay, and I seconded the order. I would sip it slowly, knowing that I would be driving, and also knowing that it probably would be as far as you could get from a decent glass of wine, but desperate times called for desperate measures. We watched the waitress saunter off on her high heels, much more adept at navigating the crowd in a skimpy costume and heels than I could ever imagine being; I can barely get up in the middle of the night to use the bathroom without sustaining some kind of injury, especially if Crawford's giant shoes are in my path. I didn't want to look around because I wasn't sure on what my eyes might fall, so I focused on Kevin. "Let's ask the waitress what she knows," I said.

He trained his eyes on me, apparently coming to the same conclusion about the safest thing to look at. "Sounds like a plan." Something must have been going on behind my head, because he closed his eyes as he spoke. "I bet she knows her. Sassy seems like she's pretty popular, given the number of fans on her Facebook page."

"Who'da known, Kevin? All our hard work in our respective fields and what do we have to show for it? Not a fan page on Facebook," I said. "That's for sure."

Kevin mulled that over.

The waitress returned with our drinks and set them on the table. I put a twenty on her tray. She didn't ask us if we wanted any change so I gathered she was keeping whatever was thrown upon her tray; that was one way to bolster your income, I suppose. "Would you like a lap dance?" she asked Kevin, who nearly choked to death. She turned to me. "You?"

"Actually, we are looking for someone," I said.

"Are you cops?" she asked, going pale.

"No," I said, my nervousness taking over and making me give far more information than was necessary. "I'm a college professor, and he's a banquet manager at a catering hall."

"And a priest," Kevin added.

Now she was really confused. "Is this some kind of kinky role-playing thing?" she asked. "I'm just trying to make enough money to buy my kid an Xbox. I don't need any trouble."

"No," I assured her. "We're really a professor and a banquet manager, but we are looking for someone."

She raised an overly tweezed eyebrow. "Sassy Du Pris?"

She tried to look impassive, but fear passed across her face.

"You know her," I said.

"She was supposed to dance tonight," she said, her voice dropping to a whisper we could barely hear.

"We know," I said. "What happened?"

When it was clear she wasn't going to give us any more information without some prompting, I slid another twenty onto her tray.

"She had a fight with the manager. Over money."

Money. Sassy's reason for being and the reason we were mired in this mess.

"She wanted more," she continued. "Said she had a huge fan base."

Kevin nodded enthusiastically. "She does!"

"I thought they had worked it out, but she never turned up for her first night. Not sure what happened," she said.

Kevin pulled out his wallet and threw a wad of cash onto the woman's tray. "Thank you. You're a lovely woman with a lot to offer," he said. I wasn't sure how he knew that, but whatever. "You need to get out of here as soon as possible and get a job that allows you to wear clothes." I knew he was trying to be helpful, but I could see that she was a little offended.

"Do you want a lap dance or what?" she asked. The money on the tray disappeared but since she was wearing so little, I wasn't sure where it went.

I pushed a twenty-dollar tip into her cleavage and thanked her for asking, telling her that we would think about it.

She shrugged. "Suit yourself," she said as she wandered off.

"We're not really going to think about it, right?" Kevin asked. He waved his hand in front of his face. "Weren't cigarettes banned in dining establishments like four years ago?"

I trained my eyes on the stage, looking for signs of Sassy. "You consider this a dining establishment?"

I was mesmerized by what went on on the stage. Maybe I *was* middle-aged. Maybe it was just that never in my life, even in my shot-putting days, had I ever looked or been able to move like the women up there. Never mind the six-inch high heels. Between the swirling lights, the pounding music, and the bare flesh, I didn't know which end was up and found myself getting sucked into a vortex that smelled like cheap vodka and even cheaper perfume that made my head spin.

One woman was more talented than the next, if you considered talent being able to dance upside down on a shiny pole, then shimmy down and land in a logic-defying split, level with the faces of the patrons at the bar. These girls didn't get enough credit for their physical fitness, that was for sure. Maybe Max had a point. Maybe exotic dancing was a viable career that could net you good money, flexible hours, and a daily workout. I wondered exactly what kind of training went into this kind of dancing and decided that I was way too old for those kinds of gymnastics, as fun as they looked.

I don't know why we stayed so long, but it was kind of like rubbernecking at a car wreck. I took a long swig from my glass of wine, and even though my inclination was to gag, I held it down. "Ready, Kevin?"

His eyes were trained on a spot behind—and above—my head, and I got a sinking suspicion that what he was looking at wasn't something, or someone, that would make me happy. Rather, watching the color drain from his face, I was sure that coming here had been a colossal mistake that was getting ready to bite me in the ass.

I turned slowly and took in the sight of my husband and Carmen, who was now blocking my view of the stage. Clearly, we had some explaining to do.

THIRTY-THREE

CRAWFORD DIDN'T SEE the humor in the situation, but Carmen did. Her belly laugh was audible over the blaring dance music, so loud that several patrons, even in the far reaches of the club, turned to see what was going on. What they saw was a hot-looking woman laughing at a less-hot woman and a pudgy man while a tall, stern-looking guy presided over the entire encounter.

"I thought you had court?" I asked.

"I thought you were going straight home?" he asked.

Tit for tat. "Well, I decided that I wanted to see where Sassy worked," I said, telling only a half-truth. I also wanted to tell her to leave us all alone and go back to whatever rock she had crawled out from under, but that didn't seem like something I wanted to say out loud at that particular moment.

He didn't look amused. I looked around. Suddenly the bar area was much more sparsely populated, as was the main stage area, Crawford and Carmen's cop pheromones clearing out the joint. The burly bouncer, the one who had taken Kevin's and my cover fee, ambled over.

"Is there a problem, officers?" he asked, assuming that Kevin and I were part of the SWAT team that had descended upon the Elegant Majestic. "This is a classy place," he said. "We don't want any trouble."

"It *is* very classy," I agreed. Kevin, the mute, stood beside me in dumbfounded confusion.

"Oh, shit, *papi*, they made us," Carmen said, her surprise

as fake as most of the breasts in the bar. She stamped her boot-clad foot. "I never thought that anyone would be able to see through your disguise," she said, giving Crawford the once-over.

His "disguise" consisted of khakis, loafers, and an oxford shirt. All he had ditched from his regular work uniform was the tie and blazer. The bouncer looked at Carmen and then Crawford, waiting for their explanation of why they were casing the place, but neither gave it up.

Crawford placed a drink order with the bouncer, pulling up a chair in front of the table that Kevin and I had commandeered when we arrived. He looked at Carmen. "We are officially off duty."

Carmen fell heavily onto the leather banquette next to me. "Oh, thank God. I thought we were going to have to frisk every dancer in this place until we found this Sassy person."

"She's not dancing tonight," I said.

"We know," Crawford said pointedly.

"Oh," I said.

He pointed at Kevin. "What are you doing here?"

In the year since Kevin had given up the collar, so to speak, Crawford had slowly started treating him like he treated everyone else: like a perp.

Kevin stammered a bit, not used to the interrogation that came with being friends with Crawford. "Well…she…" He pointed at me.

"Forget it," Crawford said, looking around for the bouncer. In his place was our original waitress, who came tottering back with two beers and two more glasses of wine, which she placed on the table, backing up into Crawford, her ample behind—although no match for Carmen's—coming into contact with his nose. He backed up in turn, grimacing.

"Do you take credit cards?" I asked, before realizing

I didn't have one on me, my possessions locked up in the glove box of my car.

"They're on the house," she said, smiling.

I shot Crawford a look he couldn't decipher. I threw my head in her direction and rubbed two fingers together. Finally, while she waited expectantly, he pulled out his wallet, peeled off some bills, and placed them on her tray.

She thanked him. "You remind me of my dad. He was a cop, too," she said before sashaying off.

Crawford downed most of his beer. Carmen pushed hers toward him. "I'll drive. Drink this before you spontaneously combust."

After he had consumed most of the second beer and settled down, Crawford turned his attention back to Kevin and me. "So, you two brain surgeons want to tell me what you're doing here?"

Kevin decided that remaining silent was the best way not to incriminate himself.

"What do you think, Crawford?" I asked. "I wanted to get some info on Sassy. If I got to see some creative interpretative dance while I was at it, all the better."

Carmen stifled a giggle.

"Why did you lie about going to court?" I asked.

"Because I knew if I told you where I was going, you'd go there, too," he said, as if it were the most obvious thing in the world. Which I guess it was. He looked helplessly at Carmen. "You talk to her."

"Listen, *chica*. We've got this under control. Girl's got some crazy background, and we're going to try to have a nice chat with her, in a controlled setting, to see if we can figure out what she wants so badly and why she'll do anything to get it."

"She wants the money," I said.

Carmen knew that, too. "Right—but it's our job to figure out why and get her to lay off." She pointed a finger at me, the French manicure impeccable; woman had a lot of style. Not my style, but style nonetheless. "Not yours."

"Why do you think she allowed her headlining act to be advertised?" I asked. "Even if it did get canceled?"

Carmen raised an eyebrow at me. "Maybe to smoke someone out who might have some information about the money? Someone who wanted to see her? Talk to her?"

In other words, me.

Crawford chimed in. "Maybe because she's dumb?" He arched an eyebrow in my direction.

Kevin was going to have some kind of seizure if we didn't get out of the club, and he didn't need to use words to tell me that. The lone trickle of sweat running down the side of his pudgy face was evidence enough. I slapped him on the back. "Ready, Kev?" I looked at Crawford. "See you at home?"

"See you at home," he dutifully intoned. "Carmen and I will just finish up here and then call it a night. Don't wait up."

"I never do," I said, sleep being as important to me as the air I breathed. I gave his hair a tousle as I walked past him, knowing that he hated that as much as my amateur sleuthing. "Later."

Kevin left the club as fast as his legs would carry him and was standing by the car before I had even gotten through the front door. I took a whiff of the sleeve of my sweater and found it ripe with the smell of smoke and some-thing else that was a combination of all odiferous and bad things. I was just about to remark to him about how bad our car ride home would smell when I saw someone come up behind him, unbeknownst to the terrified former priest, and put a long bare arm around his neck.

"Well, if it isn't the lovely Sassafras Du Pris," I said, sounding bolder than I felt.

In her ubiquitous heels, she stood a foot taller than

Kevin, and was solidly built. Kevin's eyes grew wider, and I felt bad that I had dragged him into this caper, even though he was a willing, if initially reluctant, participant.

Sassy's voice wasn't what I expected. Sure, it sounded southern, and yes, it was all lady, even though the look of her suggested "drag queen," but it was higher and thinner than I'd thought it would be, more Minnie Mouse than Demi Moore. "Where's that fucking money?" she asked.

"With the public administrator," I said.

"Don't mess with me," she said.

I decided to keep her talking because that was my best shot at having Crawford and Carmen come into the parking lot before she did something stupid. Sassy, however, had other plans.

There were a lot of things that were shiny about Sassy—her nails, her hair, the bling around her neck and that hung from her ears. Oh, then there was the gun she pulled out from her jeans pocket and held against Kevin's temple. That was the shiniest thing of all.

THIRTY-FOUR

OF ALL OF the things I had done in the name of getting to the truth, this had to be the dumbest. As I watched Kevin go from terrified to catatonic, looking like he was going to faint, I rued the day I ever thought I could have a reasonable conversation with a woman who was hell-bent on finding money we didn't have.

"Just do what she says," Kevin said when he saw that it wasn't a done deal that I would follow her into a waiting van, parked at the far end of the lot under a light that had burned out long ago. My first instinct had been to run, but I knew enough about Sassy to know what she might be capable of; her reputation definitely preceded her. I followed Kevin's sage advice and traipsed along after them, looking behind me to see if either Crawford or Carmen had emerged from the dingy, stinky club and would be inclined to save us, but the parking lot was vacant. The sound of our shoes on the pavement was the only sound in addition to the low rumble of the van, a vehicle obviously in need of a new muffler. I thought about my phone, locked up in the glove compartment of my car, and then thought longingly about the time machine I thought about constantly and always wished I had invented, the one that would transport me back to a time when I didn't make rash, idiotic decisions, dragging my friends along for the dangerous ride.

Sassy opened the back of the van, a cargo area with no seats; after that, she took Kevin's brand-new iPhone, the one he loved so much, stomped on it with her high heels, and left it for dead in the parking lot. Apparently, Kevin hadn't taken my advice and locked his valuables in my glove box. I looked at her. "Where are you taking us? And you do realize that we'll be rolling around back there?"

She pushed Kevin into the van in response to my questions, and he fell in with a thud, banging his knee hard. It was at this point that I was grateful he had gotten so chubby; maybe the extra pounds would protect him—and me—as we were tossed to and fro around the metal-encased hold. As Sassy raised a hand to push me as well, I stepped up toward the van, grabbing both sides of the door and hoisting myself in; I didn't need her help. I was an experienced kidnap victim. Once in the van, I looked around for something to hold, but there was nothing—just a strap hanging from the ceiling that wasn't long enough for us to grab to keep from rolling around when she took a corner.

She leaned in and in her squeaky voice admonished us, "If you can't keep quiet, I will kill you."

Kevin trembled beside me, and I put a hand on his knee to calm him. "Don't worry."

Sassy jumped in the front seat and slammed the door, gunning the engine. Kevin looked at me, some color returning to his cheeks. "'Don't worry'?" he hissed through clenched teeth. "What would I have to worry about? A crazed stripper just held a gun to my temple, and God knows where she's taking us. I bet it isn't church, though." He put his hands beside him to hold himself steady and dropped his head. "We're going to die."

"We're not going to die," I said, a confidence coming over me that had no legitimate source. I didn't know why, but I didn't think Sassy was going to hurt us. Well, at least not mortally. Kevin, on the other hand, didn't look so sure.

After a harrowing ride through the streets of Yonkers and its environs, Sassy pulled the car over, coming to an abrupt stop that threw me against the opposite wall of the van. I didn't have a watch and neither did Kevin, but it seemed like we had been driving around for over a half hour. Kevin managed to stay put when she came to a stop, having decided to stand and grab hold of the short strap dangling from the ceiling. After it was clear we were at our destination, I stood, rubbing my butt.

"That's going to hurt tomorrow," I said.

"If we even have a tomorrow!" Kevin said dramatically. It appeared that he was taking his anger about the situation out on me, a really uncool turn of events to me.

"God, when did you turn into such a drama queen?" I asked.

He sputtered, trying to come up with a response, but he had nothing.

I glared at him. "You had every right to say no when I asked you to come," I said.

"Oh, I did?" he asked. He did a passable imitation of my voice and vaguely New York–tinged accent. "'We'll be home early. It will only take a few minutes. I just want to talk to her,'" he said. "That's what I was supposed to say no to? Never in my wildest dreams would this happen," he said, throwing his arms out wide to indicate the inside of the dingy van.

"Listen, you're bored and unhappy with your new life and you came along for the ride. It's not my fault," I said as Sassy opened the back of the van. I peered out to see where we were; it looked like classic Westchester woodland, the kind where bodies were laid to rest, never to be found again. I shuddered slightly, hoping Kevin wouldn't notice. Maybe I had been wrong about Sassy and her intentions.

"Oh, great," he said. "Now we're going to sleep with the fishes."

I jumped off the end of the van and looked at Sassy. "Would you please tell him that we're not going to sleep with the fishes?"

She shrugged. "You might."

Kevin followed me out of the van. We stood at the edge of the parking lot, a light blinking on and off under a very dark sky, a bridge off in the distance; the van lights were still on, and they illuminated the hardened face of a woman who was probably once very pretty and who reminded me of someone else, someone whose identity wasn't coming to me now. An actress? I studied her to get a sense of whether she really wished us any harm or just wanted to scare us into giving her information that we didn't have.

If it weren't for the circumstances, I would have commented on the gorgeous night and the dark silhouette of the trees around us, but I kept my mouth shut.

She waved the gun around menacingly, but to me, her heart didn't seem to be in it. I decided to take control of the situation by offering up what I did know.

"Sassy, we do not have the money. After Chick died, it went to the public administrator, and it will be months, even years, before we find out who gets it."

She looked confused but didn't say anything.

"Did you kill Chick, Sassy?" I asked.

"No!" she said and then began crying, big, horrible sobs that came from the tips of her Lucite-heel-shod toes. "I loved him. I would never hurt him."

Kevin had no idea what I was talking about, not knowing about the note we had found in Chick's apartment. I waited to see if she had more to say.

"He divorced me. Right before he left. Everyone thought I left him, but it was the other way around. If it was up to me? We'd still be married." She scratched at her head, and it became apparent that what I thought was a weave was really a wig. She stripped it from her head and threw it into a small stream right off the parking lot. Underneath all that synthetic hair was a lovely round head topped with a short pixie cut that made the really trashy Sassy look about ten years younger and closer to a teen than a middle-aged woman. "God, I loved him." She looked at me beseechingly. "Is he really dead?"

"He's really dead," I said. I looked at Kevin, shaking uncontrollably beside me. I put my arm around him. "You have to believe us about the money because—"

"I'm a priest!" Kevin blurted out suddenly, finding his voice.

Sassy went to her knees like a sack of potatoes that had been dropped from a second-story window. "Oh, God!"

"Right! Oh, God!" Kevin said.

Standing there, I was reminded of a dog Max used to have, a giant, showy Afghan with the inexplicable name of Juniper who Max claimed was the toughest dog she knew. How she knew this was anyone's guess, but to me, Juniper was all bark and no bite. Sure, she sounded some kind of weird alarm every time someone rang the doorbell, and yes, she would jump on top of you the minute you gained entry into the house, but her tail was always between her legs, and at her core, she was extremely docile. The attempted burning down of the house notwithstanding, Sassy seemed the same way to me—a physical oddity with a strange and loud voice, but not someone who would do more than jump on top of you if the situation called for it. I think in the years since she and Chick had separated, Sassy had lost a little of her sass. The gun, to me, was like Juniper's teeth, big, shiny, and sharp but never to be used for anything that didn't have to do with food.

She was overwrought at the thought that she had kidnapped a priest and stayed on her knees. The gun clattered noisily to the ground, and I lunged for it, grabbing it before Sassy had a chance to compose herself. She reacted too late; the gun was already in my hand and out of her reach by the time she realized she had dropped it. "Let us go and this will all be behind us, Sassy."

"I need that money," she whispered from her position on the ground.

"Why? Why do you need the money so badly?" Then I remembered something that immediately made me feel less sympathetic toward her. "Why do you need money so badly that you would break into my house and poison my dog?" I asked.

She looked up, and now that the bad wig was gone, I could see her face very clearly. She looked shocked. "I would never harm an animal."

"My dog almost died," I said.

She stood. "I'll cop to trying to break into your car the other night and then breaking the window later, but I would never hurt your dog." She looked at me, her head cocked. "Your husband is a big guy. Kinda stiff, though."

"He's a cop," Kevin helpfully added.

For some reason, I believed Sassy was telling the truth about what she'd done. "Oh, jeez," Sassy sobbed. "I know. First a cop and then a priest. Do I have luck or what?"

I didn't really care if Sassy was unlucky; she was a pain in the ass and might have been the person who had set out to poison my dog. "Who poisoned my dog? Who broke into my house?" I asked her.

"I have no idea," she said, going toward the front of the van. "Did Chick ever say anything about me?"

I thought back to the birthday party, the supposedly joyous event that had set all of this ridiculousness in motion. "He referred to you once as his 'dear, sweet Sassy,'" I said.

She mulled that over, and ultimately it seemed to make her happy. "I don't know. Something screwed him up. I don't know what it was."

"Drugs? Alcohol?" I asked, going for the usual suspects in the "screw up" department.

She shook her head. "No. That wasn't it. I think he met someone else," she said. "Why else would he have left me?"

Looking at her, and knowing a bit about her background, gave me about a hundred answers to that question even though we had just met. The fact that he had found one woman, perhaps two, was a bit of a stretch, but who was I to judge? Maybe she was right. I didn't think we'd ever know. I think Chick was just your run-of-the-mill whack job. Frankly, I didn't care. Spending so much time on the subject seemed like a waste to me.

"He left me. He left me with nothing. It was supposed to be ours together. We were going to get back together. He told me that when he called me after he disappeared."

"What was supposed to be yours together?"

Her eyes narrowed. "Not too smart, are you?"

Kevin leapt to my defense. "She's very smart."

She ignored him. "The money, stupid. The money was supposed to be ours."

THIRTY-FIVE

THAT WAS ALL we learned about Sassy Du Pris, because right after telling us that she thought she and Chick would share in some ill-gotten gains—gotten from where was still anyone's guess—she took off in the van, leaving Kevin and me to try to find our way back to Yonkers and the car we had left behind at the Elegant Majestic. Since I was in possession of the gun, I guess she figured it was better to leave than to find out whether or not I had the stones to use it. (I didn't.) She left us no wiser as to why she needed the money or where she and Chick had gotten it from in the first place.

He told her they were getting back together, and she believed him. Things hadn't turned out quite the way Sassy had planned.

The night was pitch black outside the dimly lit parking lot, and, as is often the case, I had on the wrong shoes for this mission and its unintended end. Kevin and I stood and looked around the deserted park, curiously named Turkey Mountain, according to the sign.

"Where are we?" he asked.

"Turkey Mountain, apparently."

His voice sounded like he was on the verge of tears. "Where, pray tell, is Turkey Mountain?"

I tried to make light of it. "Well, if you had your iPhone, we could probably look it up."

"You," he said, his voice quavering, a finger pointed at my chest, "are not as funny as you think you are. You should really think about dropping the sarcasm. It's not attractive."

"That's not the first time I have heard that," I admitted. Under the circumstances, I could not disagree with him. I looked around in the darkness to see if there was someone, anyone, in the distance, maybe a moonlight hiker or someone with a really bad sense of direction who had started out that morning and was only now returning to the parking lot, but the whole area was completely desolate, which is just how Sassy had planned it. Across from the preserve, however, was a steep incline, and up that incline, it appeared, was a development. I grabbed Kevin's hand. "Come on. There are houses across the street."

He stood where he was, smack in the middle of the parking lot, looking a lot like he wasn't going to come. Eventually, when he realized that staying there would end up in a night alone in a nature preserve, he relented and followed me down the dirt road to the street, where nary a car passed by, the hour for driving home from local train stations long past. We crossed the street, one I had never been on, and entered the development, where only a few lights twinkled in the distant windows of the houses that dotted the perimeter.

We wended our way up a very steep hill, our feet making the only sounds in the tranquil night air. It felt as if it were getting colder by the minute, and the persistent ache in my toes reminded me once again—as Crawford always reminds me—that high-heeled boots weren't appropriate for the task at hand. Seriously, though, who knew that we would be kidnapped, tossed around the back of a cargo van, and then going on a trek in the middle of the night in a town that we had never visited and that seemed to consist only of hills? We were silent while we trudged along, Kevin's heavy breathing a reminder to me that one, he was out of shape, and two, he wanted to be anywhere but here. I tried to make conversation to pass the time.

"How are things at the catering hall?"

"Really, Alison? This is what you want to do? You want to have a conversation about work?"

"It would be better than listening to you seethe beside me," I said. "That's getting kind of old."

"I'm not seething," he said. "Besides, you can't hear someone seething."

"Yes, you are, and yes, you can." I stumbled over an uneven patch in the road, my toes banging painfully against the front of my boots. "I know what seething sounds like. Crawford seethes a lot."

"I can't imagine why."

We continued on in silence, my attempt at conversation obviously unwelcome. Finally, after a good ten-minute uphill trek, we arrived at a house where the inhabitants seemed to be not only awake but having some kind of gathering at which everyone was having a festive time. I looked at Kevin. "What do you think?"

"If it gets us off of Turkey Mountain, then I'm all for it."

"I don't think we're on Turkey Mountain anymore."

He sighed. "I was being figurative, Alison. I know we're not on Turkey Mountain anymore."

Someone was a little crabby, but I didn't let that stop me from marching up to the front door and ringing the bell. As soon as the bell sounded, the house went quiet, except for some scuffling noises and sounds of windows being opened at various levels on the three-story structure.

I looked at Kevin. "Maybe this wasn't the best house to pick?" I asked as a hooded figure raced past us and down the street, the footfalls heavy and rubber-soled. Several other figures—some male, some female—also drifted by, some running faster than others, whispers carrying across the still night air. After a few minutes of watching people vacate the house in droves, the front door opened, and we were confronted by a tousle-headed blonde, who stood inside the screen door in the hallway, her hands on her hips. She looked more defiant than an innocuous doorbell ring should have inspired, given that the house had been filled with people just moments before. "Hi," I said. "Our car broke down," sort of true, "and we need to use the phone to call someone to pick us up," all true, "and were wondering if we could come in?"

"What do you think I am? An idiot?" she asked. She couldn't have been more than fifteen, with an attitude of a thirty-five-year-old. Behind her, a voice slurred, "Who is it, Brianna?"

"Cops," she said and slammed the door in our faces.

I looked at Kevin, dumbfounded. It was the second time that evening we had been taken for cops. Well, I did have a gun. After I regained my composure, I put my finger on the doorbell and kept it there until Brianna answered again. I pulled the screen open and put my foot on the threshold. "First of all, we're not cops. Secondly, if we were, you would be in big trouble."

She rolled her eyes. "Wouldn't be the first time. Although I've never seen you two before."

"That's because we're not cops. Listen, young lady," I said, using my professor voice, "we are stranded, and I'd like to use your phone. Please let me know why that is a problem."

The sass came out in full force. Her head bobbed back and forth like a chicken's, and she waved her finger in my face. "It's a problem because I don't know you and I'm not supposed to let strangers in my house when my parents aren't home. Now move your foot and get off my property before I call the cops on you."

Leaving my foot where it was—and hoping she wouldn't go ahead and slam the door anyway—I looked up the street and saw not one other light. Finding a sympathetic ear at this hour, when everyone obviously was asleep, didn't look promising. I looked at Kevin. He gently pushed me out of the way and spoke to Brianna.

"Brianna, is it?" he said, standing in front of me. "My name is Father Kevin McManus, and my friend and I here are stranded, having had an unfortunate incident at Turkey Mountain." He pointed across the main road to the nature preserve.

Brianna rolled her eyes. "I'm still not letting you in, priest or not." She closed the front door in our faces and left us standing there, not sure if she was returning. Just as we were about to give up and pick another house, where we would have to wake up the occupants to get some help, she returned, holding a portable phone. "I'll let you use it on two conditions," she said, obviously having consulted with the slurry-voiced male inside the house. "First, that you don't tell anyone what you saw here."

Since we weren't sure what we saw, that wasn't going to be a problem.

"Second, that you use the phone and then wait at the bottom of the hill."

We didn't have any choice but to agree, because we needed to tell someone, namely Crawford, where we were. Apparently, someone was partying on a school night, and that was a no-no when you were only midway through your teens. I wondered where this snotty girl's parents were and if they knew what went on the minute their backs were turned.

I took the phone, keeping my eyes on the girl as I dialed Crawford's cell. He picked up midway through the first ring. "Hi, we're fine," I said, cutting to the chase. I put my hand over the receiver. "By the way, where are we?" I asked the lovely Brianna.

She rolled her eyes again. I wanted to warn her that if

she continued to do that, her face might stay that way. "Uh, Yorktown Heights?" she said, as if I already knew the answer to the question I'd asked.

"We're in Yorktown Heights. Do you know where that is?" I asked, trying to carry on a perfectly normal conversation in spite of the fact that Crawford was squawking like a chicken that had been run over while crossing the road. "It's about forty minutes north of us. You'll need to take the Taconic, I think," I said, taking some comfort in relaying these instructions calmly to him. "Yes, we're fine," I reiterated. "No, she didn't hurt us."

Brianna's eyes grew wide. "Of course I didn't hurt you," she said, taking umbrage.

I put my hand over the receiver again. "No, not you," I said.

"Is that Sassy?" Crawford asked.

"No, it's Brianna."

"Who?" he asked.

"Never mind," I said. "We're at"—I stepped back to see the number above the door—"43 Mount Pleasant Road in Yorktown. You have a GPS in the Crown Vic, right? We'll be at the end of the street. There's some kind of main drag that intersects with Mount Pleasant, but I don't know what it is."

"We'll find you," he said. "Stay put!" he added, knowing that there was always the chance that Kevin and I would be distracted by something shiny and wander off, never to be heard from again, until maybe the spring thaw, when our intertwined remains would be unearthed by hikers on Turkey Mountain. I shook my head to clear it of that image; where had that come from?

Brianna held her hand out for the phone. "Remember what I said."

"Okay, and you remember what I am about to say," I said. I paused dramatically for effect, something that would be lost probably on Brianna but which made me feel like my advice would be taken to heart. "Just say no." I handed her the phone. "Thank you for your help."

She slammed the front door again. I grabbed Kevin's arm and pulled him along on the journey back down to the end of the street. At the corner was an old, dilapidated stone wall, fortunately still sturdy enough for us to sit on. I swung my legs back and forth to keep warm, my jacket not really doing the trick. My heels banged against the stone, the only sound we could hear. Since the party at Brianna's had been broken up by us in an unceremonious fashion, the neighborhood was deadly quiet.

After sitting for twenty minutes in silence, Kevin finally spoke. "I miss being a priest."

"I know you do." It would be obvious to even the most casual acquaintance that Kevin was a little lost at sea these days. "Are you thinking about going back?"

"Maybe," he said, "but I want to do something different. Maybe go away."

My heart sank a little bit. "Like where?"

"Latin America, maybe. Africa?"

"Wow, really far away."

"I really want to make a difference. Being the chaplain at St. Thomas was cushy but not really significant in terms of helping people." We both chewed on that silently for a while. "Know what I mean?"

I did. I also knew that Kevin was really at loose ends. I didn't want him to make a rash decision, but it sounded like he had given this some thought. "I do."

Another half hour went by, and I felt like Crawford would never find us. We sat in silence, Kevin not really wanting to talk about his plans any further, even though I tried to get more details. I didn't want to think about him being thousands of miles away; even the thirty that separated us now didn't allow us to get together as much as we would like. I always knew he was there, though, right before the Bronx ends and Long Island begins, and that was comforting in and of itself.

It was freezing. I resisted the urge to complain and tried to put out of my head exactly how lousy I would feel in the morning after having gotten no sleep. In the distance, I saw the lights of some cars, and I prayed that someone was finally arriving to get us.

"Max is upset with you," Kevin said finally after the protracted silence.

I turned to face him.

"She is upset that you never saw her father in the hospital," he said, "and that you have been so wrapped up with Bobby's family and Christine. She feels like you don't care about her anymore."

"That's not true," I said quietly. I was so hurt by that pronouncement that I didn't even have the energy to refute Max's claims with anything approaching conviction. "That's not true at all."

"I tried to tell her that, but she won't listen. She's very upset, Alison," he said. "I think you have to make it right."

"She's been freezing me out," I said. "She wouldn't even talk to me after I found out about Marty."

He fell silent again as we focused on the road in front of us. Coming up the desolate street was a police car, the lights on top turning lazily, the siren quiet. I jumped off the stone wall, not expecting Kevin to follow me or even be able to keep up as I ran to meet the car, but he surprised me by running right alongside of me, as anxious to get to the police as I was.

The car pulled over at the corner of the main road and Mount Pleasant. The cop in the driver's seat, a young African American guy in uniform, almost looked surprised to see us, while his partner, an older white guy with a paunch that hung over his utility belt and nearly grazed the dashboard in front of him, looked over and said, "You the lady with the cop husband?"

"That would be me," I said, letting out a sigh of relief.

"Guy's ready to have a stroke," the older cop answered; his name was MacGyver. No joke. I wondered whether, if I gave him a paper clip, some crazy glue, and a rubber band, he could catapult me back to my town, where I would do nothing but go to school and then return home, content to never find out why Chick Stepkowski had two hundred and fifty g's that Sassy Du Pris wanted. Or why Tim, Christine's new husband, maybe wanted it, too. Or why his kids looked like trolls.

We stood by the side of the police car, wondering if the cops were going to take us back to the Elegant Majestic or even let Crawford know that we were safe. I also wondered why it had taken them so long to get to us; surely Crawford had called right away? Or was this another one of his passive-aggressive attempts at teaching me a lesson about not sleuthing? It didn't matter. After a few seconds of uncomfortable silence, I asked them if they would take us back to the strip club.

"What do we look like?" MacGyver asked. "A taxi service?"

Kevin let out something between an outraged croak and a sob; it was hard to tell which one dominated the strangled noise. I put my arm around him. "Please?"

The cops burst out laughing; seems we had happened upon the comedy duo known as Stearns and MacGyver, comedians by day, cops by night. "Oh, your husband's on the way. Don't worry," Stearns said and popped the locks on the door. "Hop in. We'll take you to the station."

Kevin and I jumped into the backseat, the Plexiglas between the front and back seats separating us from two cops for whom our plight was the most hysterical thing they had ever witnessed. In a few minutes, we were at the

police station, where Carmen and Crawford were standing in the parking lot next to my car, Carmen looking far
more distressed than Crawford, who was becoming used
to my disappearances. I guessed that Crawford had driven
my car here and Carmen had drawn the short straw and
taken the smelly Crown Vic.

From a distance, Crawford looked nonplussed. When I
got up close, I could see the grim set to his mouth and his
bloodshot eyes, which were a dead giveaway that not only
was he upset, he was ticked off. At whom was anyone's
guess. I was hoping it was Sassy.

Kevin got out of the police car and dramatically knelt
and kissed the ground in thanks, the events of the evening
finally taking their full toll on him. Carmen rushed over
and knelt beside him, asking him if he was okay.

"Breathe, *padre*," she said. Stearns asked her if she
needed a bus, cop-speak for "ambulance," thinking that
Kevin had gone into some kind of swoon.

I walked over to Crawford, and he hugged me, uncharacteristically, his penchant for public displays of affection
being virtually nonexistent. "What the hell happened?" he
asked into my hair, now a frizzed-out mess under my baseball cap after the evening's festivities.

"I guess we were kidnapped by Sassy Du Pris," I said.
He held me at arm's length. "You don't seem upset."

"I never thought she was going to hurt us," I said, "and
she didn't." I leaned against the car. "I don't know why she
did what she did, and I don't know why she wanted the
money so badly, and I honestly don't know why I was so
sure she wasn't going to hurt us." I put a hand to my head.
"Man, I'm tired. Are you tired?"

I was getting to that point where laughter turns to crying, and the word "punchy" didn't even begin to describe
my muddled mind.

Kevin turned to Stearns. "She had a gun, and she was

going to use it on us if we didn't do what she said," he said, but it sounded like he was making an excuse for getting in the van rather than indicting Sassy on any kind of charge of violence.

"This is pretty serious stuff," Crawford said, echoing my thoughts and the understatement of the year.

When I was sure no one was looking, I handed Crawford the gun.

MacGyver approached Crawford, his belly mesmerizing me as it swayed to and fro over his belt. "Hey, Detective?"

Crawford turned and looked at him.

"They've got the van. It's at a rest stop near the Bear Mountain Bridge."

We waited.

"But no driver."

THIRTY-SIX

IT WAS A long night. The Yorktown police took our statements and then compared them and then asked us to go over what had happened one more time. By the time they were done, I wasn't sure exactly what had happened and when, but I did know one thing: I had one more thing to tell them.

As we were leaving, Officer Stearns was at the front counter of the police station. "Officer?" I said, getting his attention.

"Yes, ma'am?" he responded, turning to face me.

"There's a house on Mount Pleasant, number 43 if memory serves, and a young lady named Brianna lives there."

He looked at me, an odd expression on his face. "Right, Brianna MacGyver." He pointed toward an office off the lobby. "Sarge's girl."

"Oh," I said, tensing when I realized where this was going. Crawford tightened his arm around my waist, and Kevin shot me a look that told me he thought we were getting into dangerous territory, never mind breaking a promise we swore to keep when Brianna handed us the phone.

Stearns waited. "About Brianna?"

"Well, she's a lovely girl," I said. "She let us use the phone so that we could call my husband."

Crawford says that every time I use the word "lovely," I'm lying. He's right.

Stearns looked relieved. He hadn't known what I was going to tell him, of course, but something had given him the impression it wasn't going to be good.

Crawford asked me if I was done remarking on the off-spring of the officers in attendance and I assured him that I was. Anything to get us out of this godforsaken town and its police station.

Once we were in the car, Crawford turned around, his arm on the back of his seat, and looked at Kevin. "So how did you end up in this mess?" he asked, shooting a look at me.

Kevin, exhausted beyond belief, couldn't even string a sentence together anymore after admonishing me about keeping Brianna MacGyver's secret. "Oh, I...I...guess..."

"Sounds like you don't know," Crawford said, helping out. "Where's your car?" I gave Crawford the location of the diner, one that he was familiar with but didn't know that I was, too. "This was carefully thought out," he said, almost sounding impressed.

I stared out the window the whole way to the diner, wondering how Sassy could have driven a van to a remote location, even more remote than Turkey Mountain, and then disappeared again. Before tonight, it was almost as if she didn't really exist, our interaction with her had been so intermittent and brief; now, even after the evening that I had had, I was sure she wasn't an apparition. She was the real deal, but definitely more sympathetic than I had expected, despite her penchant for breaking into things and stealing giant man clothes.

We dropped Kevin at the diner, and he ran to his car at top speed, jumping in and driving away, his face a blur as he passed us.

"Looks like he's anxious to get home," Crawford said, turning off the car and then turning to face me. He sighed. "I thought you didn't want anything to do with this?" he asked.

"I didn't," I said, "but once I found out that she was

tracking us down and thinking that we had the money, I had to find her and let her know that that's not the case."

"How did you find out she was headlining?"

"Same way you did."

"You got a call from an informant?" he asked.

"No. We stalked her on Facebook."

He put a hand to his chest. "Thank God. Because if I thought, even for a minute, that you now had paid informants working for you, I might have to reconsider this whole marriage thing."

I feigned shock and hurt. "Really?"

"Yes, really," he said, starting the car again and backing out of the spot. "Maybe you can leave this alone now?"

"Sure," I said, preoccupied. "Of course. Whatever you say." I was thinking about everything Kevin had told me, how he wanted to go back to the priesthood and how Max was angry at me, two things that would require a lot more in terms of brain cells than I had to devote to them at the moment. Crawford didn't seem to notice that I wasn't really listening to his diatribe—one that had the hallmarks of one of his usuals, including asking me to mind my own business, stay out of the way of police, leave well enough alone…blah, blah, blah. While he nattered on, I texted Max to ask how she was doing and to see if she had any information about her father's arrangements. I knew I wouldn't hear, given the hour, but hoped that she would at least text me back in the morning, which was rapidly approaching.

We made it home in record time, and I was in bed just minutes after walking through the back door. Crawford followed behind me, rolling into my body and pulling me close. "You need to promise me that you'll stay out of trouble."

I yawned loudly, tears of exhaustion leaking out of the corners of my eyes. "You got it, chief."

"I'm serious, Alison. It seems like we have a conversation like this every few months. What will it take to keep you at school and out of everyone else's business?" he asked.

I was so tired I didn't even have a witty response.

"You have to drive me to work tomorrow because my car is still at the precinct."

I responded by yawning again. "So that means we get up at six."

It was three. Three hours before I had to get up. I tried not to focus on that or the hand that was slowly creeping up the front of my T-shirt. Ultimately, resistance was futile, and by the time I actually fell asleep, I could hear the sound of newspapers hitting various front steps all up and down my street. It didn't take any of my incredible skills of deduction to know that the day ahead of me was going to stink, big-time.

THIRTY-SEVEN

MARY LOU BANNERMAN was waiting for me at my office door, an eager smile on her face and a bag in her hand that looked suspiciously like it had come from my new favorite bakery near her home. On the floor, next to her feet, was a cardboard coffee cup holder with two of the biggest cups of coffee I had ever seen wedged into its slots. I didn't know whether to burst into tears or drop to my knees; after only sleeping a couple of hours and then braving rush-hour traffic to get Crawford to work on time before heading to St. Thomas, I was a basket case. The sight of this wonderful, thoughtful woman, armed with my breakfast, was a sight for sore eyes.

"Good morning," she said in a chipper voice.

"Good morning," I said, wondering, with the sunlight streaming through the back windows of my office, if I would be able to take off my sunglasses at any point during the day. First there was the issue of the giant dark circles under my eyes, and then there was the light sensitivity that accompanies sleep deprivation. Not a pretty picture overall. I opened my office door and peeked over the top of my sunglasses to get a sense of how bad this might be. Bad. I turned to Mary Lou. "You're going to have to excuse me. I need to keep my sunglasses on for at least the beginning of our conversation. I didn't get much sleep last night, and I have a raging headache."

She clucked sympathetically. "I hate when that happens. Insomnia?"

"Something like that," I said cryptically.

"This may not be the best time, then," she said.

I settled in behind my desk, wondering when she was going to offer me what was in the bag.

"To go over some questions I had about my story?" she asked, looking so enthusiastic for my help that it almost broke my heart. She was trying so hard but didn't have the confidence yet to write with the training wheels off, so to speak, still feeling a little self-conscious and thinking that she didn't belong. To her mind, she was not a writer and didn't have any business in a class with young adults. Every time class ended, I attempted to disabuse her of both notions and encouraged her to come see me for help. I just wished that today hadn't been one of the days she did, the coffee and whatever baked good was in the bag notwithstanding.

It was hard to look positive peering out from behind big black sunglasses, but I did my best. I peered over the top again; nope, still sunny. "Sure, Mary Lou. What questions do you have?" I hoped they weren't hard to answer; I had nothing in the tank.

She pulled out a big sheaf of papers and started thumbing through them, identifying places where she was stuck or where she had a question about how to proceed. All told, there were twenty different queries that we miraculously managed to get through before I had to go to class. About midway through, I was able to take off my sunglasses without feeling like someone was driving a steak knife through each eye, and Mary Lou's sharp intake of breath at my appearance didn't go unnoticed by me.

The only thing that reminded her that she still hadn't given me either the coffee or the muffin or scone in the bag was the persistent rumble of my stomach after we had finished going through her story.

"Oh! I forgot," she said, handing me the coffee and the bag.

Inside was a giant piece of crumb cake, powdered sugar covering the brown peaks that dotted the top. I nearly wept with joy. "Thank you, Mary Lou. This looks delicious," I said, daintily breaking off a piece. The minute she left my office, I was going to shove the entire piece in my mouth and wash it down with scalding hot coffee, those two things in combination in my stomach being the only way I was going to get through the day. I stared lovingly at the crumb cake, trying to tell her with my mind that she needed to leave so that we could be alone.

Mary Lou had other plans, namely finding out how I was doing. "Are you okay?" she asked, leaning forward in her chair, her hands clasped together between her knees. "I mean, really okay?"

It wasn't until she asked that I realized I wasn't. I was tired, overwrought, and grieving Max's father. I was holding it together, but barely. Someone showing a little compassion, like she was, was dangerous, and I feared that if I opened my mouth, I would crumble. I nodded and smiled in an effort to assure her that I was absolutely fine.

"You just look so tired," she said. "I hope you're not burning the candle at both ends." Her smile was sad. "You look like you need a hug."

That was the last thing I needed but what I got anyway. That's when it hit. Soon I was sobbing in this wonderful woman's arms, my tears wetting the shoulders of her very soft, and very expensive, cashmere pullover. I was thankful that I hadn't had time to put on makeup that morning, because if I had, I would probably have been stuck with a drycleaning bill for God knew how much, since my crying jag was likely to ruin her sweater. My best friend was bereft, her dear father dead, but she was also angry with me for a variety of infractions. Over the last several weeks,

I decided, I'd felt a little adrift socially, with a bunch of people surrounding me from the dark recesses of my husband's former life—his life before me—and that left me seeking solace and comfort anywhere I could at that particular moment.

"There, there," she said and stood up straight. I was still in my desk chair, and she had leaned over to hug me, folding her tall frame to fit in the small space between my desk and the filing cabinet. She went back to her seat. "Now why don't you tell me what happened and why you are so sad?" she asked.

Crying to Mary Lou Bannerman wasn't my intention, and it was something I would never have foreseen doing, but she was there with a sympathetic ear, a compassionate look on her beautiful face, and a willingness to hear my entire sordid tale.

Not being strong enough to use better judgment, I just let the whole thing out, squalid detail by squalid detail.

I started at the beginning, all the way back to when Crawford was married and had a bunch of crazy brothers-in-law and no Alison Bergeron in his life, and ended with the night before and my best friend—the former priest—being taken on a major boondoggle to a strip club to chase a woman named Sassafras who may or may not have been a murderer. When I got to the part about Turkey Mountain, Mary Lou's eyes lit up.

"Lovely place," she said. "My husband and I hiked there all the time."

I agreed but also reminded her that being there in the dead of night in high-heeled leather boots with a hysterical man, looking for signs of life, was not the best way to be introduced to the nature preserve's loveliness. She saw my point.

"This Sassafras woman," she said. "Did she hurt you?"

I shook my head, a few tears dropping onto the folder

in front of me on my desk. "No. She just wants to find out where the money is and why she can't get at it."

"Do you think maybe she's the person who poisoned your dog?"

"I asked her, and she denied it." I thought about that for a moment. "What did she have to gain by denying it? She had already vandalized our car, stolen my husband's bag of backup work clothes, and kidnapped us. Poisoning a dog is the least of her offenses, it would seem."

"Maybe…"

I rested my head on my folded arms, my voice muffled. "I just want to be left alone."

She chuckled. "Then maybe you shouldn't have gone looking for her."

"Not you, too," I said, groaning. "I just wanted to tell her the story from my perspective and see if I could get her to leave us alone. As you now know, that was a mildly misguided plan."

"Maybe you should write a short story about it?" she asked, her tone still light. She was trying to cheer me up and doing a passable job at it.

I lifted my head and smiled, then dropped it back down so I could think in the warm embrace of my own arms. I had to pull myself together to get through the next few hours of teaching, if not the entire day. Finally, I raised my head, blew my nose and wiped my eyes, and took a huge bite of the crumb cake, figuring at the very least it would make me feel better. Exhaustion coupled with hunger was a deadly combination, I had learned over the years, so I scarfed down the generous slice, slurped up some more coffee, and steeled my resolve for the day.

"Thank you, Mary Lou," I said, standing. "I'm terribly sorry for that outburst. I don't know what came over me. That was extremely unprofessional."

The sun glinted off the big hunks of diamonds, beautiful

studs, in her ears. "You needed a friend. I just happened to be here." She picked up her bag. "Your secret—or should I say secrets?—are safe with me."

"Please, Mary Lou," I said. "This is embarrassing."

She smiled her beatific smile again. She lifted a finger to her lips and turned them slightly as if she were locking them shut. "Not a word will be spoken." She started for the door and then stopped. "It's really reassuring to know that someone like you has problems."

"Someone like me?"

"Yes, someone who seems like she has everything together. The great job, the wonderful husband, lots of friends. You've got it all."

I did? Where she had gotten this impression I would never know. I only had some of it, and even some of that wasn't very good.

"Now I see you've got your crosses to bear, and some of them are very heavy," she said and opened the door. "Take care of yourself. I'll see you later."

Maybe that was her way of telling me to count the blessings that I had. Besides wanting to repair my relationship with Max—the first blessing that I asked for—the only other blessing that I really wanted at this point was for someone to find Sassafras Du Pris and to make her stop her reign of terror, her quest for something that would never in a million years be hers.

By the end of the day, I had one of my wishes.

THIRTY-EIGHT

I LEARNED THROUGH the obituaries online and then a text from Fred that Marty Rayfield would be laid out—as my mother used to put it in her usual eloquent fashion—at a funeral home with which I was familiar up near the Rayfields' home. The viewing, as Catholics call it, was from seven to nine, and a quick flurry of texts between me and Crawford confirmed that he would meet me at home by six so that we could head up there together. I raced through the door at six-oh-five and he wasn't there, so I didn't have to listen to him lecture me about that. I do leave myself enough time, that is, if enough time means always being five minutes behind schedule. I clipped on Trixie's leash and dragged her toward the front door, something that she wasn't overly enthusiastic about because she could hear the rain hitting the pavement, making the prospect of her evening constitutional less than desirable.

"Come on, Trixie," I said, pulling. She responded by sitting heavily on the floor and digging her heels in, the only result of my pulling being that she was now surfing along the tiled hallway on the fake Persian area rug that ran from the front door to the stairs. Let me tell you, Home Depot replicates Persian rugs like nobody's business. The rug bunched up in front of the door and onto my feet, and I stepped to the side. I finally gave up. "It's your bladder," I said, unclipping the leash and putting it back on the counter in the kitchen.

Crawford walked in a few minutes later. "Does Trixie need to go out?" he asked.

"She's on strike," I said. I brushed some rain off the shoulder of his jacket. "It's raining. She won't go out when it rains, remember?"

He shrugged and looked at the dog. "It's your bladder."

She looked at the two of us, nonplussed. In a showdown between owner and animal, animal always got her way even at the expense of her own comfort. At least in this house.

I grabbed an umbrella from the hook next to the back door and raced across the backyard to Crawford's car. He called out to me to clean off the seat before I got in; when I opened the door, I saw a large envelope on the seat with *Rayfield Family* written across the front in his big, looping handwriting. I picked it up. Mass card.

"How did you have time to get a Mass card?" I asked. "Thank you, by the way."

"I stopped at one of the four thousand churches in the Bronx while I was working and picked it up. It's a really nice one. I spared no expense," he said, backing down the rain-slicked driveway. "You know where this place is?"

I gave him some sketchy directions, thinking that I remembered the funeral parlor from when Max's grandmother died, about fifteen years previous. Turns out I had no idea where it was, and after driving around a tiny hamlet for what seemed like three days, when in actuality it was only twenty minutes, Crawford pulled over and did what most men wouldn't think of doing: He asked for directions. The woman walking her dog in the pouring rain didn't look happy for the interruption, but she obliged, telling us to make one left turn at the end of the street and drive one hundred feet to the funeral parlor parking lot.

I gave myself a little head smack. "Right! Left on Hamilton."

Crawford was not amused, even though he was as

exhausted as I was. Whereas I had entered the land of the
punchy, he had landed in the land of the bad tempered,
and I realized that this was not the time for jokes, even if
they were at my own expense.

The funeral parlor was a grand Victorian affair, high on
a hill with an unobstructed view of the Hudson River. On
any other night, I would have stopped to admire the view,
but the rain was the kind that was cold and pelted against
your skin, so getting to the lobby was job one. I wasn't surprised to see that the parking lot was filled with cars or that
the lobby was teeming with people; Marty Rayfield had
been a colorful, popular figure in the town in which Max
had grown up and in which he had lived all of his adult
life, and people came out to support the family. It was my
hope that Max was now focused on the proceedings of the
next few days, too much so to still be angry at me for any
perceived slight.

We don't always get what we hope for.

After we signed our names to the guest book, we made
our way into the cramped viewing room—actually two
rooms, a small area that had probably been a parlor back
when this funeral home was an actual home. In the first
room sat assorted Rayfield family members, including
some of the rambunctious children I had met at Max's
birthday party a few weeks earlier. In the next room, separated from the first by an arched doorway, was the coffin
in which Marty was laid out, dressed in a black suit, white
shirt, and colorful tie, a small smile playing on his lips.
Whoever the undertaker was here either knew Marty well
or had a sick sense of humor; I wasn't sure how Max felt
about Marty smirking for all eternity, but to me, it was a bit
jarring. Max and her mother sat side by side in giant comfy
Queen Anne chairs, Gigi looking gorgeous and composed,
Max looking small and sad. Fred hulked in a nearby doorway, looking like he wanted to be anywhere but here. He

had once told me that he didn't understand the whole concept of a wake with a body on full display, and obviously, even though he spent a good deal of time around dead people, he didn't like to do it in his off hours.

Crawford and I waited in line to approach the casket and finally got there—several of the mourners ahead of us having paused so long it seemed like they were reciting the Declaration of Independence to Marty's dead body. We knelt side by side to pray. I looked at Marty and was flooded with memories ranging from the first time he met me and asked me to watch out for his daughter while we were at school, a task that proved to be incredibly challenging for an eighteen-year-old with not a lot of life experience herself, to my wedding day, when, without a father, I was without someone to walk me down the aisle aside from my very traditional mother, who thought that Uncle Phillippe would be a fine stand-in. He would have been if I had actually known him. Marty to the rescue. We were an odd pair, this little, elfin man and the statuesque bride beside him, holding on for dear life, but together we walked down the aisle. At the altar he whispered in my ear, right before lifting my veil from my face to give me a kiss, "You could walk away right now and no one would blame you." He knew, as did most everyone in the church, that Ray Stark wasn't the right man for me, or for anyone for that matter. He was a liar and a cheater, and a bad one at that, arousing my suspicions almost immediately after saying "I do." He was all wrong for me and I was blind to that fact, so intent on making my mother happy in the knowledge that her only daughter had married before she died. Marty had gently tried to coax me into changing my mind before the wedding, and although that one last-ditch effort in the church angered me at the time, in hindsight I found it to be incredibly courageous and knowing. He only wanted the best for me, and he knew the best wasn't a handsome, yet delusional, fellow professor with a taste for any woman who wasn't me.

Crawford and I got up, and I wiped my eyes, turning to face Max and her mother. Gigi was her usual gracious self, wrapping me in her thin arms, the scent of her perfume filling my nose and bringing with it a wave of nostalgia. She touched my face with her hand, the skin thin and papery but soft.

"He loved you like a daughter, Alison," she said, and I resisted the urge to go into a complete hysterical meltdown. He wasn't my father, when all was said and done, he was Max's, and for her, I had to hold it together.

I bent down and gave Max a kiss, but her body stiffened. "Nice of you to come," she said, the words innocuous enough but the tone portraying something else. Crawford stood behind us, his hands clasped in front of him.

"And Bobby," Gigi said, grabbing his hands, not tall enough to give him a kiss.

He gave her an awkward hug, looking like he was afraid he might break her in two. "So sorry for your loss, Mrs. Rayfield."

"Please, dear, call me Gigi."

He didn't, and I knew he wouldn't. I looked at Max and tried to discern exactly what had happened to make her so edgy with me. "The funeral is Saturday?" I asked.

She nodded, still cold. "Ten o'clock. You won't be investigating any major crimes at that time, will you?"

I decided to play it straight and not banter with her like I normally would, even under these circumstances. "No. I'm free. I'll be there."

She didn't acknowledge my response, greeting the person behind me instead and giving him her complete attention. I stood there in an uncomfortable silence for a few seconds before Crawford's hand on my back let me know it was time to move on. I looked over my shoulder at him, searching for any sign that he might know what was going on. Obviously, this wasn't the time to ask Max.

Fred was moving toward the back door of the funeral home and out to a balcony that overlooked the river. We followed him and stood, clustered together, under the big yellow-and-white-striped awning that protected the wooden structure. I didn't think it was fair to ask him at that time either, so we made small talk until Crawford decided that it was acceptable to bring him up to speed on the previous night's adventures.

Fred raised an eyebrow, his forehead wrinkling like that of a Shar Pei. "Really? She threw you in a van and took you to what? Turkey Mountain?" He shook his head. "Did I really hear all of that correctly?"

"Unfortunately, yes, you did," I said.

"I assume nobody got hurt?"

I did a mental assessment of my physical state. "A little banged up from riding around in the back of a van, but other than that, feeling fine."

"Where did they find the van?" he asked Crawford.

"Rest stop near the Bear Mountain Bridge."

Fred closed his eyes and played out some kind of scenario in his head. "She must have been meeting someone. No way to get too far from there, at night, if you don't have wheels."

Crawford followed his train of thought. "Or she had another car stashed up there."

Fred looked over the top of my head, and I turned around to see Max's face in the glass of the back door. "Gotta go," he said. "Keep me posted?"

He and Crawford embraced, something I rarely saw them do. "Will do, partner," Crawford said and then took my hand, leading me down the side steps to the parking lot.

Once we were in the car, he stated what I was thinking. "You haven't been there for her, at least not enough to satisfy her." I started to protest but knew that it was a waste of breath. No matter what I felt, she was hurt, and like Kevin had said, it was up to me and only me to make sure that the situation was rectified.

He turned on the car, but we couldn't go anywhere; the windshield was completely fogged up and opaque. "I know I've asked you this a million times, but why do you think you can get to the truth when no one else can?"

He *had* asked me a million times, but I still didn't have a good answer. "Maybe because I was deluded so long by Ray that I want to make sure I always know what's right? What's true?"

"Or maybe you're just nosy?" he asked, smiling.

"Maybe."

"Or maybe you read too many Nancy Drew novels and think that the amateurs are smarter than the detectives?"

"Maybe."

A small clear patch began to form on the windshield, starting at the bottom and slowly rising to the top. As it did, Crawford continued to put forth theories, some sort of on the money, others ridiculous. "Maybe you're bored with teaching?"

"Most definitely."

"Maybe you thought that when you married me life would be one constant episode of *McMillan & Wife*?" he asked, referencing a show from our youth in which Rock Hudson and Susan Saint James were married and solved crimes together.

"More like *Hart to Hart*," I said. "You're definitely more Robert Wagner than Rock Hudson."

"Good point," he said. The windshield was almost clear. "Leave it alone, Alison. Please. For everyone's sake."

I was tired, hungry, and very, very sad. I felt tears welling up but wouldn't let them spring forth. "I will." If spending time investigating things even tangentially related to me impacted my relationships this much, it would be wise to leave things alone. It was time to subvert my longing for excitement and answers and all things related to amateur sleuthing and go back to the life that I had, the one that was sort of boring but suited me—and him—to a tee. The life in which strippers took off your wallpaper and murders only took place during prime time on your favorite TV shows.

We were just about to put the car into DRIVE when his phone trilled. I waited while he listened, using few words to respond to the caller on the other end.

"When?" he asked. "Where?" He snapped his phone shut and put it back in his pocket. "Forget everything I just said. Change of plans."

"What happened?"

"Sassy Du Pris was found at the bottom of a ravine by the Bear Mountain Bridge."

I waited, knowing what was coming next.

"She's dead."

THIRTY-NINE

SEE, THIS IS why I don't hike: You never know what you're going to find on some densely wooded, deserted path. One day it might be an antique Indian arrowhead and the next a dead stripper. You just never know.

My plan to stay indoors and not venture out unless absolutely necessary was starting to look better and better.

The call had come from MacGyver, who figured we would want to know about Sassy's untimely passing given the events of the night before. We were not far from the scene of the crime, as they say, so instead of going to get a slice of pizza before returning home, something we had planned originally, we headed north about twenty minutes and pulled into the very same rest stop where Sassy Du Pris had left the van, disappearing into the night without a trace. It was hard to know, given her straight trajectory down from the rock wall at the edge of the rest stop, whether she had jumped, fallen, or been pushed, but what was certain was that she had fallen a great distance, hitting rocks and tree branches on the way down, and had died almost instantly from her injuries.

You know you have been nosing around too much when you have a personal relationship with the medical examiner for the county. Mac McVeigh stood by the rock wall, looking over the edge, waiting for the crew that was transporting Sassy's body back up the hill so that he could do what he needed to do to get her logged in and on her way to the ME's office down county. He didn't look terribly busy, standing and waiting, so I called out to him.

"Alison?" he said. "Now, what in God's name is your connection to the deceased? Or were you and the husband out for a moonlit stroll?"

"Mac, you know me better than that. I don't stroll in the moonlight if I can help it." I peered over the side of the wall, where I spied a bunch of rescue workers struggling mightily with the stretcher that would carry Sassy up to the rest stop. If it weren't such a macabre scene, I could have enjoyed the beauty of the night. The rain had stopped, and in its place was a hazy fog that danced along the teeny whitecaps of the Hudson.

Mac read my thoughts. "Gorgeous night. Just wish there wasn't a dead body to keep us company in it."

Crawford was talking with a couple of the responding county cops, listening intently. He walked over to me and filled me in on what I already knew, which was about the same as what the cops knew. "Hiya, Mac," he said, shaking the ME's gloved hand. "What are we thinking?"

"Hard to tell," Mac said. "I'll know more, obviously, when we get her to the morgue. Poor thing. It's wet and cold. I hope she hasn't been down there too long."

Crawford filled him in on the timeline from the night before. Mac looked at me, his pale blue eyes wide. "Kidnapped? Alison, how do you get yourself into these situations?"

I smiled sadly. "That's the question Crawford and I have been asking ourselves repeatedly over the past few hours. I'm afraid we don't have an answer."

Mac put a protective arm around me. "Someone needs to be your personal bodyguard."

"Are you volunteering for the job?" I asked.

He laughed. "With bodies stacked up for me like pancakes at IHOP? Hardly."

After much struggle, the rescue workers were able to get Sassy's body up the hill and onto the pavement. Crawford asked me to wait in the car.

"Why?" I asked, but as I saw Mac start to unzip the body bag, the temporary klieg lights illuminating everything as if we were in an operating room and not on the top of a mountain at night, I had my answer. I dutifully walked back to the car and got in, facing away from the action, staring at the beautiful Bear Mountain Bridge in the distance, twinkling merrily on a night where death had taken center stage.

FORTY

ANOTHER DAY, ANOTHER round of research on Sans-a-Flush.

I know I had promised Crawford I wouldn't do any more sleuthing but after seeing Sassy Du Pris's dead body being hoisted up a hill, I just couldn't resist taking one last peek into the world of porta-potties that my search engine could provide. Driving to work, I had heard an advertisement on my local sports radio station (a leftover preset from when Crawford had last used the car) about a company that will go through everything related to your identity or place of business and push down negative links that might impact your sales or revenue or anyone's general impression of you as a person or company. I scrolled through a few pages and hundreds of links before I hit the jackpot.

Right there, in black and white, was news of Sans-a-Flush's bankruptcy filing, a standard Chapter 11, back in 2003, less than two years after Chick's departure. Seems like the company had gone down the tubes and fast after Chick had hightailed it out of New York for parts unknown. I wondered if the two events were related and if even a Chapter 11 filing meant anything beyond just bad money management by the extended Du Pris family, the ones who actually ran the business. Since I didn't know anything about filing for bankruptcy, thankfully, I shot an e-mail to the director of the Business Department, Glen McConnon, who knew a little about a lot of things, making him the perfect go-to guy for this kind of question. I didn't need to know the particulars of a bankruptcy filing, or at least I didn't think I did, and I figured he'd be the best person to start with anyway, bankruptcy lawyers being in short supply here at St. Thomas.

I hit send and sat back, hoping that his response would come sooner rather than later, I also hoped that a scurrilous rumor about my finances—specifically a Chapter 11 filing—didn't circulate around campus. Why else, in Glen's mind anyway, would one need to know about bankruptcy? Too late. The message sent, I figured I would deal with that later.

I also sent Tim a message, thinking that as a hedge fund manager, and one with more than a passing acquaintance with the Stepkowskis and Du Pris families, he might have some information. Moments after I hit send I got an undeliverable-message notice in my in-box. I checked Tim's e-mail address against the card he had given me when we first met and saw that I hadn't mistyped it. I sent the message again. It came back undeliverable once again.

I pulled his card closer and studied the phone number, then punched it into my phone. A receptionist answered, using someone else's name. "Tim Morin, please?" I asked.

"Mr. Morin no longer works here," she said. "Can I direct you to one of our other fund managers?"

"When did Mr. Morin leave?" I asked.

"Two weeks ago," she said. "Can I direct your call elsewhere?"

"No, thank you," I said, staring at the phone. Not one word had been uttered about Tim no longer being at Westcore, and that certainly cast a certain light on the phone call that I had overheard at his house. Did Christine even know?

I put that aside for the time being, this new information being too much to sort through after the night I had had. I tried not to focus on how sleep deprived I was or the fact that Max was still in a snit over my not being as attentive to her as I usually am, an accusation that cut to my very core. Was there a kernel of truth in there? Is that why it hurt so much?

There were the unreturned calls and my not visiting her father before he died, and yes, I had been late to her birthday party—but was this the point we were at now? Every transgression documented, every minute late to an event charged against some mental friend calculator?

We would have to get through the funeral and the days following, and then we'd hash it out. This was my last mystery, I would tell her, and even if I tripped over another dead body—unlikely, given my profession—I would stay far away from any situation that held a lingering question, a mysterious subplot, or the hint of suspicion. I was hanging up my sleuthing shoes and calling it a day.

That would make her happy. Maybe.

According to the local news, Mac had turned in a swift pronouncement on Sassy: suicide. There had been a note and no evidence of foul play. She had jumped to her death from the rest stop and, according to a little tidbit Mac had read in her suicide note and shared with me via e-mail, done so in order to spend eternity with Chick, the only man she had ever loved.

So what we had was a case of unrequited love, two people hell-bent on getting some money and hightailing it out of Dodge. Seemed to me there were some missing details, but as I was done with my investigation for the time being—or forever—I would never be able to fill in the blanks.

Tonight was the night I was going to get out of here on time, pick up some dinner, and take a load off in front of the television. One night of no sleep was bad enough, but two? Things were going to get mighty dicey if I didn't log in a good eight hours before the funeral the next day. I steeled myself for a day of teaching, preparing to leave my office for my first class. The phone rang before I had a chance to get out the door, and I picked it up, thinking it was Glen with an answer to my question about bankruptcy.

Christine. Oh, jeez. "Alison, Bobby just called me and told me about Sassy. Is it true?" She sounded more than a little relieved.

"It's true," I said. "Saw her body with my own eyes." Sort of. Saw her body bag with my own eyes, but her body was definitely in there.

"God, I'm so relieved," she said, and I waited for the questions about my well-being after having been kidnapped by her. They never came. Either Bobby hadn't told her or she didn't really care now that Sassy, her archenemy and burner-down of houses, was dead.

"She seemed to really love your brother," I said.

Her gasp led me to believe that Crawford, your typical "just the facts, ma'am" kind of cop, hadn't told her about the kidnapping. "You met her?"

I filled her in. Suffice it to say, she was horrified.

"But you're okay?" she asked.

"I'm fine," I said. "Exhausted, but fine."

"Oh, Alison, I can't apologize enough for getting you involved in this whole thing. You must really think that my family is a bunch of cavemen."

They weren't as evolved as cavemen, but I kept that observation to myself.

"I'm so, so sorry, Alison. Really I am."

She sounded so distraught that I couldn't do anything but assure her that it was fine. "It's over now, Christine. There has been a lot of collateral damage in the wake of Chick's…passing," I said, knowing that she still believed he had been murdered and not taken his own life, "but let's just all move on. How does that sound?"

"That sounds great," she said. "Maybe during the Christmas break, you and Bobby would come up for dinner?" she asked, her tone hopeful.

I responded instantly, knowing that any hesitation whatsoever would hurt her feelings. "Of course!" I said, far more enthusiastically than I actually felt. I figured when the time came, I could find an excuse. Hanging out with Christine and Tim—except when absolutely required and necessary, say, when the girls were involved—was very low on my list.

"Tim got a panini press for himself and all he wants to do is make sandwiches," she said, laughing. "I can't believe it took him this long to buy one, but there you have it."

At the mention of Tim, the sandwich king, and his new panini press, I thought back to the conversation I overheard at their house about his wanting the money. All I could muster was a weak chuckle about Tim's latest purchase. Did he want the money to finally pursue his dream of making sandwiches all day long for the well-heeled Greenwich crowd? Or did he just want a nice little nest egg, more robust than the one he presumably already had, for the little trolls in the event he checked out early? Or, now that he was out of work, did he need the money just to survive? Who knew? I tried to wrap up the conversation, having a few classes awaiting me interspersed with lunch, a coffee break at some point, and then office hours. After that, sleep. Lots of sleep. Then all of this would make sense, or so I hoped.

"Is Tim there, Christine?" I asked. "I want to ask him a quick question about my money market account."

She laughed. "Here? Alison, he won't be here until after ten. He's working on a big deal at the office and has been out every night for the past two weeks. I'm really hoping it closes soon so we can get back to normal."

I immediately felt sorry for her. He wasn't at work, and God knew where he was; I had a feeling he wasn't scoping out locations for the sandwich shop. I hung up and immediately did another search on Westcore, finding out that it was still a robust and functioning hedge fund, and one for which money seemed to keep rolling in, if the gorgeous Colonial with its chef's kitchen was any indication.

So, where did Tim go every day?

I decided I would deal with that later, opting instead to send Max a text message telling her that I was thinking of her; I knew she wouldn't respond, with another day of the wake ahead of her, but it made me feel better. Over the course of our two-decade-plus relationship we had had our ups and downs, I reminded myself. I got mad at her. She got mad at me. It always blew over. Until now. This time felt different, as if her hurt were really emanating from her core and generated by something much more portentous than just our usual topics of squabbling. The death of her father and my inability to be there for her when she was going through everything that went along with such a tragic event was on a par with all of the things I had already gone through: the death of both of my parents, my first husband's infidelity and then our contentious divorce, his murder. She had been with me through all of those life events and then some.

I, however, had dropped the ball in the biggest way imaginable and couldn't have felt worse if I had donned the proverbial hair shirt.

I put my head in my hands and fought back the urge to cry. "Pull yourself together," I whispered. "You'll work this out, too."

I wasn't so sure, though, and that was the most painful thing of all.

The funeral was the next day, and I had to think that once it was over and the process of living her life began again in earnest, I'd at least be able to talk to Max, if not get us back to the way we were.

I went through the motions of teaching my classes, ate lunch by myself at a corner table in the cafeteria, and held office hours, just as I had planned. By the end of the day

I was beyond exhausted, the last several minutes of my office hours dragging on, a time on a Friday afternoon when no one was likely to appear. I could barely keep my eyes open, but I knew it wouldn't look good if a student happened by only to find me slumped over my desk, drool running from my mouth onto a stack of uncorrected papers. I rallied and, as soon as the clock hit five minutes to five, started to pull my things together so I could get home. I had no idea if Crawford was coming home early, late, or on time, his schedule being completely unpredictable, so I didn't get my hopes up. I'd see him when I'd see him, just like always, and maybe if he was late, I could squeeze in a nap that wouldn't interrupt my regular sleep but would allow me to have an actual conversation with him that wasn't punctuated by loud yawns.

The knock at my office door nearly made me burst into tears, the identity of the knocker most likely someone who wanted to spend some time setting up the outline for a paper that was due the following week. I don't know when I had gotten so conscientious, but there you have it. Whereas in the old days, I might have been known to fall silent, pretending that I wasn't behind the frosted glass of the decades-old mahogany door, these days, I was the model professor, always available, always willing to help. It crossed my mind that I could fold myself in half and hide under my desk until whoever it was went away, but guilt got the better of me. My best friend was already suspicious of my moral fiber; if word got around school that Professor Bergeron hid under her desk so that she didn't have to deal with students, my shaky reputation would take another hit, crumbling once and for all. I shoved the rest of the papers in my bag and called out to the person on the other side of the door to come in, hoping that usual social cues like me donning my coat and jangling my keys would hasten his or her departure.

It was Mary Lou Bannerman. With a large cup of something hot, if the steam coming out of the little hole on the plastic lid was any indication. I smiled. In spite of my exhaustion, seeing her was just the lift I needed. She brandished a manila envelope as well as a wide grin.

"What's that?" I asked, referring to the cup.

"It's the beginning of my manuscript!" she said, obviously excited and proud.

It wouldn't be in good taste to ask after the cup again, so I expressed my delight over her pages instead. "Will you read it?" she asked.

"Now?" I asked, my enthusiasm waning.

"No, silly," she said, putting it on my desk. "Whenever you get a chance. I had a burst of creativity last night and just started writing." She pointed at me. "You were right. When you're ready to write, you're ready to write. It just flowed out of me."

Finally, someone appreciated my wisdom. I stared pointedly at the cup she was holding, protected by a wide cardboard ring that would keep the hot in and off her hand.

"Oh, and this is for you," she said, handing it to me. "Chai tea. From the cafeteria, not some fancy coffee shop, I'm afraid."

I looked at my watch. After all my years teaching here, I had no idea that the cafeteria was open at five on a Friday. "Really? They're open?"

She looked momentarily flustered. "I have an in there," she said. "I've made quite a few friends among the staff, and once they heard it was for you," she said, throwing her arms wide, "well, the world was my oyster, so to speak."

Nice to know I had friends in high places, or at least ones where you could get a burger after closing time. I opened the cup and inhaled deeply. "Thank you, Mary Lou. I was starting to fade."

"Do you have five minutes?" she asked, sitting down in her usual spot across from my desk.

How could I say no? I sat back down behind my desk and sipped the tea. Chai wasn't my favorite, but it definitely hit the spot at the end of a long day, not to mention week. I fingered the envelope on my desk. "I'll read this first chance I get, Mary Lou. Was it difficult writing about the topic?" I asked, referencing her husband's murder.

"I'm not there yet," she said. "I'm talking about how we met."

"How *did* you meet?"

"At work," she said, a slight flush coming to her cheeks. "He had his own company, and I was an assistant to the director of marketing."

I took another sip of my tea.

"I know I'm married again and very happy, but can I confess something?" she asked, her blue eyes shining. Tears? Or a glimmer of what was past? "He was my soul mate. I will never love anyone the same way again."

I stared at her, not sure why she was sharing these feelings with me. Had I blurred the line between student and professor so much that I was now in the business of listening to confessions of the lovelorn? Probably. I could do nothing now but sit and listen, my head feeling heavy, the lack of sleep catching up with me and making me inert. I took a bigger sip of tea, which seemed to perk me up in the short term but wasn't doing a lot to counter my feelings of exhaustion overall.

She dropped the manila envelope on my desk. "The synopsis and some pages. I would love your opinion. It's all in there."

I stood, not really wanting to have this conversation in the confines of my office. Outside, darkness was settling over the campus, and the last student stragglers, the ones who hadn't immediately left the building after their last class ended, were scurrying back to their dorms to prepare for whatever that particular Friday held in store. I put the remaining papers in my messenger bag and asked Mary Lou if she'd like to continue our conversation on the way to my car; all of a sudden, a heat was creeping up my neck, and I felt like I needed to get out of my office and into the chilly night air.

She followed me out of the office area and into the stairwell. As soon as I hit the outside and the cold air, I got lightheaded and grabbed on to the new banister that now ran along the back steps. Mary Lou chattered away, oblivious to the fact that I was dead on my feet. I took another sip of tea, now a comfortable temperature. With each passing step, I felt slower and slower, my legs feeling leaden as I navigated the stone stairs. We reached the top and headed toward the parking lot.

"Do you feel that way about your husband?" she asked. The way she said it indicated to me, even in what was becoming a weakened state, that she had already asked me at least once before but I hadn't answered.

I stared back at her, not sure how to respond. Of course I felt that way about Crawford, but did I really need to get that personal with her? Suddenly I realized that even if I wanted to answer, I couldn't. My tongue was thick and unmoving in my mouth, and I attempted to lick my lips.

"Are you sick?" she asked, a look of such great concern on her face that it made me nervous.

I opened my mouth to speak, but nothing came out. I felt my knees give out and I hit the macadam, pitching forward and breaking my fall with my hands. The combination of the cold ground and the rough surface was doubly bruising, and I felt the pain course through my hands and up my arms, an insult to the nerve center in my brain. The papers that I had been packing to take home escaped from my bag and skittered off the side of the parking lot, my eyes following them, not really understanding what I was seeing.

"Professor Bergeron?" she asked, her tone frantic.

A student hurrying by stopped when he saw me falter and go to the ground. It was Meaghan's boyfriend, and even though I was having a hard time telling which end was up from my perch, I could see in his eyes that he was thinking about continuing to move rather than help me, but something got the better of him. His conscience, maybe? I didn't know, but he scurried over and helped me up.

"Are you okay?" he asked.

"Thank you, Alex," I said, finally nailing his name, even in my altered state. He was a big guy, so getting me off the ground wasn't too much of a chore, even with his heavy backpack over one of his shoulders.

He looked worriedly at Mary Lou. "She doesn't look good. Is she alright?"

Mary Lou looked behind her. "I'll take care of it. Thank you for coming to our assistance," she said.

"Are you sure?" he asked. "Should I call her stepdaughter?"

"Her stepdaughter?" Mary Lou asked, as if Meaghan's existence weren't something she had considered. Now she looked worried.

"Yes, her stepdaughter. She's my girlfriend," he said, giving me a glance that told me that he knew I wasn't pleased with the relationship.

"No," she said. "Thanks again. I'll take it from here."

I really wasn't able to form a coherent sentence, so I stood idly by, my hands scraped and bloodied, while this exchange played out between Mary Lou and Alex. After a few more questions from him and reassurances from her, he wandered off uneasily.

Behind me, I heard the sound of a car coming up the one-lane road that wrapped around campus and served as the exit on this side. It came to rest on the far side of the road, just below the cemetery and what I hoped was the ever-watchful spirit of my old friend, the late Sister Alphonse. Still unsteady on my feet, I attempted to grab the papers that were on the ground, but the action proved too hard. I looked at Mary Lou and, with every ounce of energy that I had left, attempted to tell her something.

"I don't feel well," I managed to get out after only getting one errant piece of paper back into my bag, my limbs heavy and shaky, my mind muddled.

The car was still idling by the curb, and I saw Mary Lou give it a nervous sideways glance.

"Who is that?" I asked, hearing an edge of hysteria in my voice. Between the way I felt physically and the way she had suddenly stopped talking, choosing instead to cast her gaze about shiftily, I had a feeling that things were about to change for the worse.

The driver's door of the car opened, but it was too dark for me to see anything except that the figure who got out was large and male.

Mary Lou put a hand on her hips and looked displeased. As the figure got closer, she got more agitated. Finally, when he had made his way to us, she looked at him and in a voice dripping with disappointment and despair asked him one question that left me even more baffled.

"Briggs, what did you do?"

FORTY-ONE

HE WAS STILL in his work clothes, a chef's jacket and black-and-white-checkered pants, black professional cooking clogs on his feet. This, more than anything, more than the fact that we were leaving campus for parts unknown, more than the fact that he had thrown me in the back of the car as if I weighed no more than a large sack of potatoes, and more than the fact that he kept calling Mary Lou "Mom," confused me. I looked at the scenery whizzing by, unable to tell what road we were on or where we were going. I remember seeing the river to the right of me at one point, leading me to believe that we were headed into the city, or maybe toward New Jersey.

Crawford was right: I sure did get kidnapped a lot. What was it now, five? Six? Eight? Who could remember?

My brain was fried, and I couldn't tell if the words I were thinking were actually coming out of my mouth. The last thing I thought—"and I wanted to fix you up with my stepdaughter!"—must have left my lips because Briggs looked in the rearview mirror and gave me a little smile, responding with "I *am* a catch." Sure he was, if I wanted Meaghan with a guy who looked like Ryan Gosling but acted like Ted Bundy.

I wasn't sure how long we drove, the sound of Mary Lou's impassioned pleas to him to not hurt me filtering into my head as we wended our way north, as it turns out. Although I thought the river was on my right, it was actually some other body of water, smaller but wider. I groaned when I saw that we were back at a place I hoped never to see again, the inexplicably named Turkey Mountain, the place where Sassy had taken Kevin and me. How I had ended up back here, who Briggs actually was, and why this was all happening were thoughts that were swirling around my addled brain.

He stopped the car just a few spaces away from where Sassy had stopped the car when we were here together. He turned and looked at me, and I saw that although he was handsome, he had mean eyes, the kind his smile never reached; the kind that looked like there was nothing behind them. "Ready to take a walk?" he asked.

I really wasn't. I was ready to curl up on the backseat of the car and take a nice long nap. Despite Mary Lou's protestations, though, he was insistent on getting me out of the car and into the wild, going so far as to grab my arm and drag me out onto the pavement, where gravel embedded itself into any exposed body parts. I was thankful that I had put on tights that morning but not that I had worn high heels.

Another day, another kidnapping, and another pair of inappropriate shoes. I stumbled along the gravel path that led to an entrance to the preserve and went to my knees as I failed to navigate the dip in the earth. Briggs pulled me up by the back of my coat and threw me forward. It took all my will and coordination not to fall again.

I couldn't run and I couldn't hide, as they say. I knew, because it was jutting out from the pocket of his chef's coat and into my back, that Briggs had a gun, and he seemed just itching to shoot it. Anyway, where exactly would I go? Behind that big tree over there? Or the one right next to it? Too many choices and not enough brain cells.

I would have liked to see the look on Mary Lou's face, just to get a sense of what she might be thinking, but taking my eyes off of my own feet for too long would result in another fall. If my screaming joints were any indication, another fall would push me into a whole different level of pain, one that I couldn't withstand without crying, something that I wouldn't do in front of this strange man.

We got to a little bridge and I decided that I had had enough. I turned to Mary Lou. I summoned up whatever brainpower I had left. "So are you in on this?" I asked. "Did you buy that tea in the cafeteria so that he could drug me and the two of you could get me up here to what? Kill me? Bury my body so that no one would find me until the spring thaw?"

She surprised me by starting to cry. Good Lord. I was the one in high heels being frog-marched through a nature preserve, probably to my death, and here she was bursting into tears. Great. "I'm so sorry, Professor Bergeron."

Briggs gave me a little push. "Back off, Briggs," I said. "If you're going to kill me, I'd like to get some information first." I was surprisingly calm and collected and actually a bit more clear-headed than I had been in the car. I wondered what he put in my tea and if, in smaller doses, it would just take the edge off a bit.

"If you had just told my aunt where the money was," he said, exasperated, "we would have left you alone. Now, I have to do this," he said, throwing his arms wide in reference to the great outdoors.

His aunt. Even with some kind of drug in my system, it was all starting to come together. Sassy. "Yes, it's very inconvenient that you have to drive me to the middle of nowhere—"

"It's actually Yorktown," Mary Lou added helpfully.

"Okay…Yorktown…to kill me, but why? The public administrator has the money and will probably have it until the people in the Stepkowski family tire of asking about it or hire a lawyer to get it back. My money's on the lawyer part because I think every single one of them is champing at the bit to get it."

Briggs shrugged. "You were as good as anyone. You found his body. You're married to his sister's ex. You live in that shitty little house, so you'd probably want a piece of the pie even to get rid of that crappy siding. Seriously," he said, "you need to step it up with the landscaping. Although it did provide good cover."

How did I end up on a home improvement show all of a sudden? "If you're going to kill me, please don't insult me first," I said. "That's what's called adding insult to injury." Suddenly, or at least suddenly given the current condition of my brain, I realized what that comment about the landscaping meant. "You poisoned my dog," I said, gasping.

"I didn't poison it," he said.

"Her."

"Fine. Her. I just made her sleep for a while."

"You nearly killed her," I said. I thought about how I could get my hands around his ample neck and squeeze the life out of him. "Did you make Chick take all of those drugs, too?" I asked, making a logical leap, at least in my own head.

His confusion was masked a bit by his anger over my stalling. "That guy offed himself. Plain and simple."

"Why would he do that?" I asked, because I still didn't know.

"Guilty conscience?" he suggested. "Okay, enough. I hated that guy and I don't want to talk about him anymore. Where's the money?"

"For the last time," I said, trying to sound as convincing as possible, "I do not know."

He pulled the gun from his pocket. "I still don't believe you."

I looked at Mary Lou. "You're not writing a novel, are you?"

She continued crying loudly. "Well, now that I've taken your class, I would really like to!"

Finally, a good evaluation. Too bad I'd be dead before I'd see it. I tried to take an analytical approach. "Listen, Briggs. I don't have the money. I won't get the money. If I had to take a guess, I'd say Christine will eventually get the money and, knowing her, will probably split it between her brothers and the girls." And the trolls, maybe. "I will never see a dime of that cash, nor do I want to."

"I still don't believe you," he said, taking the safety off the gun. "I think you know more than you're letting on."

"Why would that be?" I asked.

"Because Meaghan told me about the money he gave her. For her birthday," he said. "I think there's more where that came from."

"Meaghan told you about the money she got for her birthday?" I asked. When this was over, I was putting her in timeout.

"She was going to buy new skis. And an iPad." He laughed. "What that kid won't tell you for a free chocolate chip cookie."

So that's what it took to get her to talk. I'd have to tell Crawford.

I backed up a little and got my heel stuck in the space between the two wooden slats on the bridge. I wiggled my heel back and forth to get it loose, but it was stuck in there good. "If you don't believe me, then you're not very smart," I said, bending down to pull my shoe out of the slat. It was released with a resounding *thwack*, and as I held the shoe in my hand, I realized that what I had was a weapon. A beautiful, suede-covered weapon, but a weapon nonetheless. I handled the shoe, feeling the heft of it—my feet are big—and looking at the heel, a slender piece of wood covered with fabric that came to a tiny point at the end. I lifted my foot as if I were going put my shoe back on but grabbed Mary Lou around the throat, holding the point of the shoe against her carotid artery, now doing the salsa against my palm. Doing so required focus that I didn't have and strength that seemed to have left me but that I was able to summon in one last-ditch effort to save myself. When all was said and done, I was going to need a very long nap.

"So I have an idea who you are, but I'm not entirely sure," I said to Briggs, wondering if he had given me some kind of truth serum. Suddenly, I just wanted to tell the truth. "I don't know who this woman is exactly either," I said, digging the heel into Mary Lou's throat, "or what connection you have to her or to me or the Stepkowskis, but if you don't throw that gun as far as you can, and you look pretty strong, so I'm guessing you can throw it pretty far, I will plunge the heel of this shoe into her throat." This last part was almost a growl, and mostly true. "I don't have the money. For the last time."

A voice, female and small, came from inside the preserve. "But I do."

FORTY-TWO

"HELLO, SISSY." A small figure, but one that I recognized, came out of the woods, a miner's hat strapped to her head, the light blinding me momentarily. "Alison, you can put the shoe down," Christine said, standing at the other end of the slat bridge. "They're not going to hurt you." Next to her were three giant duffel bags, one stacked on top of the other, almost as tall as she was. "I hope big bills are acceptable," she said. "It was easier to carry that way."

I took my arm from around Mary Lou's neck but kept the shoe handy. I knew it wasn't any protection against a gun, but seeing Christine had made me let down my guard. I hoped it wasn't to my own detriment. Mary Lou staggered off, coughing and choking, still crying; the hold I had around her throat had been pretty tight, judging from the way she was rubbing at her neck.

Briggs asked Christine if she had come alone.

"Just like you asked," she said. She pointed toward the parking lot. "Do you see any other cars there?"

I hadn't even seen hers, so I wouldn't know if there were more than just the car we had arrived in.

"No, really, Alison," Christine said. "You can put your shoe back on."

"What the hell is going on?" I asked, donning my beautiful pump, the one that I was thankful I hadn't had to plunge into Mary Lou's neck. I would have ruined a perfectly good shoe and ended my day on a particularly sour note, and neither of those things appealed to me.

"Why did you bring her?" Christine asked. "I thought we had a deal."

"Insurance policy," Briggs said. "Just in case you had changed your mind."

Christine took a closer step, leaving the bags behind her. They looked like they weighed more than she did, and I wondered how she got them this deep into the woods. Even though we could still see the parking lot, it was a pretty long way to drag what looked like really heavy duffels. "Do you want to tell them or should I?" In her sneakers, puffy down coat, and miner's hat, she looked like a kid playing war in the woods rather than the mother of two and stepmother of four.

I looked at Mary Lou and then Briggs, who had returned the gun to his pocket. "Please. Someone. Anyone," I said. "The suspense is killing me."

No one spoke for a minute, and then Christine explained. "Alison, this is Sissy, Sassy's sister."

"Say that three times fast," I said.

"Briggs is my son," Sissy/Mary Lou said.

"Of course he is," I said. It didn't really matter. "Can I go?" I asked, knowing that I could return to Brianna Mac-Gyver's house, break up another party, and use the phone. "I honestly don't care who anyone is or what they have to do with this. I'm just really, really tired." Suddenly, exhaustion took complete hold of me and I sat down on the bridge. "What did you put in my tea, anyway?" I asked. "I'm exhausted but in a good way."

"Ativan," Briggs said. "It's an anti-anxiety drug."

"Ah, that explains it," I said, curling up in a ball on the slats. "I should be more anxious given that you were going to kill me, but I couldn't care less." I got comfortable on the bridge. They could continue their conversation as long as they wanted; I was taking a nap.

"You'll have to come and get the money," Christine said,

knowing now that I didn't care what the story was or what anyone had to do with anything. "I can't lug these bags again. They're too heavy."

"It's all of it?" Briggs asked. "The whole two hundred and fifty thousand?"

"All here," she said.

"Where did you get it?" he asked. "I thought it was with the government or something."

"I married well," Christine said, and I could hear the smile in her voice.

"You married a guy who could come up with that kind of money quickly?" Briggs asked.

"I did," Christine said. "Fortunately, he's a really nice guy, too." I could hear her moving on the bridge, her feet coming to rest beside my face. "He gave me the money to give you so that you would leave us alone," she said.

I wasn't so sure about that. Old Tim didn't have a job anymore.

"Once the public administrator released it, we would have our money back," she said.

Made a certain amount of sense, but Briggs wasn't buying it.

"Chick stole that money. From my father. There's no way the public administrator will ever give it back," he said.

Christine had an answer for that, too. "Whatever happens, we're even. And I can rest easy, knowing that the money that you think my brother stole is now back with you. Where it belongs." She took another step forward. "Go get the money. I kept up my end of the bargain, and now you have what you want."

Mary Lou was still weeping somewhere in the vicinity.

"Why shouldn't I just kill you?" he asked.

"Because you got what you want. Killing me might make you feel good for a little while, but when all is said and done, it won't bring your father back. Or your aunt."

Mary Lou let out a tortured sob. I thought back to our earlier conversation where she professed her love for her late husband. It had never occurred to me that she might be related to Sassy, but I would ask Christine about that later.

I kept my eyes closed, drifting in and out of an Ativan haze. If this went on much longer, I would get a full night's sleep. Finally.

"Let us go," Christine said quietly, leading me to believe that we were at some kind of standoff. I didn't care; any energy I had had been used up grabbing Mary Lou and holding the stiletto to her neck. Now, I just wanted to go to sleep, letting the darkness envelop me in a sweet peace. "Take it. Go. I will never say another word."

"How do I know that?" Briggs asked.

"Because it would tarnish everyone's memory of my brother," she said, "and I could never do that, even now that I know what he did."

I wanted to raise my head and ask, "What did he do?" but I was too tired.

Footsteps marched past my head, dangerously close, and the bridge swayed gently with the moving feet. I heard the sound of a zipper being opened and the rustling of paper. "It better all be here," Briggs said.

"It's all there," Christine said, using her inside, calm-mommy voice. "All of it. Now go. Not another word. Live your life. It's all in the past now."

"Mom, you take one bag," Briggs said. "I'll come back for the last one." He went by me again, this time dragging one of the duffels. Mary Lou followed behind, her weeping still audible, dragging another one of the bags.

When they reached the end of the bridge, their feet now making squishing sounds in the marshy muck of the preserve, the area was bathed in a harsh light and a voice, which in my befuddled state sounded suspiciously like Crawford's but wasn't, blared through some kind of PA system, the origins of which were a mystery to me. "Stop. Drop the bags. Police."

I sat up and rubbed my eyes, shielding them against the glare. "Nap over," I said to a bewildered Christine. I couldn't see what was going on, blinded by the light, but I could hear scuffling as the police swarmed the area, taking down Briggs and Mary Lou. "Who are these people and what's their fascination with nature preserves?"

Christine helped me get to my feet and I rocked back on my heels, a little unsteady still, but managing to keep myself upright. "I'll explain everything in the car," she said. We walked off the bridge, finding Briggs and Mary Lou facedown in the muck, their hands cuffed behind their backs. Mary Lou was still wailing.

"We just wanted what was ours," she cried.

Christine stopped and turned. I had never seen her so angry, her face so filled with rage. It came on in an instant, and she lashed into Mary Lou. "You could have gotten everything you wanted if you had just waited. I told you. I told your sister. I told your son. But you had to take matters into your own hands and drag Alison along for the ride. That wasn't part of our deal. And now you're really in a heap of trouble." The police in the area stopped what they were doing and looked at her. "You lost your sister and I lost my brother in all of this mess. Isn't that enough?"

Two police officers—a duo in a sea of blue—pulled Briggs and Mary Lou to their feet, dragging them with no regard for their personal comfort to the waiting police cars. Christine and I followed after assuring one of the officers—a young woman who looked like she was fulfilling her life's dream by being in the middle of this dragnet—that we were fine and didn't require medical attention. Though who knew? I was still as high as a kite. I suspected my injuries, the ones I had sustained from falling in the woods, would make their presence known once I was first, sober and second, fully awake.

Crawford was pulling into the parking lot as we emerged from the woods, pulling his Passat into an empty space on two wheels. He was breathless, red in the face, and completely flummoxed when he got out of the car, stuttering all sorts of accusations and recriminations to one of us, I wasn't sure which.

"I…I…" he started. "Her… You," he said, pointing at Christine, "I expect more than…I expect more from you."

Where did that leave me?

"I know," she said. "I should have let you know, but I never thought Alison would be involved. They told me they wanted the money, so I contacted the police in Greenwich and they put me in touch with the FBI. They set the whole thing up." She crossed her arms across her chest. "Then Briggs called me and told me he had an insurance policy. That's when I knew this wouldn't go according to plan."

"You're not getting the money, are you?" I asked, suddenly feeling so sad that tears were forming in my half-shut eyes. It was the Ativan talking. "So Tim can't open his sandwich shop?"

Christine turned toward me. "What?"

"The sandwich shop. Tim's Fancy Sandwich Shoppe," I said, giving a little wave as a flourish to emphasize just how fancy it would be. "That's the name I came up with, anyway."

Crawford looked at Christine and she mouthed "Ativan."

"He doesn't work at Westcore anymore," I blurted out, much to everyone's surprise.

Christine's mouth fell open. "What?" she repeated.

Crawford looked at me. "Yes. What?"

"I don't think I should say anything else." I closed my mouth. "Ask Tim," I said to Christine after a brief pause.

Crawford turned his attention back to the matter at hand.

He looked back at his ex. "I expect these sorts of things from her, but you?"

"Hey, what's that supposed to mean?" I asked, my senses not dulled enough to notice that he seemed to think I was a bad influence.

He wrapped his arms around me. "Forget it. Tell me later. I am pretty sick of Turkey Mountain and driving all the way up here every few nights."

"It's actually the town of Yorktown," I said.

"Whatever." He looked at Christine again. "You sure you're okay? Do you want someone to take you home?"

She pointed toward the car that held Mary Lou and Briggs. "Now that they're gone, I'm fine. I'm sure someone here will want to talk to me about this whole thing, and once that's over, I think I'll go home and collapse."

I leaned into Crawford, suddenly too tired to stand. "Was there really two hundred and fifty thousand dollars in those bags?" I asked.

She shook her head. "Nope. Xeroxes of money. No actual money."

"So Tim didn't pony up the cash?" I asked.

"There are very few people who could get that kind of money in a short amount of time, Alison," she said, the implication being that I didn't know a lot about money. She was right; I didn't. That was just fine with me.

Something occurred to me. "Hey, how did you know we were here?" I asked.

"Believe it or not," Crawford said, "I got a call from Alex Most."

"I have no idea who that is."

"Alex Most? Meaghan's boyfriend?"

"That's his name?"

Crawford was starting to get impatient; nothing like trying to explain a simple story to a woman under the influence of a most excellent drug. "Yes. He was worried after he ran into you and Mrs. Bannerman—"

"You mean Sissy."

"Okay, Sissy, and he called Meaghan. He said you didn't look well. She called me after she called her mother, who obviously knew where you were headed."

"So Mr. Super Senior and Christine saved my bacon?" Crawford had had enough of my comedic stylings. He motioned to one of the cops standing on the perimeter. "We're going to get going soon, so if you need something from her, get it now." The cop raced over. Even in a situation like this, where he had absolutely no jurisdiction, Crawford took over, which explains why his retirement lasted all of two days. The cop asked me to come over to his car so he could get my statement, as incomprehensible as it would be, given my state of mind. I took a seat sideways, my feet still in the parking lot. What can I say? I don't like being in the backseat of police cars.

My statement was short: They picked me up. They took me here. Christine showed up. No, I'm not hurt. I want to go home.

The cop, not as handsome or as friendly as the other Yorktown cop, Stearns, looked at me sadly. "We may need to get more from you tomorrow or the next day."

"That's fine," I said. "I'm really tired." The night suddenly felt chillier than it had, and I started to shiver. Coming down off an Ativan high after being hauled up north to a nature preserve was starting to take its toll. Crawford came over, stripped off his jacket, and wrapped it around my shoulders.

"Let's go," he said.

"I need a time machine," I mumbled, half asleep.

"What?"

"A time machine. Let's go back in time," I said.

He opened the door to his car and helped me get in,

pulling the seat belt across and buckling me in, something he had been doing since we first met. "To when you didn't have another wife and she didn't have crazy brothers and—"

"I don't have another wife," he said, putting his hand over the belt to make sure it was tight enough.

"You know what I mean."

"Well, if I didn't have another wife, I wouldn't have the girls, and you know how I feel about them." His face was inches from mine. "I couldn't live without them," he said softly.

"I know," I said, suddenly sad. It was the Ativan talking, but still, I was engulfed in a profound despair. "I think I want my own."

"Your own what?" he asked, even though I had a feeling that he knew what I meant. He wanted to hear me say it.

I waved my hand around, at a loss for words. "You know. My own."

He smiled and pulled me close. "I know. I want more of my own, too."

"So you're open to getting another dog?" I asked, not out of it enough not to ruin the moment with a bad joke.

"You'd better be kidding," he said into my hair.

"I am," I said.

"Don't change your mind."

"I won't," I said, feeling surer about that than about any other thing in my entire life.

FORTY-THREE

I DIDN'T KNOW you could have a hangover from antianxiety meds, but there you have it. Another lesson learned. I woke up on that Saturday morning with a pounding headache and only the briefest of recollections of what had happened the entire day before. Crawford was standing over the bed in his best black suit, the one he wears to weddings and funerals, and it occurred to me that we didn't know anyone getting married but we did know someone who had died.

"Marty's funeral," I said, my mouth coated in loose cotton, or so it felt. I turned over and pulled his pillow over my head.

He pulled the pillow off of me. "I made coffee. Get up, because we have to drive up north and we don't have a lot of time," he said. "Tell me what you want to wear and I will get everything together while you shower."

He's a good guy, that Crawford. I told him I wanted my black wrap dress, sheer hose, and any pair of black pumps he laid his hands on in the closet. There were a lot in there, and trying to describe exactly which ones I wanted would have taken far too long. I certainly didn't want the ones that I had worn the night before, one of which I had held against Mary Lou's throat with all intention of using it as a weapon, and hopefully, he would know that.

While I showered, I tried to piece together what had happened. The door was open, so I called out to him as I soaped up. "Did I get kidnapped again or was that a bad dream?"

"You got kidnapped again." A drawer slammed. "What color pantyhose?"

"Sheer!"

"What do those look like?"

"Find a pair that looks like your skin and pull them out."

"Gross," he said. I didn't know if he thought the stockings actually looked like skin or he was reacting to the state of my drawer. "You have a lot of athletic socks." Clearly the latter.

"And you have giant boxer shorts." I poured some fragrant shampoo into my hair and lathered. "There's no way to fold those things."

He made a sound of triumph. "Got them!"

As I massaged my scalp, bits and pieces of the evening started coming back to me. "Did I tell you I wanted a baby last night?" I asked tentatively, not liking the long silence that came after my question. "Crawford?"

"What?"

"Did you hear me?"

"Blah, blah, blah, boxer shorts. That?"

"No, the other part. About the baby."

More silence followed. Finally, he came into the bathroom and peeked over the top of the glass shower door, something he can do easily at his height. "Oh, that."

"Well?"

"So is it another dog or a baby? You were kind of sketchy on the details."

I leaned my head back under the showerhead and rinsed off. "Baby."

"I'm in." He smiled. "Totally in." He handed me a towel.

"Just promise me that they won't look like trolls. You know, like Tim's kids."

"No troll DNA on my side. Can't speak for the cheese-making Canadians on your side. I've never met any of them.

From what I hear, though, they all have bad hair and really long arms."

I pulled the towel around my body and tucked in the ends. When I got out of the shower, Crawford was waiting to give me a big hug. "I never thought we'd get here," he said.

I'm usually the last one to the party, so I wasn't surprised to hear him say that. "Promise me it won't hurt. Promise me there's some kind of instruction booklet that comes with a baby."

"Sorry. No can do on both accounts. Hurts like hell from what I've been told, and you literally fly by the seat of your pants." He held me at arm's length and studied my face. "You sure about this?"

"I really am," I said. I was, too—and it felt good.

THANKS TO CRAWFORD'S excellent driving skills—and ability to avoid speed traps—we made it to Marty Rayfield's church in record time. I had been to this church once before for another friend's funeral and knew it well. Parking was a nightmare, so Crawford dropped me in front and drove around the block looking for a place.

One thing I remembered about this church was its pithy sayings, posted on the sign in front of its doors. Today's would have made me laugh out loud if the mood hadn't been so somber. HUNGRY? SOUL FOOD SERVED HERE! I thought about Marty and how he would have loved that. He was a man who enjoyed a good pun and who wasn't averse to busting his own out every now and again.

Several limousines lined the curb in front of the Gothic building, and their doors opened almost simultaneously, Rayfields spewing forth and onto the sidewalk. Max's brothers, their wives, their children, and assorted aunts and uncles started to assemble at the steps to the church, and I scanned the crowd for my best friend. She was the last one out of the first limo, Fred standing by her side as she emerged from the deep backseat of the long black car. The day was unseasonably mild, and her black cashmere swing coat was open, revealing a fitted black dress that, in turn, revealed a very curious detail about Max's usually very slim, very taut shape.

If my eyes weren't deceiving me, I would say that my friend was just a little bit pregnant. That, or last night's burritos hadn't properly digested.

I didn't stand on ceremony, nor did I wait to see if she was mad at me. I rushed up to the car and, pushing myself between her and Fred, grabbed her in a hug. At first resistant, she finally relented and softened, falling into me and letting out a sob that she seemed to have been holding in for an eternity. Then she punched me in the shoulder.

"I'm really mad at you," she said, but her heart wasn't in it.

"I know."

"I wasn't even expecting to see you. Heard you got kidnapped again. Twice."

I shrugged. "Just another day in the life of a boring college professor."

"We have to talk. Not today, but soon."

"Whenever you're ready," I said and pointed to her belly. "Seems like I've missed a lot."

"More than you know," she said. "I figured my not drinking was a dead giveaway but sometimes you're really dense, you know?"

Yes, I knew.

"Dad always liked you best, you know." She was only half-kidding; she'd let my comment about the belly slide, indicating to me that she wasn't ready to talk about it. Or that she didn't want to ruin something so happy with the events to take place.

"That's only because I was the good girl."

She arched an eyebrow. "You think?"

"I know." I laid my hand lightly on her belly. "The tattoo, the blue hair, the nose piercing…shall I go on?"

"You need to stop," she said, but she was talking about something else. "Before someone…before you get hurt."

"Too late for that," I said before realizing I didn't know what she was talking about. "I need to stop what?"

Her eyes filled with tears. "Everything. The sleuthing. The mystery solving. The getting into everyone else's business. You don't have time for anything else," she said. "You don't have time for me."

So there it was. She was feeling neglected. Who could blame her? I had spent so much time on other pursuits the past several weeks that I had left her in the dust, and if I knew anything, it was that a neglected Max was an unhappy Max. Just as she was once the only person I had in my life, it seemed like now I was the only one she needed. Or the one she needed the most; I couldn't tell which it was.

There was nothing more to say, at least not at that moment. Her father had to be buried; there was time to repair what had been broken between us. "I'm going to go inside and grab a pew," I said, starting off toward the front doors.

She grabbed me by the shoulder. "No, you're not. You're sitting with my family," she said. She took my hand, and together we waited curbside for Marty's coffin to be removed from the hearse. I gave her hand a hard squeeze, which she returned, and then we all fell in line behind the beautiful mahogany box, Max grabbing hold of her stoic mother with her free hand. Her blond hair done up in an elaborate chignon, Gigi resembled an older Grace Kelly, her very expensive handbag dangling from her thin wrist. In the distance, hurrying past what was once the parochial school that Max had attended and was now a parish hall, was Crawford, his coat flapping behind him as he made his way to the church. He went behind us and snuck in a side door, leaving me to process behind the casket with the only family I had ever had since losing my parents.

Before we got inside the church itself, the casket taking up most of the space right inside the door, she leaned over and whispered in my ear. "Nice dress."

That's how I knew we would be good again. We always were.

FORTY-FOUR

Mary Lou Bannerman, if that was even her legal name, wasn't going to win any writing awards, but her story was compelling and illuminating nonetheless. It helped clear up a few things for me, loose ends that kept me awake at night as I listened to Crawford snoring contentedly beside me, his duties as stud wearing him out.

Mary Lou was on probation; Briggs, not so much. The mastermind of the extortion/kidnapping plot was most likely going to go to jail for a long time, and I certainly wasn't doing anything to stop anyone from putting him away.

I was back at school and keeping a low profile, brown bagging my lunch so I didn't have to look into the sad eyes of Marcus, the person who had gone to bat for the hiring of Briggs, spending long stretches in my office by myself, and only leaving to teach my classes. It was a lonely existence but one that I needed to maintain if I were to keep my job. I had definitely worn out my welcome at St. Thomas, bringing dishonor to a school for which, deep down, I had great affection.

It was late in the day and I was tired, but I was also champing at the bit to read Mary Lou's pages. I had made a copy, having turned over the original manuscript of what was really only a synopsis and a few pages, an outline really, to the authorities, curious to see just what had driven Mrs. Bannerman to try to get as close to me as possible and what she had to do with this whole charade turned nightmare.

*I wasn't surprised when my parents adopted Sassa-
fras; after all, she had nowhere else to go. She was
a sweet kid with a wild side, but her heart was in
the right place and even though more than a decade
separated us in age, we became close.*

*She always called me Sissy, not because I was now
her sister, but because that's what I was: a big sissy.
"No guts, no glory," she used to say before bringing
me into her latest scheme, something that usually involved lying to my parents.*

I resisted the urge to correct grammar and punctuation
as I read the story of how Sassy came to be part of Mary
Lou's genteel family and what really happened to her husband. It had all the earmarks of a southern tragedy.

*She arrived in New York when she was twenty, look-
ing to live with me and Bob, but he wouldn't take her
in. I tried to help her find a job because even though
my family was well-off, Sassy had been cut off. Her
lack of direction, dropping out of school, and inability to stay out of trouble had caused my father to stop
giving her money and she had nowhere else to turn.
I helped as much as I could but it wasn't enough.
She turned to exotic dancing to make ends meet. The
money was great and she was very talented, from
what she told us. I didn't think dancing was a career
but she was bringing in more money in a week than
I had ever seen.*

And then she met Chick.

Seemed like we were getting to the good part.

*What kind of man supports a woman in a career
like that? Someone like Chick, obviously. They were*

married on a beautiful Saturday, in a beautiful church, and had a reception at a beautiful restaurant.

They seemed to be madly in love even if their lifestyle choices weren't what my family and I chose for ourselves. The rest of his family seemed nice, his sister especially, but he was a ruffian, despite his job standing at Sans-a-Flush. He put our company on the map, but he also was partially responsible for its descent into bankruptcy, using money from various accounts to support his and Sassy's lifestyle. Bob, by then the CEO of my father's company, decided that the best course of action was to fire Chick.

The day Bob died, a gorgeous day in 2001, he wasn't supposed to go to work that day, but my father wanted Chick gone. Chick was stealing, my father said. Chick was bad news. Bob went to work to fire Chick. I kissed him good-bye and wished him luck. Bob liked Chick but got to thinking that he might be up to no good just as my father suspected. On that day, Bob traveled to his office to meet Chick. When he got there, he found Chick emptying his office and taking things he shouldn't, files of work, ideas for new marketing directions, and in the midst of all of that, some of the company's financial records. And checks. Signed by Bob. The ones he had been using to keep him and Sassy in the lifestyle they wanted.

Bob and Chick fought. Not physically, of course, but loudly and violently in their way, Bob trying desperately to talk Chick out of doing what he planned. After Chick left, Bob had a massive coronary right there at the offices, right where he had given Chick his start, right where he had built an empire, and died.

Chick Stepkowski murdered my husband.

Why Chick had taken his life was still a mystery. Guilt over the fact that his intrusion at the Sans-a-Flush offices had in some way contributed to Bob's death? I didn't know and I didn't care. As involved as I had been in all of this, I was not invested in Chick, in Mary Lou, or in the Du Pris family at large. I just wanted all of them to go away and leave me alone with my boring existence, my recalcitrant students, my hectic teaching load, and my Crawford.

I do love Michael, just not in the way I loved Bob. I married him because I don't know how to be alone. And that makes me very, very sad.

I looked out the window and stared at my favorite sight, the St. Thomas cemetery, the one that was the final resting place of the nuns who had passed on, including my favorite, Sister Alphonse. If I had been a nonbeliever before, I was rapidly coming around to the idea that maybe Alphonse was now my guardian angel. So much had happened, and yet I was still safe. For me to think that she had had some hand in my well-being was crazy, but for me to think that she didn't have a hand in it was also crazy. How could I have avoided so many dangerous scrapes without some divine intervention?

As I mulled this over, I spotted a figure that I had come to recognize coming down the stairs in front of the cemetery. How she had gotten past security at the front gate—everyone now had her picture—wasn't all that mystifying; the security team, and I use that term loosely, was not known for its crack enforcement. As an extra precaution, Crawford's brother, Jimmy, my go-to for all legal matters, had requested a restraining order, but she had probably plied the gate guard with an applesauce loaf or a few cupcakes; they could be bought that easily. Mary Lou Bannerman was not supposed to come to my place of work at any given time, something that was in effect until her probation ended, sometime in the next decade.

I was frozen in my chair. St. Thomas, for Mary Lou, was completely off-limits. I had a few choices, all of which swam through my head. Calling security was an option, but really, what could any one of the guards—most of them overweight, legally blind, old, or some combination of those traits—do if she had come to hurt me, armed with God knows what? Call Crawford? I wasn't sure where he was or what he was doing, so I decided that texting him was the best way to get his attention. I knew that I had a few seconds before she arrived in my office, so I tapped out a quick SOS to my husband, somewhere in the Bronx, doing something that was probably as unsavory as protecting me from Mary Lou Bannerman, someone I wasn't sure was even dangerous. These days, though, I wasn't taking any chances.

When she arrived, I was standing behind my desk with a thick first edition of *Anna Karenina* brandished over my head, prepared to throw it if necessary. She stood outside my open office door, knowing that what she was doing was not kosher under the terms of my order of protection. My arms were getting tired; *Anna Karenina* was heavier than I thought.

"You can put the book down," she said. "I'm not going to hurt you."

"How did you get on campus?" I asked.

"I walked." She smiled. "No one looks twice at a middle-aged mother when she enters a college campus."

"But everyone has your photo."

She shrugged. "Lot of good it did." She rested her hand on the doorknob. "Can I come in?"

"Absolutely not," I said, my arms coming down a little farther from the weight of the book. "What do you want?"

"Put the book down, Alison," she said, smiling at Sister

Evelyn, shuffling past to her corner office. To Sister Anna Catherine, who was also passing by, what was going on both inside and outside my office was completely normal. The convent must have let their subscription to the local paper lapse, keeping Sister Anna Catherine and all of her compadres in the dark about my latest exploits and what the appearance of former student Mary Lou Bannerman might mean.

"I just wanted to say I was sorry for what happened," Mary Lou said, taking a step closer to the office.

"Stay there. Not another step."

"I really am," she said. "Can I give you a hug?"

"Again, absolutely not," I said, wondering what it was about this woman that allowed her to not take a very direct hint. "Get the hell off campus, Mary Lou. I've already let Crawford know that you're here, and if he gets here before you leave, you're going to spend the night in jail for sure."

The crying started again. After my night in the woods with her, I had been hoping I would never hear the keening cries of Mary Lou Bannerman, her sadness apparently the only thing that mattered. "I'm so sorry."

"You should be," I said, finally putting down the book. "You have a nut job of a son, and I could have been killed. Your sister was no picnic, either. I just want you and your family to go back to Crazy Town, where you all belong." I sat down, suddenly feeling the exhaustion that had plagued me for the past few weeks returning. "All I wanted to do was throw a nice birthday party for my stepdaughters. Nothing fancy," I muttered. "Just a little cake and champagne and presents. I wish I had never thought of it."

"Why are you so angry at me?" she asked. By her tone and the plaintive look on her face, it appeared that she really didn't know.

I didn't feel like explaining to her that getting drugged, kidnapped, and threatened usually made people angry at one another, even if the person asking the question wasn't the one who actually did the drugging, kidnapping, or threatening. I fixed her with a look that I hoped communicated what I felt without having to say a word.

"He stole our money. Bob's money. It wasn't fair," she said. "We'd been looking for him for years. When we found out he was back, through Sassy, we just had to find a way to get the money back."

"Did you kill him?" I asked, thinking of Christine's fervent conviction that he had been murdered.

"No," she said, tears filling her eyes. "We would never do that. Do you understand why we wanted the money so badly? It was ours," she said. "That company was our future. Our family. When Chick took that money, it left us with nothing. My father was crushed. Everything we had was flushed away."

That was a good way to put it.

"And what about Sassy, Mary Lou? Why did she kill herself?"

Her face crumbled. "I don't think I'll ever know. To be with Chick, maybe?"

"Fine. It was yours. But you dragged so many people into this mess than were necessary." In the distance, I heard sirens. "The jig is up, Mary Lou. They're coming for you. Again."

A voice came from behind her, the accent definitely Polish, the tone definitely harsh. "Don't move a muscle, lady."

I peered out around Mary Lou and saw Sister Anna Catherine—Sister Perpetua beside her—holding a giant dagger aloft. I recognized it as the one the Theatre Department used in last semester's production of *Hamlet*. She was little but powerfully built, and hoisting the dagger didn't seem to give her as much trouble as holding a large volume of Russian literature aloft had given me. Perpetua looked like she would really enjoy smashing someone over the head with the giant rolling pin in her right hand, the one that she was slapping menacingly into the palm of her left.

You can't make this stuff up.

Perpetua used a softer tone. "We're going to have to ask you to leave, dear. Professor Bergeron really shouldn't be in your presence."

It was really the other way around—Mary Lou needed to stay away from me—but who was I to quibble with weapon-wielding nuns? It was nice to know they had my back. Here all along I thought it was a dead nun protecting me. Seemed I had a whole army of Jesus's brides on my side.

The sirens got closer, but Mary Lou's visage never changed; she was as unconcerned as one could be by the impending arrival of law enforcement. "Will you accept my apology?" she asked finally.

"No!" I said. "No, I will not accept your apology. I will not ever be friends with you again. I don't want your lousy sandwiches or your scones." The last part was a total lie. I would always want her sandwiches and her scones, but as our relationship had moved to a different plane, having any just didn't seem like it was a realistic expectation anymore. Her face fell. "Just leave me alone. Go away."

Sister Anna Catherine brought the dagger down with a loud clang, scaring all of us. "I'm going to ask you one more time. Leave."

Mary Lou's face crumbled. "I'm going," she said. "I never meant to bring you into this. I just wanted to find out what you knew about where the money might have been."

"Why, Mary Lou?" I asked. "Why did you want the money so badly?"

"Because we're bankrupt. We have nothing."

"Sell one of the Chanel bags," I said. "That'll net you a mortgage payment." I set the book down. "This is not my problem." I stepped back toward the window, keeping Anna Catherine in my sights. She was strong, but how good was her aim?

"That money would have saved all of us," she said. "Me. Sassy. Briggs. It was ours, and he took it."

"Why me?" I asked.

"You were close enough to the family to know something even if you didn't know a lot. I wanted to get close to you to find out what you knew."

I had invested time and emotion into Mary Lou, buying the line of crap she was selling, and now felt betrayed—and angry. "You used me. You almost got me killed." I took a deep breath. "Oh, and by the way? Your story stinks."

I don't know what part of that made her cry the loudest, but she let out a huge, gasping sob, a sound that made it seem like I had stabbed her through the heart. Figuratively, I guess I had and for that, I felt kind of bad. I had to remind myself of what had transpired so that I didn't completely forgive her or God forbid, apologize for my rudeness.

I looked outside and saw Crawford, a guy not known for his speed, hurtling down the back steps, Fred on his heels. "There's my husband. You'd better go."

It was too late, though. Mary Lou dithered just a few seconds too long and was soon being given a stern talking-to by Fred as well as a recitation of her Miranda rights. Crawford, on the other hand, was mesmerized by a little nun brandishing a dagger. He had his gun trained on Mary Lou while Fred cuffed her, but his eyes uncharacteristically strayed toward Sister Anna Catherine.

"Please put the knife down, Sister," he said.

"It's a dagger, Detective," she said, still holding on tight with both hands.

Sister Perpetua let out a little giggle. "Hello, Detective Crawford."

"Hello, Sister," he said to Perpetua while retraining his

eyes on Mary Lou, someone who I think was less of a threat than Anna Catherine. "Sister, please put down the dagger."

She let it clatter dramatically to the floor. "'O happy dagger!'" she exclaimed.

Perpetua offered a little tsk-tsk. "That's from *Romeo and Juliet*, Sister."

"I know," Sister Anna Catherine said testily. "It was the most fitting response, however, to Detective Crawford's request."

Fred, too, was transfixed by two tiny nuns holding what they considered deadly weapons. He pulled Mary Lou up by the cuffed hands finally and started to march her out of the office area. Thankfully, it was late in the day, so the number of rubbernecking professors was smaller than usual, and Mary Lou was perpwalked out of the St. Thomas Humanities Department with only a few openmouthed stares to follow her. Sisters Anna Catherine and Perpetua drifted off to their offices; I called out a hearty "Thank you!" to them before they each closed their doors.

Crawford came into my office. "Are you alright?"

"Fine," I said. "Just exasperated. Will this ever be over?"

"Well, now that she's blown the order of protection, she may do some time." He turned and looked out into the office area. "I thought that little Russian nun was going to cut her."

"She's Polish." I jammed a bunch of papers into my messenger bag. "And she teaches in the Nursing Department, so she could probably cut her and not leave any evidence."

He considered that intently, then returned to one of his favorite topics. "You hungry?" he asked.

"You hungry?" I echoed. "That's what you have to say after all of this?"

He smiled sheepishly.

"You're finished working?" I asked.

"I was until I got your SOS text. Fred will process Mata Hari over there," he said, pointing out the window, where I spied Fred pushing Mary Lou's head down as he stuffed her into the back of a squad car, "so we are free to go. What are you in the mood for?"

I thought that over for a minute. "A hot shower followed by a vacation to a remote island, one where none of your extended ex-family resides or visits."

"I don't think I can arrange that right this minute."

I rested my head on a stack of papers and collected my thoughts. I could feel his eyes on me. "You're still hungry, right?"

"Starving."

"Meet you at the Chinese place?"

"Sounds like a plan," he said.

Beyond my office, I spied Joanne Larkin by the Xerox machine and realized, with everything that had gone on, that we hadn't really resolved our conflict. I didn't want Meaghan to have a grade tainted by the suspicion of cheating, nor did I want to be blackmailed by Joanne into keeping my silence. After Crawford left, I went on the Web site for the publisher that distributed the textbook Joanne used, created a fake password and ID, and downloaded what the publisher considered a reasonable multiple choice test to be given midway through a term. I don't know why it hadn't dawned on me sooner or why I had been so passive, but it hadn't and I had.

Now the jig was up and Joanne was going to do things my way.

I approached her, noticing a bottle of Wite-Out resting on one side of the Xerox machine; pages of what looked like a previously mimeographed test were flowing through the giant copier. While she waited, she mulled over a pull in the sleeve of her sweater, this one festooned with an image of Garfield.

"Hi, Joanne," I said.

"Alison," she said, a sneer developing on her lips.

I leaned in close. The events of the last several weeks had worn me out, and I felt like I had nothing to lose. "So here's how we're going to play it," I said, handing her the test. "You're going to let Meaghan take this test and give her a grade that befits her performance. You're going to tear up the previous test. We will never speak of it again. And you will never threaten me or my stepdaughter again or there will be hell to pay," I said.

"What if I don't?" she asked.

I opened the top of the copier and pulled out the page she was copying, a test that had seen better days and that had been created, obviously, before the Internet had been invented. The type was blue and from an old-fashioned typewriter, not a fancy font from one of the several hundred Macs that were on campus and that most of us used to create our tests and reports. I folded the page in quarters and slipped it into my skirt pocket. "Then I have this, and it will find its way to the dean of your department."

"There are no rules against reusing tests," she protested.

"There are when they find their way into the hands of former students who sell them to current students," I said. Her eyes were growing wide. "That's right, Joanne. Your tests are being sold. I wanted to keep this from you, seeing if we could reach some kind of agreement on Meaghan's situation, but you wouldn't have it. So now you know." I had kept it from her because she had been so unreasonable and not knowing what she might do to my stepdaughter had stupidly kept my mouth shut. That time was gone now and she knew it.

She took the tests out of the copier and threw them into the recycling bin by Dottie's desk. "I had no idea."

"Well, now you do," I said, waiting for an apology that never came.

"Please excuse me. I have some work to do," she said, scurrying off.

MEAGHAN GOT A C− on the retaken midterm and a C+ for the term, and never had I felt so proud of any grade she had received. Alex broke up with her after the term was over, saying that her Stepmother seemed crazy and it would never work between them. Meaghan took a vow of celibacy and devoted herself to her academics and basketball, becoming the high scorer for the season for the St. Thomas Blue Jays.

"See what you can do when your put your mind to something?" I had asked, bearing her withering glance with ease, now that I had some experience with the care and feeding of teenaged daughters. She knew she owed me, and that was something that I would keep in the back of my mind until it was absolutely necessary. The time would come when she would have to pay the piper, so to speak, and hopefully, that would keep her on her toes, just where I wanted her.

FORTY-FIVE

MARTINA ALISON RAYFIELD-WYATT was born on a cloudless spring day, the color of her eyes matching the sky above. I was there for the birth, something, in hindsight, I should have taken a pass on. When I've seen births take place in movies, the mother is screaming or moaning or threatening everyone around her. Martina's birth was soundless, with just a wild-eyed Max looking at everyone encouraging her to "push!" with such deadly intensity that it was beyond frightening. It didn't help that I kept asking Max at inopportune moments how much it hurt, just to get a handle on whether it was as bad as it looked. It hurt pretty bad, judging from the hold she had on my fingers. Then there was the blood…and the other stuff. I hit the ground when a giant mass resembling a platypus burst forth to great fanfare in the delivery room, the word "placenta" being bandied about. That was all I needed to hear. Here I thought that once you had the baby, it was all over. You put on your silk bed jacket, ordered room service, and accepted visitors. Your husband handed out cigars in the waiting room. Before long you got up, put on your makeup, and went home. I didn't realize that what came next made some of the dead bodies I've seen look positively sterile. When I came to, it was all over—for real this time—and Max was holding what looked like a football with eyes and ears. A beautiful, perfect football that had grabbed hold of her finger and wasn't letting go.

Fred was uncharacteristically chatty. "That's my girl!

e said, bending over to get a look at a baby who had his
erfectly round head and Max's bow lips. It was hard to tell
ow much she had gotten, genetically, from her Samoan
African American father and Irish American mother, but
ime would tell. I said a silent prayer that she wouldn't
row up to be a six-and-a-half-footer with a bad attitude,
ust like her dad.

Crawford was in the waiting room when I came out. I
ave him two thumbs up. "It's a girl," I said, "and she looks
ust like you. What's up with that?"

"Very funny," he said, giving me his fake smile. "How's
Max?"

"Cranky."

"So how is that different from any other day?"

"I'm going to give her a pass," I said. "She just passed
watermelon through her hoo-hah. We're going to cut her
ome slack." I sat down on one of the vinyl couches in the
vaiting room. "You didn't tell me it looked like a scene
rom *Apocalypse Now* when you had a baby."

"Yes, I may have left that out." He pulled me close, kiss-
ng my head. "You hungry?"

"Is the pope Catholic?"

"Last time I checked." I was starving. Seeing a live birth
ad taken a lot out of me.

"Tim's Fancy Sandwich Shoppe?" I asked.

"That's not what it's called," he said.

"Yes, but it's what I like to call it," I said. Tim's midlife
risis had turned out surprisingly well. His sandwich
hop—the Earl of Sandwich—had opened in Greenwich
nd had become a bit of a hot spot with the locals, so much
o that he was thinking of opening another location in an-
ther part of town. Yes, he had quit his job and not told
is wife, but his newfound fame and success as the Earl
ad put him back in her good graces, and things seemed
o be better again. Seemed that old Tim had done quite

well in the hedge fund business so even if the shop hadn't done well, they were set for life. He had a silent partner as backup, too; the guy had been on the phone with him the night I had overheard his conversation about the money. I was really in the wrong business. I had a soft spot for his eggplant rollatini wedge, and the minute Crawford mentioned sandwiches, my mouth began to water. "I should really call Kevin before we go," I said.

"How much is that going to cost me?" Crawford asked.

"A call to Botswana? Well, we'll probably need to refinance the house, but he really should know about Max's baby," I said. I got a little light-headed. "Seriously, that birth stuff is not for the faint of heart," I said, dropping my head between my knees.

"You think you can still go through with it?"

I patted my growing midsection. "Do I have a choice?"

* * * * *

REQUEST YOUR FREE BOOKS!
2 FREE NOVELS PLUS 2 FREE GIFTS!

⊕ HARLEQUIN®

INTRIGUE®

BREATHTAKING ROMANTIC SUSPENSE

YES! Please send me 2 FREE Harlequin Intrigue® novels and my 2 FREE gifts (gifts are worth about $10). After receiving them, if I don't wish to receive any more books, I can return the shipping statement marked "cancel." If I don't cancel, I will receive 6 brand-new novels every month and be billed just $4.74 per book in the U.S. or $5.24 per book in Canada. That's a savings of at least 14% off the cover price! It's quite a bargain! Shipping and handling is just 50¢ per book in the U.S. and 75¢ per book in Canada.* I understand that accepting the 2 free books and gifts places me under no obligation to buy anything. I can always return a shipment and cancel at any time. Even if I never buy another book, the two free books and gifts are mine to keep forever.

182/382 HDN F43C

Name	(PLEASE PRINT)

Address	Apt. #

City	State/Prov.	Zip/Postal Code

Signature (if under 18, a parent or guardian must sign)

Mail to the Harlequin® Reader Service:
IN U.S.A.: P.O. Box 1867, Buffalo, NY 14240-1867
IN CANADA: P.O. Box 609, Fort Erie, Ontario L2A 5X3

**Are you a subscriber to Harlequin Intrigue books
and want to receive the larger-print edition?
Call 1-800-873-8635 or visit www.ReaderService.com.**

* Terms and prices subject to change without notice. Prices do not include applicable taxes. Sales tax applicable in N.Y. Canadian residents will be charged applicable taxes. Offer not valid in Quebec. This offer is limited to one order per household. Not valid for current subscribers to Harlequin Intrigue books. All orders subject to credit approval. Credit or debit balances in a customer's account(s) may be offset by any other outstanding balance owed by or to the customer. Please allow 4 to 6 weeks for delivery. Offer available while quantities last.

Your Privacy—The Harlequin® Reader Service is committed to protecting your privacy. Our Privacy Policy is available online at www.ReaderService.com or upon request from the Harlequin Reader Service.

We make a portion of our mailing list available to reputable third parties that offer products we believe may interest you. If you prefer that we not exchange your name with third parties, or if you wish to clarify or modify your communication preferences, please visit us at www.ReaderService.com/consumerchoice or write to us at Harlequin Reader Service Preference Service, P.O. Box 9062, Buffalo, NY 14269. Include your complete name and address.

HIDIR13R

Reader Service.com

Manage your account online!

- Review your order history
- Manage your payments
- Update your address

*We've designed
the Harlequin® Reader Service
website just for you.*

Enjoy all the features!

- Reader excerpts from any series
- Respond to mailings and special monthly offers
- Discover new series available to you
- Browse the Bonus Bucks catalog
- Share your feedback

Visit us at:

ReaderService.com